Praise For Bette Lee Crosby's Novels

Emily, Gone

"Heart-wrenching and heartwarming. A page turner until the end."

— Ashley Farley, bestselling author of *Only One Life*

"An extraordinary book that raises questions about love, family, faith, and forgiveness. This one will stay with me for quite some time."

— Camille DiMaio, bestselling author of *The Way of Beauty*

"A beautiful story that will being you to tears! The writing is flawless! Definitely one of the most beautiful books I've read this year!"

— *Book Nerd*

A Year of Extraordinary Moments

"One of those rare books that makes you believe in the power of love. Filled with memorable characters and important life lessons, a Southern treat to the last page."

— Anita Hughes, author of *California Summer*

"Throughout this book, the author beautifully explores the theme of letting go of the past while preserving its best parts . . ."

— *Kirkus Reviews*

The Summer of New Beginnings

"This women's fiction novel is full of romance, the power of friendship and the bond of sisters."

— *The Charlotte Observer*

"A heartwarming story about family, forgiveness, and the magic of new beginnings."

— Christine Nolfi, bestselling author of *Sweet Lake*

"A heartwarming, captivating, and intriguing story about the importance of family . . . The colorful cast of characters are flawed, quirky, mostly loyal, determined and mostly likable."

— *Linda's Book Obsession*

"Crosby's Southern voice comes through in all of her books and lends a believable element to everything she writes. *The Summer of New Beginnings* is no exception."

— *Book Chat*

Spare Change

"Skillfully written, *Spare Change* clearly demonstrates Crosby's ability to engage her readers' rapt attention from beginning to end. A thoroughly entertaining work of immense literary merit."

— *Midwest Book Review*

"Love, loss and unexpected gifts . . . Told from multiple points of view, this tale seeped from the pages and wrapped itself around my heart."

— *Caffeinated Reviewer*

More than anything, *Spare Change* is a heartwarming book, which is simultaneously intriguing and just plain fun."

— *Seattle Post-Intelligencer*

Passing Through Perfect

"This is Southern fiction at its best: spiritually infused, warm, and family-oriented."

— *Midwest Book Reviews*

"Crosby's characters take on heartbreak and oppression with dignity, courage, and a shaken but still strong faith in a better tomorrow."

— *IndieReader*

The Twelfth Child

"Crosby's unique style of writing is timeless and her character building is inspirational."

— *Layered Pages*

"Crosby draws her characters with an emotional depth that compels the reader to care about their challenges, to root for their success, and to appreciate their bravery."

— Gayle Swift, author of *ABC, Adoption & Me*

"Crosby's talent lies in not only telling a good compelling story, but telling it from a unique perspective . . . Characters stay with you because they are simply too endearing to go away."

— *Reader Views*

Baby Girl

"Crosby weaves this story together in a manner that feels like a huge patchwork quilt. All the pieces and tears come together to make something beautiful."

— Michele Randall, *Readers' Favorite*

"Crosby is a true storyteller, delving into the emotions, relationships, and human dynamics— the cracks which break us, and ultimately make us stronger."

— J. D. Collins, Top 1000 reviewer

Silver Threads

"*Silver Threads* is an amazing story of love, loss, family, and second chances that will simply stir your soul."

— *Jersey Girl Book Reviews*

"Crosby's books are filled with love of family and carry the theme of a sweetness for life . . . You are pulled in by the story line and the characters."

— *Silver's Reviews*

"In *Silver Threads*, Crosby flawlessly merges the element of fantasy without interrupting the beauty of a solid love story . . . Sure to stay with you beyond the last page."

— Lisa McCombs, *Readers' Favorite*

Cracks in the Sidewalk

"Crosby has penned a multidimensional scenario that should be read not only for entertainment but also to see how much, love, gentleness, and humanity matter."

— Gisela Hausmann, *Readers' Favorite*

A
MILLION
LITTLE
LIES

Also by Bette Lee Crosby

A
MILLION
LITTLE
LIES

A Novel

BETTE LEE CROSBY

A MILLION LITTLE LIES
Copyright © 2020 by Bette Lee Crosby

Cover design: damonza.com
Formatting by Author E.M.S.
Editor: Ekta Garg

ISBN-978-0-9981067-8-6

BENT PINE PUBLISHING
Port Saint Lucie, FL

Published in the United States of America

To the women of my PSL Posse
There can be no finer gift
than that of friendship.
Thank you…

Joanne Bliven
Kathy Foslien
Lynn Ontiveros
Trudy Southe

*"Which is worse—a lie that draws a smile
or a truth that draws a tear?"*

Bryan Bedford
Miracle on 34th Street

SUZANNA

Sun Grove, Florida

In the weeks following her mama's death, ten-year-old Suzanna Duff learned to lie as convincingly as any con man who'd ever walked the earth. When neighbors came with cakes, fruit baskets, and casseroles, she smiled politely and said she and her daddy were doing just fine. Never once did she mention that on the few nights when he did manage to make it home, he came in rip-roaring drunk and in a thunderous mood.

To Suzanna her lie was not a deception but a necessary altering of the truth; a way to shade the ugliness of her life and make it appear somewhat normal. She was following in her mama's footsteps, smoothing the road she had to travel, avoiding questions or confrontation.

They were tiny little lies that seemed harmless, rather like a game of Let's Pretend or Charades. She signed her daddy's name on her report cards, told tales of a vacation that never took place, and boasted of a kindly grandmother who didn't exist. But as time passed the lies grew larger, more substantial and solid. They built one upon another like the stones of a pyramid until they reached the pinnacle and left her with nowhere to go.

Now she fears it would be impossible to undo what has been done. Every waking moment her conscience urges her to tell the truth and be done with it. Do it for Annie, the small voice whispers, but Suzanna is wary of the consequences so she turns on the radio and sings along to silence the thought.

She knows the truth will cause a great deal of unhappiness and hurt those she loves. That's something she won't do, so she builds lie upon lie, pretending to be someone else, answering to a name that's not hers, and constantly looking over her shoulder. She dreads the day when the truth comes knocking at the door, and it will. She's almost certain of it.

It seems ironic that after so many years, the situation she now finds herself in began not with an outright lie but a mere slip of the tongue, a simple omission of truth.

SUZANNA DUFF

May 1960, Sun Grove, Florida

The sky was still dark when Suzanna Duff eased herself from beneath the weight of Earl's arm and inched her way to the far side of the bed. Hesitating a moment, she listened for the sound of sleep to return. He wheezed, gave a groan, then turned on his side and went back to snoring. Believing it safe enough to make her move, she climbed from the bed and silently crossed the room.

His pants were tossed over the chair, the same as always. She cradled the belt buckle so it wouldn't fall to the floor or clank against the wood of the chair, slid her hand into the pocket, and pulled out a folded wad of bills. Not stopping long enough to count how much he had this time, she tiptoed from the room and made her way down the hall to where Annie was sleeping.

Suzanna kneeled beside the bed and pulled out the things she'd stashed there a day earlier: sandals, a pair of jeans, a tee shirt, and the old brown suitcase that had once belonged to her mama. She dressed quickly, slid the folded bills into the pocket of her jeans, then leaned over the child and whispered, "Wake up, baby, we've got to go."

Annie was seven but smarter than most. She'd already learned that when her mama held a finger to her lips, there was a need for silence. She sat up, rubbed the sleep from her eyes, and in a hopeful voice asked, "Can Bobo come too?"

Eyeing the stuffed dog the child held in her arms, Suzanna gave a reluctant nod.

"Okay, but if you bring Bobo, you've got to promise to carry him yourself."

Annie grinned, showing the spot where her front teeth were missing. "I promise."

It was almost three miles to the highway and there was a possibility she would have to carry Annie part of the way, so Suzanna took nothing she didn't absolutely need. It meant leaving behind the photo album she cherished, the milk pitcher that belonged to a grandma she'd never met, and most of their clothes, but it was a choice she'd made; not an easy choice, but one she was determined to stick to. Suzanna knew that somewhere out there was the life she was supposed to live but it wasn't here, and it sure as hell wasn't with Earl Fagan.

Route 70 was a narrow road frequented mostly by grove trucks hauling oranges or cattle off to market. One lane ran west, the other east, and on any given day you could stand there for twenty minutes with nothing but overloaded citrus haulers passing you by splatting grapefruits along the road. Suzanna hoped that would not be the case this morning. In fact, she was counting on it. Before noon, before Earl woke and discovered them missing, they had to be long gone from Sun Grove. East or west made no difference; they'd go whichever way a driver was headed, then head north once they were safely away from Earl.

Stopping alongside a clump of palmetto bushes, Suzanna set the suitcase a few feet back from the road and told Annie to squat down beside it.

"Pretend we're playing hide and seek," she said and then stepped out onto the road, craning her neck to catch sight of a vehicle headed their way. After several minutes, a tanker headed west came into view. She crossed the road, stood on the westbound side of the blacktop, curled her mouth into a sexy-looking smile, and stuck her thumb out.

The tanker rolled by without slowing.

After the tanker, there were two fully loaded citrus carriers, a Buick headed east, and, behind it, a red pickup that slowed and rolled to a stop twenty yards past Suzanna. Grabbing the suitcase and motioning for Annie to follow along, she hurried toward the truck.

"Thanks for stopping," she said as she yanked open the door.

The driver, a man with sun-weathered skin and dark stubble covering his chin, gave a nod. "Where you headed?"

"Jersey." Suzanna stuffed the suitcase behind the seat then hoisted Annie up.

A look of surprise flickered across the trucker's face. "Where'd she come from?"

Catching the sound of apprehension in his voice, Suzanna scrambled into the seat and closed the door before he had time to change his mind. "Don't worry, she's a good kid and won't be any bother."

With his forehead furrowed and a look of concern settling on his face, he pulled back onto the road, drove for a mile or so, then asked, "What's your name, kid?"

"Her name's Annie," Suzanna answered before Annie had the chance. "And before you go getting any weird ideas, I'm her mama."

"Let the kid answer for herself." He glanced down at Annie. "That true? Is she really your mama?"

Annie nodded.

"You don't have to be afraid of telling the truth. If she's stealing you away from your family, speak up. I'll see you get back to where you belong."

Annie giggled. "Mama, he said—"

"I heard what he said," Suzanna replied. She looked across with an icy glare. "You've got balls suggesting a thing like that. I appreciate the ride, but that doesn't give you the right to—"

"Hold on, missy! I'm just concerned for the kid's welfare. Most parents with children travel by car or on the bus; they don't stand out on the road thumbing—"

"If they've got money enough for a bus ticket, good for them," Suzanna snapped.

No one said anything more, and several minutes lumbered by before he broke the silence.

"Sorry. I was thinking about my own kids. Maria and me, we got three girls, and I worry about them all the time. The youngest, she's eight." He pointed to a snapshot rubber-banded to the visor. "That's them," he said and smiled.

The rigid set of Suzanna's mouth softened. "Sometimes I'm too touchy. No harm done."

He introduced himself as Joe, said he was only going as far as Georgia, then started talking about his family and how his girls were growing like weeds.

"Before you know it, they'll be married and gone," he said sadly.

An easy exchange of words followed, but Suzanna offered little about her haphazard life and nothing about Earl. She glossed over the past and focused on the future.

"Once we get to Jersey, I'm gonna look for a job taking pictures or maybe designing ads like you see in magazines."

"Nice," he said. "How'd you get into a profession like that?"

"Well, I'm not actually in it yet." She looked over with a mischievous grin. "But I figured I could fudge it a bit. You know, everybody's got to start somewhere. I'm real creative, and I've got an eye for design."

"Good for you." He laughed. "Good for you."

Shortly after they crossed the Georgia line, he asked where they were going in Jersey.

"Hoboken," Suzanna answered.

The sorry truth was she'd left home knowing only that she had to get away from Earl. Beyond that she had no plans; at least nothing concrete. Gladys, a onetime friend she'd worked with before Annie was born, had moved to Hoboken three years ago. They'd stayed in touch for a while, but the last postcard was almost two years ago. She had to hope Gladys hadn't married or moved on since then.

Forcing a smile, she said, "We're planning to stay with a friend 'til I get a job. Once I'm set with a steady income, we'll find a place of our own."

Not long after they'd passed through Ben Hill County, Joe turned off the highway and headed west. Fifteen minutes later, after a long stretch of sparsely-traveled road, they came to a sign that read, Welcome to Cousins, Georgia – Population 16,897.

The center of town was a lineup of stores: the Ben Franklin five-and-dime, a Piggly Wiggly market, a barber with a revolving pole out front, a quilt shop, and several others. Halfway down the street, Joe pulled over in front of the bus station, a squat brown building one quarter the size of the Piggly Wiggly.

"Sorry, missy," he said, "this is as far as I go."

"Maybe you should drop us off back by the highway," Suzanna suggested. "It'd be easier to catch a ride."

He shook his head, not letting his eyes meet hers.

"Not a good idea," he said. "With a sweet little girl like Annie, you ought not be hitchhiking. You got lucky this time, but there's no telling what…" As his words drifted off, he reached into his pocket, pulled out a billfold, and handed Suzanna a 20-dollar bill. "This here's enough for a bus ticket—"

"I'm not looking for charity!"

"And I'm not giving any. I just don't want it on my conscience if something happens to one of you." He pushed the 20 dollars into Suzanna's palm then grinned. "There's probably a northbound bus leaving sometime today, and you'd be a lot better off taking that than chancing it on the road."

Suzanna hefted her suitcase from behind the seat, then stood watching as he drove off.

With his 20 dollars and the 18 dollars she'd taken from Earl's pocket, she had enough for a bus ticket but money would still be tight. They had a thousand miles yet to go; they'd have to eat, and if Gladys wasn't around they'd need a place to stay, a motel room maybe. Taking those things into consideration, 38 dollars didn't seem like very much.

With Annie's hand in hers, Suzanna reluctantly walked into the bus station. At least they could freshen up in the ladies' room. Then, depending on cost and scheduling, they'd either buy a bus ticket or start hoofing it back toward the highway.

❦

As Suzanna stood at the ticket window, the clerk adjusted his glasses and peered across the counter. Glancing down at Annie then back to her, he said, "Fourteen-forty for an adult. She rides for free."

As she was digging through her pocket for the singles she'd taken from Earl, he added, "Next bus is tomorrow, 10:30 a.m."

"Tomorrow? You don't have one leaving today?"

"Afraid not. The New York-New Jersey bus is once a day, 10:30 a.m."

"What about if we're willing to make a transfer?"

He shook his head. "Too late. The last northbound passed through 11:15. The only others we've got today are a 4:30 headed for Chicago or a 6:15 to Omaha."

"No thanks," Suzanna said and turned away.

"You want the New Jersey ticket?"

"I'm thinking about it."

She walked to the far end of the waiting room and plopped down on a bench; Annie sat beside her. With the sun blistering hot, the walk back to the highway would be a long one, but sitting in the bus station overnight was not much better. Besides, they hadn't eaten all day, and she could hear Annie's stomach rumbling.

She looked down with a half-hearted smile. "You're hungry, aren't you, baby?"

Annie nodded. "Starving."

As Suzanna sat there considering which was the better of the two really bad options, she spied a flyer left lying on the bench.

WILLIAM G. PARKER MEMORIAL LUNCHEON the heading read, and beneath it was the photo of an elderly gentleman. The copy went on to list all of the man's achievements then said that anyone who had ever been fortunate enough to cross paths with William Parker was invited to attend. The luncheon was to be an open-house buffet held at the Elks Club on Main Street.

Open-house buffet?

Suzanna called over to the ticket window. "Is this Main Street?"

When the clerk nodded, she inquired how far it was to the Elks Club.

"Two blocks down, right hand side of the street," he answered.

Believing that providence had for once stepped in and was squarely on her side, Suzanna smiled. Fifteen minutes later, they walked out of the station with her wearing the one dress she'd thought to pack and Annie outfitted in a fresh pair of shorts. The tattered brown suitcase was now stashed in a bus station locker.

"We'll go to this luncheon, have ourselves a nice big meal, then find a park and pretend we're camping out," she told Annie. "Tomorrow morning we'll wake up nice and fresh, come back to the station, climb on the bus, and be in New Jersey before you know it."

As they started down Main Street, Annie asked, "Mama, is there gonna be cake?"

"I'm pretty sure there will be cake; maybe even pies as well."

"Oh, boy!" Annie grinned and quickened her step.

IDA PARKER

Cousins, Georgia

This was the day Ida Parker had been dreading. Today she would say one last goodbye to the man she'd loved for over a quarter of a century. She leaned heavily on the railing as she mounted the five steps leading to the Elks Club building.

Inside the foyer she stopped in front of the large brass easel and stood looking at the collage of photos. Bill, when he was alive and well—playing golf, sitting behind the wheel of a boat, laughing with friends—and in the center, a larger shot where they stood arm in arm, him with a grin that stretched the full width of his face, her holding a bouquet of flowers. Their wedding day.

His temples already had a tinge of silver, and a fan of laugh lines cornered the edge of her eyes. It was a second marriage, but they'd never seemed old to one another. They'd laughed and loved the same as all newlyweds. He'd called her beautiful and teased her for worrying over a few extra pounds. She in turn had promised to love him even after his hair had turned white as snow. That was 25 years ago, but she remembered it as if it were yesterday.

Their love had remained steady and strong for all those years, in good times and bad. It had withstood the onslaught of Tommy's anger and the heartbreak of him taking away their only granddaughter. Ida shook her head sorrowfully.

"Such a waste," she murmured. "Such a terrible, terrible, waste."

Turning away from the poster, she moved into the clubroom and was quickly surrounded by friends and neighbors.

"You know we're here for you," Agnes Shapiro said. "Whatever you need…"

Wally Hawthorne echoed the thought, adding that he'd be coming over to mow the lawn, then asked if Tommy knew that his dad passed away.

"I doubt it," Ida replied. "Bill hadn't seen or heard from Tommy since Darla Jean's christening. We never knew where he'd gone or how to get in touch with him."

Wally wrinkled his brow. "Damn shame. Bill took good care of that boy after Maggie died. Tommy had no cause to turn his back on his daddy the way he did."

He wasn't saying anything Ida hadn't thought a thousand times over, but today it was too painful to allow those memories to take hold of her. She thanked Wally for his thoughtfulness, then turned and started across the room.

Ida was the cause of Tommy leaving, but never, not once, had William blamed her. In fact, when she suggested they stop seeing one another, he'd refused to even consider the thought. Tommy is acting like a spoiled child, he'd said. He doesn't understand how painful loneliness can be. Give him time, and he'll see this is a good thing. As time had proven, it was a good thing, but Tommy never did come around. Not long after their wedding was announced, he left town with his wife and baby.

With Bill now gone, remembering how he clung to the thought that Darla Jean would one day find her way home was more painful than ever. Ida could feel her heart pushing up against her chest and the echo of Bill's voice in her head. Her steps slowed, and she came to a stop. Regardless of what her daddy thinks, he'd said, there will come a day when she'll want to know her family, and she'll come back here looking for us.

Ida was lost in thought when Lynn Olsson took hold of her arm.

"There you are," Lynn said and wrapped Ida in a warm hug. "Marsha Lambert is planning to start a Tuesday afternoon bridge game, and I suggested it might be just the thing to get you out of the house. I know how much you miss Bill, but you can't just sit around and do…"

As Lynn rambled on they were joined by several others offering help or advice on how to manage, but standing there in the midst of all those well-meaning friends, Ida felt as alone as she could possibly be. She didn't want to join a bridge club, attend a library luncheon, or be part of a crochet club. She wanted what she'd lost—a family.

❦

The young woman stood at the door for a moment, looked around, then stepped inside the crowded clubroom. She was more visible than most because of what she was wearing: a flowered sundress. It was not only the dress. She also stood a head taller than the other women in the room and had a child with her, a girl dressed in shorts and a yellow tee shirt. Most of Bill's friends were businessmen or senior citizens.

From the corner of her eye, Ida saw the woman sit the girl in a chair, bend down, and speak to her. The child nodded, and the woman turned and started across the room. She walked with a deliberate stride, not stopping to chat as she made her way through the gathering.

Ida continued to watch for a few moments, then caught the woman's eye and smiled. There was a slight flicker of hesitation; then the woman ducked her head and smiled back.

She was a scant arm's length away when Ida realized who she was. Her hand shot out and grabbed the stranger's arm as she passed by.

"Darla Jean," she said in a whispery thin voice. "Your granddaddy knew you'd come."

Suzanna winced and stood there with her eyes wide and her cheeks growing crimson.

"I'm sorry, truly sorry. I didn't mean to intrude. We've been traveling and—"

"Intrude?" Ida smiled. "Darla Jean, you're not an intrusion, you're the answer to a prayer." She pulled Suzanna into an embrace from which there was no escape.

Before there was time to explain the mistake, Ida waved to the group of friends standing nearby and called them to come and meet Darla Jean, Bill's granddaughter. Moments later, they were surrounded by people chattering about how Suzanna was obviously gifted with her granddaddy's fair skin and blue eyes.

"Height too," one man said, and the woman beside him nodded.

As the crowd closed in on Suzanna, beads of perspiration rose on her forehead and the flush on her cheeks began to spread. She fanned her hand in front of her face.

"I'm feeling a bit warm," she said. "Perhaps I should step outside for a breath of air."

"You're right," Herb Meltzer replied. "It is warm in here; I'll have them crank up the AC."

Suzanna's expression was that of a trapped rabbit, but with Ida having a firm grip on her arm she was unable to break free. She gave a stiff smile, nodded politely, then craned her neck to see if Annie was still sitting in the chair where she was told to wait. Seven-year-olds were notoriously unreliable, and anything could happen in a room full of strangers.

"After all these years…" Ida stood looking up at Suzanna's face. "Here you are, all grown up, nearly as tall as your granddaddy, and pretty as a picture. Why, the last time we saw you, you were a red-faced swaddling baby." Her eyes grew misty. "When Tommy left town, I thought for sure we'd never see you again."

"I'm sorry, but I really don't understand—"

"Well, of course you don't, you were just a baby. There's no way you could remember. It was a terrible time…" She went on to tell of how Bill's son couldn't find it in his heart to forgive his daddy for getting married again.

Suzanna nervously shifted her weight from one foot to the other as she kept watch on Annie. Every now and again she nodded or gave a thin smile as Ida spoke of the bitter words that had passed between father and son. When Annie scooted out of the chair and started toward the dessert table, Suzanna finally broke free of Ida's grasp.

"Excuse me, I've got to check on my daughter," she said and hurried off.

Her intention was to grab Annie and head for the door, but Ida was blinded by her happiness and failed to notice. Step by step, she followed along still telling how Bill had continued to believe long after she'd given up hope.

Suzanna grabbed Annie from behind just as she was reaching for the chocolate layer cake.

"I told you to stay put," she hissed.

Trying to wriggle free, Annie wailed, "I'm hungry, Mama. You said I could have cake!"

"Yes, but I told you to wait until—"

Ida moved closer and touched her hand to Suzanna's shoulder.

"I'm normally not the type to butt in," she said apologetically, "but your granddaddy would have my head if he thought I'd let his great-granddaughter go hungry."

Annie stopped trying to get loose and looked at Ida quizzically.

With her smile broadening into a grin, she said, "You don't know me yet, sweetheart, but you're sure enough going to. I'm your Great-Grandma Ida."

"Grandma Ida?"

"Yes indeed," she replied with a laugh. "I'm a Parker, just like you and your mama. We're family. Parkers, all three of us."

Before Suzanna could stop her, Annie asked, "What's a parker?"

Ida chuckled. "Why, that's our surname; the name your mama had before she married your daddy."

Annie turned to Suzanna looking even more confused. "Mama, I don't understand—"

"I'll explain it later," Suzanna cut in. She glared at Annie with an expression that squelched any further bickering.

"Come." Ida motioned to a door at the side of the room. "Let's have lunch where it's quiet, and we can talk."

With a firm grip on Annie's hand, Suzanna followed along as Ida led the way through the crowd and into a cozy back room. In the center there was a round table with four chairs. Sliding a chair back, Ida motioned for Annie to come and sit. She took a bottle of milk from the refrigerator and filled a tumbler.

"Start with this," she said, "and I'll bring you some lunch."

As soon as Ida was out the door, Suzanna turned to Annie.

"Listen up," she said. "We are going to eat lunch and then go. And if this woman calls me Darla Jean, you'd better not question it. You eat, say nothing, then we leave. Got it?"

With a pouty look settling on her face, Annie nodded.

A nod was not enough. Suzanna repeated, "Not a word, do you understand?"

"Okay, Mama, okay. But why—"

Ida came through the door carrying two plates heaped high with meat, potatoes, vegetables, and squares of cornbread. Setting them on the table, she turned to Annie, "After you've eaten your lunch, you can have a nice big piece of that chocolate cake you were eyeing."

Ida poured herself a cup of coffee and sat alongside Suzanna.

"We've got an awful lot of catching up to do," she said wistfully. "I don't suppose your mama or daddy ever told you about what happened?"

Suzanna shook her head. "Not that I can remember."

A weighted sigh rose from Ida's chest as she settled back in the chair.

"It's easy enough to understand why they didn't," she said sadly. "It was a bad time for all of us, and your poor granddaddy had the worst of it…" She continued on telling how Maggie Parker, William's first wife and Darla Jean's true grandmother, was like a sister to her and how after Maggie's passing it seemed only natural she be around to comfort William.

"There was nothing sneaky about it. We were friends, that's all. But Tommy was still living at home, and every time he'd see us together he'd roll his eyes or make some snide comment. I knew the lad was peeved at seeing me in his mama's kitchen, so I suggested maybe it would be better if I stayed away, but Bill wouldn't hear of it. He thought Tommy just needed time. He said, 'Once Tommy gets to know you, he'll love you just the same as I do.'"

For an instant, a flicker of light danced in her eyes and the fan of crow's feet at the outer edges deepened. "Bill was like that, forgiving of everything, but your daddy, well, now he was just the opposite."

As Ida spoke the ridges of sorrow seemed to deepen, but her expression was one of tenderness, made warmer by the glow that comes from loving somebody. Memories of the good and bad times she and William had shared came floating to the surface as she told of how they would sit at the kitchen table drinking coffee and talking about how much they missed Maggie.

"Caroline and your daddy were dating then, and the following year when they got married he moved out. Two years went by and then a few weeks after your christening, Bill told your daddy that we were planning to get married and Tommy just about went crazy. He told Bill that if we did, he'd leave town and never again speak to either of us."

Suzanna gasped. "How awful."

"It surely was. I wanted to call the whole thing off, but Bill wouldn't hear of it." She shook her head and heaved a sorrowful sigh. "Neither Tommy nor Caroline ever spoke to us after that, and two months later they left town with you. Not a single goodbye or any word of where they were going. That was the last we heard…" She hesitated a moment then her face brightened. "Until today, when you walked in."

Annie pushed her empty plate forward. "All done. Can I have cake now?"

"You sure can. Wait here, and I'll get you a nice big piece." Ida disappeared into the clubroom a second time.

She was barely out the door when Suzanna leaned close to Annie and whispered, "After you finish your cake we're leaving, and I don't want to hear any argument about it."

"Why? This is better than the stupid bus station."

"I said no argument."

"But, Mama, she's my grandma."

Before Suzanna could argue the point, Ida returned with two pieces of cake. She handed one to Annie and set the other on the side of the table. "I brought extra in case you'd like a piece."

"Not me," Suzanna said. "I'm stuffed, but I'll join you in a cup of coffee."

The next hour flew by as Ida told how William had searched for Tommy several times.

"Not at first," she said. "Back then he claimed he didn't care if he ever heard from the lad again; said if that's how Tommy wanted it, then it was fine with him. But that was just a lot of bluster and hurt feelings. I could tell how much he missed—"

"Tommy didn't ever try to get in touch with his dad?" Suzanna cut in.

Ida blinked. "You call your dad Tommy?"

Being so wrapped up in Ida's story, Suzanna had obviously forgotten herself. She did a quick turnabout, laughed, and said, "Not really. I guess I called him Tommy because you were; to me he's just Dad."

"How is Tommy and where—"

A young man poked his head in the door. "Sorry to interrupt, Mrs. Parker, but I thought you'd like to know they're starting to clear the tables."

Ida gave a nod, and then he was gone. With a bit of reluctance, she stood and said, "Wait here; I won't be all that long. I just want to say goodbye to my guests."

Suzanna stood also. "No problem. We should be leaving anyway."

"Leaving? You can't leave now, we've barely gotten to know one another."

"I wish it could be longer, but Annie and I are on our way to New Jersey. We just wanted to come by and pay our respects—"

"Why so soon? I'm certain your husband would understand if—"

Without taking time to think about it, Suzanna said, "There is no husband. Annie's father wasn't the marrying kind. We're planning to stay with a friend in New Jersey."

"But surely your friend would understand if you spent a day or two with the grandmother you haven't seen since you were an infant."

Although it was doubtful that Suzanna could say whether it was the sorrowful look on Ida's face or the thought of sleeping on a park bench that brought about her change of mind, she wavered for a moment, then said, "I guess we could stay the night, if you're sure it's no inconvenience."

"Of course it's not. With Bill gone I'm alone in that big old house, and it's terribly lonely. I'd welcome the thought of having someone to talk with."

SUZANNA

Just One Night

As she sat there waiting for Ida's return, Suzanna thought back on their conversation and found herself almost envious of the love Ida had for the deceased William. She had not known such a love since she'd lost her mama, and now, more than ever before, she could feel the vastness of the hole that remained in her heart.

The truth was she wanted to stay just as much as Annie did, but she was afraid of the questions that would arise; questions about the man who was supposed to be her daddy. Tommy. A mean-spirited man who she imagined to be much the same as the daddy she'd grown up with. A man with bottled-up anger and very little love to give.

Thoughts of her father brought back memories of the last time she'd seen him and the terrible row they'd had. By then she was big and round with Annie, so there was no more hiding the pregnancy. He'd railed over what he called her deplorable condition and said she was an embarrassment that he wanted gone from his sight. She'd packed a bag and left, hoping he'd call her back, say his harsh words were a mistake, and ask her to stay. He didn't. Not that night. Not ever. Now almost eight years had gone by, and they'd not spoken to one another.

Suzanna was thinking of how sad it was that Annie had never known her father, her grandfather, or grandmother when the idea came to her. She could substitute her own father for the dreadful Tommy if the need arose.

She would say they were estranged and had not spoken in years. After all, it was only for one night, so what harm could it possibly cause?

By the time Ida said goodbye to reception guests and gathered her things, it was after 6 p.m. when they returned to the house. As they rounded the corner of Homer Street and pulled into the driveway of a huge grey Victorian with white trim and a wrap-around porch, Suzanna gasped. "This is it?"

"Afraid so," Ida replied. "As you can see, it's way too much house for one person."

Suzanna climbed out of the car, then stood looking up at the steep-roofed turret, towering chimneys, and muntined windows.

"It's absolutely beautiful," she said. "How wonderful it must be to live in a place like this."

Ida gave a sorrowful-sounding sigh. "It was, until Bill passed away. But being here alone makes it feel a bit like a mausoleum."

Having grown up in a house that was a handful of nails from falling down, Suzanna couldn't imagine being unhappy in such a grand house.

"You got any kids?" Annie asked.

Ida chuckled. "Afraid not, but if you're looking for a playmate I've got something even better." She slid her key in, twisted the lock, and before the door was fully open, a brown and white spotted dog came charging out. His bark was bigger than his body, and he had a tail that never stopped wagging.

Annie gave a squeal of delight. "Can I play with him?"

"Absolutely. His name is Scout, and he loves to play." She stepped inside and Scout followed. "There's a ball here somewhere…" She glanced around the living room then shrugged. "It might have rolled under the sofa, and Scout's afraid to go under there."

"I'm not. I can get it." Annie dropped down on her knees, lifted the skirt, and peered into the darkness. "Found it!" She scooted herself under the sofa then reappeared with dust bunnies stuck to the front of her shirt.

"Oh dear," Ida said, "I guess my housekeeping leaves a lot to be desired, but with Bill being sick for so long…"

The way her words trailed off made Suzanna wonder if there was something more to the story, something left unsaid. But, she reminded herself, she would be here for one night, so it would be better if there were no questions asked and none answered.

Once Annie was preoccupied with the dog, Ida took Suzanna on a guided tour of the house. As they walked from room to room, she mentioned tiny flaws that to Suzanna seemed invisible: the cracked leather on William's favorite chair, bookshelves in need of painting, and windows that needed washing.

As Ida told of the summer William planted hydrangeas along the front of the house and how he'd fenced in the yard so Scout would have a safe place to run free, Suzanna wondered why anyone would leave a daddy like that. It could only be someone as callous and uncaring as her own father. She'd been right in thinking of them as one and the same person.

Later that evening, with Annie fast asleep in the upstairs bedroom, Suzanna sat across from Ida Parker listening to tales of the granddaddy she never had. She pictured William a tall man with gentle hands and a kind heart and imagined herself part of the family. She could envision him buying her ice cream cones, teaching her to ride a bike, and lifting her onto his broad shoulders. When Ida told of how on her christening day the four of them had stood side by side at the altar as Pastor Henderson repeated the name Darla Jean Parker, the scene became as vivid as a movie unspooling inside her head. By the time she stirred a spoonful of sugar into her second cup of tea, she was all but convinced that, much like her own mama, the mild-mannered Caroline had been bullied and bossed about by a tyrannical husband.

It was almost midnight when she kissed Ida's cheek and said, "Goodnight, Grandma." Throughout the evening she'd told herself it was a game of pretense, something to enjoy for a day or two before moving on, but she'd turned a blind eye to the truth.

Earlier that afternoon there had been a moment when it was still possible for her to have explained the misconception, but she didn't. The thought was there, the words on the very tip of her tongue, but she pushed them back. She'd seen the grin on Annie's face and figured, what harm could it do?

That night as she snuggled beneath a quilt stitched with roses and lavender ribbons, a tiny voice at the back of her mind warned that she was opening the door to trouble.

The real Darla Jean could show up at any time, the voice said. Then what?

She won't, Suzanna reasoned. Tommy's family had been gone 25 years. There was no earthly reason why any of them would come back now.

Really? the voice argued.

Pushing aside the troublesome thoughts, Suzanna hushed the voice then turned on her side and closed her eyes. Tomorrow morning they'd be gone, and that would be the end of that. It was not something she had to worry about.

As she drifted on the edge of sleep, the voice again whispered, Really?

EARL FAGAN

Sun Grove, Florida

With the house quiet as it was and the raging headache that came from mixing beer and whiskey, Earl didn't hear the front door click shut when Suzanna left. In fact, he didn't even stir until almost 1 p.m. that afternoon. When he finally did open one eye, he saw the empty bourbon bottle on the nightstand and started to remember the events of the previous night.

"Crap," he groaned and rolled onto his other side.

This was going to be a bad day; he was certain of it. The best he could hope for was Suzanna giving him the cold shoulder, maybe go a day or two without speaking, but that was unlikely. Not after last night.

He cringed, remembering how he'd come home with a buzz on, fell over the end table, and sent the lamp crashing to the floor. There he was, face down in the middle of all that broken glass, but instead of showing some concern for him she started yelling about the damn lamp. One word led to another, and that's when she called him a hopeless drunk.

"I don't know what I ever saw in you," she said. "You're way worse than my daddy!"

Earl knew he should have ignored her and gone to bed, except he didn't. Her saying that bothered him; it was the kind of thing that got under his skin and made him feel like he'd slept in a bed of poison oak. He could already feel the blisters rising up. Instead of walking away like he should have, he gave her a taste of what she'd given him.

"Seems to me a girl who's knocked up don't have a whole lot of choices."

The worst of it was, he didn't stop there. When she came back at him with a smart-ass answer, he smacked her upside the head. Smacked, not punched. There was a red mark on her cheek, that was it. But as luck would have it, Annie saw it happen. She'd been standing in the doorway for less than a minute, but it happened to be that minute. As soon as he yelled at her for being out of bed, she hightailed it back to her room.

The kid seeing the fight is what sent Suzanna over the edge. Thinking back on it, Earl regretted the slap; he should have let her have her say, then walked off. But with Suzanna it wasn't that easy. Once a fight got going, she didn't back down. She kept right on screaming; first it was about the lamp, then she went off on this tangent about how a child can't un-see something they've already seen.

"I don't want my daughter to grow up believing it's okay for some asshole drunk to slap her around! She deserves better than what I got!"

It wasn't like he didn't try to smooth things over; he did. He even offered to buy a new lamp, something nicer than the piece of junk they had, but that wasn't good enough.

"I don't want a new lamp," she screamed. "I want a new life."

"Screw you!" he said. "You want a new life? Then go find Annie's daddy and see if he's willing to give it to you!"

Maybe he shouldn't have said what he did, but at that point he'd had enough.

Things got a whole lot uglier after that. This morning, with his head feeling like it was ready to split open, he was in no mood for rehashing the whole stinking mess. Hopefully she wouldn't drag it out for another two days.

Earl pulled himself up to a sitting position, then grunted and shook his head. Days like this, it seemed like getting out of bed was hardly worth the effort.

"Suzanna," he hollered, "bring me a cup of coffee."

No answer. That meant he was getting the silent treatment. Better than the alternative.

Tromping through the house in his underwear, he called out again. Still no answer. He expected to find her sulking in the kitchen or in the back yard with her nose in a book to prove she was ignoring him, but she was in neither of those places. He checked the laundry room, then Annie's room, but she was nowhere to be found.

With a grumble of annoyance, he turned back to the kitchen for a cup of coffee. Suzanna made a full pot every morning; she drank one cup and left the rest for him. Except this morning the pot was empty. Not just empty, but washed clean as if it had never been used.

"What the hell…" For few seconds Earl stood there letting it register. Then he slammed the empty pot back down on the counter and grumbled, "Nice, Suzanna, real nice. Watch what being spiteful gets you!"

Desperately in need of coffee, he returned to the bedroom, pulled on his jeans, then got in the car and headed for Angie's Luncheonette.

Still feeling the pinch of Suzanna's spitefulness, he ordered coffee and a sweet roll then sat there fuming. He was determined Suzanna would get payback for this morning's stunt but was not yet sure how he'd go about it. One thing was certain: this time he was not going to apologize for what happened last night.

After downing four cups of coffee and two cinnamon rolls, he was ready to take on the day. He stood and asked, "What do I owe you, Angie?"

"Seventy-five cents."

Earl liked Angie; he especially liked the way she'd lean across the counter giving him a look-see at her boobs as she poured the coffee. She was a woman who knew how to get on the good side of a man, and that was something he appreciated. Reaching into his pocket for the folded bills, he figured he'd slap a dollar down on the counter and tell her to keep the change but the money he'd had last night was gone. Not in the right pocket, nor the left. He fished through the back pockets; nothing. There was a bit of loose change in the right front pocket, but the bills were gone.

A single thought crossed his mind: Suzanna. Was it possible she'd pull a stunt as stupid as this? She'd never done it before, but then she'd never deliberately left the coffee pot empty either. The more he thought about the possibility of her taking the money, the angrier he got.

Trying to hide the anger rising up inside of him, he forced a smile and said, "Angie baby, looks like I went off without any money. Okay if I catch up next time?"

She sashayed over and leaned across the counter. "And if I'm willing to wait until next time, what's in it for me?"

Most days he would have answered such a provocative question with an equally suggestive answer but not today.

"A fat tip," he said, then disappeared through the door.

Earl went home, searched the house looking for the missing money or a clue as to where Suzanna had gone, but he came up dry on both counts. As far as he could tell, nothing else was missing, so where could she have gone with a seven-year-old kid and only eighteen bucks in her pocket?

The thought of her doing this as revenge for him being a little short-tempered settled into his brain and sizzled like an egg on a hot griddle. He had half a mind to toss her crap out onto the front lawn and let it get soaked by the evening rain. By now she probably knew what a stupid mistake she'd made, and it would serve her right to find those sopping wet clothes and have to haul them back into the house. If she didn't come back until tomorrow, all the better. By then the hot sun would bake the mud into her dresses, and they'd be ruined.

She'd be back, he had no doubt of that; if not today, then tomorrow or the next day. When the money gave out, she'd come dragging her sorry ass home. She'd have to; there was nowhere else to go. Her daddy had said goodbye and good riddance before Annie was born, and her friends, if you could call them friends, were neighbors who'd think twice about getting involved in a family spat.

Earl glanced at the clock: 3 p.m. He had to be at the bowling alley by four. With the thought of seeing her clothes scattered across the lawn still sizzling in his brain, he begrudgingly pulled his Beer n' Bowl manager's shirt from the closet and got dressed. As he stood in front of the mirror and slicked back his hair, he vowed to get even, to pay Suzanna back for the aggravation she'd caused him.

"Nobody crosses Earl Fagan and gets away with it," he grumbled then snatched his keys from atop the dresser and headed for the car.

That night when the bowling alley closed, he stopped at Maloney's for a few drinks, just as he always did. But this night he drank almost twice as much and stayed until they closed the place. As he stumbled toward the door, Maloney said he was in no condition to drive and offered to give him a lift home.

"Don't bodder." A bit of spittle shot from Earl's mouth, and the words were so slurred they were barely understandable.

With a grunt of disgust, Maloney shook his head then took Earl by the arm and hauled him off.

"No bother," he said. "It's on my way."

When they pulled into Earl's drive, Maloney eyed the house. Pitch black, no porch light, no lamp in the window, nothing.

"Seems Suzanna got tired of waiting up and went to bed."

That thought made Earl angrier than ever. "When I get hold of her, she'll get more than tired. She'll get her face bashed in!"

"Hold on now, don't go saying something you don't mean—"

Earl shouldered the car door, pushed it open, and started to climb out. Hesitating long enough for a glance back, he said, "I ain't just bullshittin'. She deserves it."

A look of concern flitted across Maloney's face. "That's jackass talk."

He climbed out of the car, circled around, and again took Earl by the arm. "Let's get you to bed before you get your fool self into trouble."

Built like a bull, Maloney hoisted Earl up the steps and into the house. When Earl started toward the bedroom, Maloney grabbed him and shoved him into the recliner.

"Stay there, and don't go bothering Suzanna when she's asleep."

"Asleep?" Earl guffawed. "She ain't asleep, she's gone. Stole money outta my pocket and took off."

"That doesn't sound like Suzanna—"

Earl cut in, saying he'd woke up that same morning to find both her and his money missing. He told of how he'd searched the house and found nothing. No clue as to where she'd gone and no note explaining why she'd leave. He didn't mention the row they'd had the night before, nor did he say that it wasn't the first time he'd whacked her across the face.

Lowering himself onto the sofa opposite Earl, Maloney shook his head sympathetically. "I'm surprised at Suzanna doing such a thing. She seemed like a nice woman, a good mama."

"She's good enough to the kid," Earl grumbled, "but when it comes to me, that's a whole other story."

With someone willing to listen, Earl went on and on telling of Suzanna's faults until smack in the middle of a sentence, he dozed off.

That was just moments after he'd told Maloney he was all but certain she'd come crawling back.

SUZANNA

The Next Morning

Suzanna never intended to stay more than just one night. It was fun pretending to be Ida's granddaughter, and sleeping in a comfy bed was far better than a wooden bench at the bus station, but when morning came her first thought was to leave before anyone discovered she was not who they thought her to be. She climbed from the bed, pulled on the dress she'd worn yesterday, and hurried across to the room where Annie had slept.

She expected to find her still curled beneath the blanket with her thumb in her mouth, but the bed was empty. Not just empty, but made, with the corners of the coverlet tucked neatly in place and the pillows plumped. A feeling of dread took hold of Suzanna's heart. There was no telling what Annie would say. Hurrying down the staircase, she called for her.

Before the answer came, she heard the trill of childish laughter coming from the kitchen. Rounding the corner, she saw them sitting side by side, their heads together and both of them grinning as if they'd shared the most delicious secret.

"Annie," she said nervously, "are you pestering Mrs. Parker when she's got a dozen other things to do?"

Annie giggled. "Mama, you're not 'posed to call Grandma Mrs. Parker."

Ida looked up. "I hope you don't mind that I told her to call me Grandma."

Trying to push back the edginess that made her voice sound high-pitched and panicky, Suzanna gave a lighthearted laugh. "No. No, of course not. Why would I mind? I just hope she hasn't made a pest of herself. Annie can talk your ear off if given half a chance."

"Not at all, she's a delight. She's been telling me how you stopped a trucker on the road and caught a ride." Ida chuckled as she stood and pulled a mug from the cupboard. "You've got your granddaddy's spunk, that's for sure. When Bill wanted to get something done, he rolled up his sleeves and did it. Nothing wishy-washy about that man. Your daddy, well, now, he's another story."

Ida shook her head as if remembering something, then set the mug on the table, filled it with coffee, and motioned for Suzanna to sit. "Breakfast is ready. We've got blueberry pancakes and country ham, but if you'd rather I can fix bacon and eggs."

A bit unnerved by Annie's chattiness, Suzanna hesitated a moment. She glanced at the clock on the wall: 8:30. Enough time for a quick breakfast, and they could still make the 10:30 bus.

"Pancakes would be perfect."

She slid into the chair across from where Annie was sitting. Ida was every bit as pleasant as she'd been last night, so apparently the tale of them hitchhiking had not aroused any new suspicions. Feeling a bit of relief, Suzanna sipped her coffee and eased back into the role of being Darla Jean. They were halfway through breakfast when Annie dropped a bombshell.

"Guess what, Mama? Grandma has pictures from when you was a baby."

Suzanna tried to smile, but it felt as though she were about to choke on the chunk of pancake she'd just swallowed. Beads of nervous perspiration rose on her forehead, and now, more than ever, she felt the need to get going.

"Wonderful," she squeaked. The word was thready and too high pitched. "I'd love to stay and see them, but we've got to be leaving in a few minutes."

The smile on Ida's face vanished. "I thought you'd at least spend a few days with me…"

She hesitated, her eyes grew misty, and when she spoke again the lighthearted sound of happiness Suzanna had heard earlier was gone.

"You and Annie are all the family I've got now. It's terribly lonely here without Bill, and this house is so full of memories…"

Annie scooted her chair closer, her small hand patting Ida's knee. "It's okay, Grandma, we're here." Glancing up at Suzanna with her face pinched into a look of determination, she said, "We don't really gotta go, Mama. You said—"

Fearful of what might come out, Suzanna jumped in. "I know what I said, Annie, but there's only one New Jersey bus and it leaves at 10:30."

"But I don't wanna go to New Jersey. I wanna stay here."

Annie was a child who could often be coaxed into doing one thing or another, but once she'd set her mind to something she could also be stubborn as a mule. Given the pinched-up pout stuck to her face, Suzanna knew she was in for a fight.

"Annie, we've already discussed this. You know I have to start looking for a job and…"

"I don't care. I wanna stay here with Grandma. She said I can have my own room and she's gonna let me—"

Ida interrupted. "I have a suggestion that might help. Instead of looking for a job right away, why don't you stay here and work for me? This house is way too big for one person, and without Bill's pension I can't afford to keep it. I'm going to put it on the market, but it would be foolish to do so right now. First, it has to be cleaned top to bottom. The windows washed, the closets emptied out, the clutter packed away, the hydrangeas cut back…"

Suzanna smiled as Ida continued listing the multitude of things that needed to be done in the house she'd seen as perfect.

"That's a very tempting offer," she finally said. "But I wouldn't feel right taking money from you. Besides, Annie and I need to get settled, find a place of our own—"

"Wouldn't that be a lot easier if you had some extra money in your pocket?"

"I guess so, but I still wouldn't feel comfortable taking—"

"Do it, Mama, please do it. Please, please!"

Suzanna looked across at the two them, the same expression of hopefulness on both faces, the same pleading looks in their eyes. It seemed unfair, the burden of such a decision being placed on her shoulders, and yet there it was. She wanted this every bit as much as either of them did. When she weighed staying or leaving against one another, the happiness of staying was light as a feather, while the thought of leaving had the weight of a boulder. Her resolve began to fade.

"I really think we should be going..." she said, but her words were weak and without much determination.

"Just for a few days," Ida pleaded. "To help with the heavy work. That bus runs every day. You could take it tomorrow or the next day or the day after that."

Annie's lower lip began to quiver, and her eyes grew teary. "I don't wanna go. I wanna stay here and make cookies with Grandma."

Suzanna felt her heart crumbling. "Please, Annie, don't make this harder than it is."

"It's not hard, Mama, all you have to do is say yes."

All you have to do is say yes. Suzanna turned her head and stared out the kitchen window as her thoughts raced back to eight years earlier when Bobby Doherty asked for the same thing. She'd finally said yes, then ended up pregnant and alone. Instead of going off to college, she'd been thrown out of her daddy's house and had to move in with Earl.

Saying yes had been a costly mistake back then, and if the truth were discovered it could be even more costly now. She not only had herself to think about; she had Annie. Saying yes had taken away her future, but it had given her Annie, a gift more precious than anything she'd ever owned. A single yes could take or give, but there was no way of knowing which it would be. Should she chance it again, or be smarter this time and move on?

Turning back, Suzanna saw the two eager faces waiting expectantly.

"We can stay for a few days," she said, "but then we have got to go."

◯◦◦◦◯

That same afternoon, Suzanna returned to the bus station and retrieved the battered brown suitcase. Ida had suggested she take the car, but Suzanna chose to walk. It was fourteen blocks from Ida's house to the station, just far enough to give her time to think.

She mulled over the potential problems of them staying, and the one that stood head and shoulders above all else was the very real possibility that Darla Jean could return at any time. Then what? Could she be arrested for impersonating the girl? Thrown into jail? And what about Annie? Would she be taken away and plunked down in some obscure orphanage? Without a daddy, that's what would happen. If the truth were exposed,

Annie would lose the grandma she had taken to so quickly, and she would be on her own.

Suzanna knew there was no getting around it; she was Annie's only family. Walking past the rows of tidy houses with freshly-mowed lawns and manicured flowerbeds, Suzanna pictured the shock on Ida's face as she stood watching them take her away in handcuffs.

Were it not for that one gigantic fear, she would remain here forever. She would gladly become Darla Jean and cast aside the miserable existence that had been her life. She would work her fingers to the bone, cleaning, scrubbing, running errands, doing whatever Ida needed done. She would do almost anything to have a grandmother like Ida, but the one thing she would not do was risk losing her child. Annie was her life, her reason for living. Her only reason for living. Regardless of what she had to do, what she had to sacrifice or give up, Suzanna was going to see that Annie had a better shot at life than she'd had.

On the walk home, she decided to work like a fiend for the next two days, get the house in tip-top shape for Ida, and then move on. To make the leaving easier, she'd tell Ida that she would write and be back for visits. She'd promise to come for Christmas, but once gone she would have to stay gone forever. Annie would be angry with her for doing it, but she would be safe, and hopefully with time thoughts of Grandma Ida would be little more than a pleasant memory.

Suzanna felt the weight of that decision settle on her shoulders like a lead cape. It wasn't what she wanted to do. It was what she had to do.

IDA

Finding Family

Once Darla Jean agreed to stay for a few days, Ida breathed a sigh of relief. Having her here at the house had changed things. The gloom that lurked in the corners of every room seemed to be disappearing; the house was suddenly brighter, happier even. The patter of Scout scrabbling up and down the stairs behind Annie reminded Ida of how it used to be. Before the cancer, before nurses came and went at all hours of the day and night, stepping softly in rubber-soled shoes, taking away hope and leaving behind bottles of pills. Back then, the house reeked of sorrow and antiseptics. The odor remained even after Bill was gone.

Then this morning Ida had opened the kitchen window and for the first time in over a month caught the musky smell of the wisteria in the back yard.

She saw that as a sign, a sure sign Bill was watching over her, telling her the time for mourning had passed, giving her the family she'd wished for. In those last few weeks, when he'd been too feeble to stand, she'd sat beside him and they'd talked for hours on end. That's when he'd told her he would always be there.

"Even after I'm gone from this earth," he'd said, "I'll still be watching over you." Afterward, he'd closed his eyes. Ida thought him asleep until a raspy breath rattled through his chest and he added, "Both you and Darla Jean."

Now he was giving her the gift he treasured most: his granddaughter.

How else could something like this happen? It was no coincidence that after 25 years Darla Jean had showed up to say goodbye to a granddaddy she'd never even known. If something like that wasn't a sign, then Ida didn't know what was.

When Annie convinced her mama to stay a few days, Ida knew this was the one opportunity she'd have. Darla Jean clearly wasn't her daddy. She wasn't anything like him. After thinking about it, Ida had come to the conclusion that Tommy had been as callous with his daughter as he'd been with his daddy, because Darla Jean wouldn't even talk about him. That in itself said a lot about her. A girl who wouldn't run down her mean-ass daddy had to have a forgiving heart.

Ida had two, maybe three days to show her granddaughter what being a family meant, and she sure as the devil wasn't going to waste that time cleaning.

Just moments after Darla Jean left to retrieve her luggage from the bus station, Ida pulled out a picture album that had been in the family for years; one that had been passed down from Bill's mama, the leather cover worn at the edges and loose pages tied together with a narrow blue ribbon. She brushed a thin layer of dust from the top and called for Annie.

"Would you like to see pictures of your mama when she was a baby?"

"Can Scout see too?"

"Of course he can. Climb up here beside me on the sofa, and we'll look through this album together."

"What's an album?"

"It's a book with family pictures that go way, way back. Some of these were taken when your great-granddaddy was a teeny-tiny baby."

Annie grinned and scooted a bit closer. "Has it got pictures when Scout was a baby?"

"There are some pictures of Scout, but I'm not sure how old he was at the time."

Having Annie curled up against her made Ida's heart feel warm, like the sun appearing from behind the clouds after a year of rain. She untied the ribbon and opened the album to the first page. It was filled with sepia-colored prints of dour-faced ladies in long dresses.

Annie pointed to a photo in the center of the page. "Who's that?"

"I believe that's your great-granddaddy's mama when she was a young girl. Some of these pictures have names and dates written on the back of them, would you like to see?"

When Annie nodded, Ida eased the photo from the corner mounts that held it in place. "Looks like I was right. See, it says right here, Lucinda Graves."

"How come she wasn't a Parker like you and me?"

"She was a Parker after she married your great-great granddaddy. Graves was her maiden name, the name she had before she and George Parker got married."

Looking a bit puzzled, Annie asked, "Do people have to change their name when they get married?"

Ida gave a chuckle and nodded. "That's how it works. When a girl baby is born, she's given her mama and daddy's surname. Then when she gets married, she switches over to using her husband's surname." With Annie still looking as puzzled as ever, Ida continued. "Take your mama for instance; she's a Parker right now because that's the name she was given at birth, but if she falls in love and gets married, then she'll use her new husband's name."

Annie looked up, her forehead wrinkled and the corners of her mouth drooping. "If Mama gets married, I won't be a Parker anymore?"

Ida left the album in her lap and turned, gathering Annie into her arms. "You're a Parker now, and you'll always be." She smiled and touched a finger to Annie's chest. "Being a Parker starts here, inside your heart, and it stays there for as long as you want it to."

Annie's lips curled into a smile. "I'm gonna stay it forever, 'cause I like being a Parker."

They went back to looking at the pictures in the album, and as Ida explained the relationship of this aunt or that cousin a thought settled in her mind. She was never going to lose touch with Darla Jean again. Never. She would try to get her to remain here in Cousins, but if that failed she would sell the house lock, stock, and barrel, and follow them to New Jersey. They were family, and what Bill couldn't do in his lifetime he'd done afterward. He'd brought Darla Jean back home where she belonged.

That afternoon, Ida went through the album twice. She explained the Parker ties to distant cousins, long-dead aunts and uncles, and showed pictures of Bill from the day he was christened up until the year he'd been diagnosed with cancer. That year they'd stopped taking pictures, and the joy of life disappeared from the house.

When Suzanna returned, Ida and Annie were still sitting on the sofa with Scout squeezed between them and piles of photos scattered about.

"Mama, look!" Annie grabbed a picture and waved it in the air. "This is when you was a tiny baby!"

A look of apprehension flitted across Suzanna's face. "How nice." She set the battered suitcase beside the staircase, then crossed the room and peered over Ida's shoulder.

"This was taken on the day of your christening." Pointing to the face of each member of the group, she said, "This is your grandpa, and that's me standing next to him. Your mama's the one holding you, and this here's your daddy, on the end."

The picture was a grainy black-and-white snapshot, taken from too far away to see the faces clearly, so Suzanna squatted to get a better look.

"Daddy looks mad in this picture, almost like…"

"He was always like that," Ida said cynically. "Mad at the world, griping about one thing or another."

Annie grabbed another photo. "This is great-granddaddy when he was little as me!"

Suzanna leaned in, squinting to see the faded photo.

Ida turned and looked up. "You shouldn't be squatting down like that, it will give you bad knees. Come around here and sit next to me." She scooted closer to Annie then patted the empty spot on the sofa.

"I thought maybe I ought to get busy with the cleaning. You said there was a lot—"

"There is, but it's nothing that won't keep until tomorrow."

"Still, the sooner I get started, the sooner I'll finish and—"

"Darla Jean, don't you start acting like your daddy. Life is too short to always be thinking about what has to be done. Relax. Take time to enjoy every minute, because once that minute's gone, it's gone forever."

Such a thought apparently weakened Suzanna's determination to get the job started. She came from behind the sofa and sat beside Ida.

One by one they turned the pages of the photograph album, with Ida telling stories of thrice-removed cousins, great aunts, and generations that were long gone before she arrived.

"Your granddaddy used to claim his mama said her great-great Uncle Harold was rumored to have come over on the Mayflower."

"Really?"

Ida nodded. She pointed to a photograph so faded Suzanna could barely see the figure standing in front of a cornfield. "This here was his boy, Fredrick. He never married and never had any children. Supposedly his sister, Helen, did, but I don't have any pictures of her."

"Are you still in touch with anyone in that family?"

"Heavens, no. There're gone. Every last one of them. As far as I know, Tommy was the last of the line. That's why Bill was so devastated when the boy left without a word about where he was going. It was a terrible thing to do."

With a flat-faced expression that gave away nothing, Suzanna nodded her agreement.

For a long moment Ida sat there looking at that photograph as if there was more to the story; then she gave a sorrowful sounding sigh and turned the page.

Annie tugged at her sleeve. "Are you sad, Grandma?"

Ida smiled, wrapped her arm around the tiny shoulders, and gave Annie a squeeze. "No, I'm not. I used to be sad about not having any family, but now that I've got you and your mama, I'm not sad anymore."

By the time they finished going through the albums and photographs, it was almost suppertime, and then after supper Ida said it was far too late to start cleaning now. Besides, it was Wednesday, which she insisted had the best lineup on television.

Once the dishes were washed, dried and put away, the three of them settled on the sofa to watch The Price is Right. Without a word passing between them, Ida patted her lap and Annie climbed up onto it. That's how they spent the evening. Annie fell asleep shortly after the Kraft Music Hall came on, but Ida never moved. She just sat there tracing her fingers along Annie's shoulder and cheek.

Later on, after everyone had gone to bed, when the house was silent and the only sounds to be heard were a night breeze rustling the trees and the faraway tinkling of a wind chime, Ida lay awake. She thought back on the evening and how good it had felt to have Annie snuggled up against her chest.

"Thank you, Bill," she said, giving her thoughts a whispery soft voice.

"You know how lonely I've been without you." She hesitated a moment and rubbed her fingers across the wedding ring she still wore. He'd placed that ring on her finger the day they were married and she could still feel the love in it, especially late at night, when she spoke to him as she did now.

"Bill, no one will ever take your place in my heart, you know that, but having Darla Jean with me eases the pain of losing you. I wish you could have known her, honey; she's everything you thought she'd be. Good-natured, sweet, not at all like Tommy. And, oh, how she loves that little girl of hers. Annie. You'd be very proud of them both, Bill, I know you would. I'm pretty certain it took a lot of doing to bring them here, but now I'm going to need your help with something else."

SUZANNA

Oh, Suzanna, Tell Another Lie

The next morning Suzanna woke early and as she was stepping into a pair of worn denim shorts, she caught the sound of Annie's laughter coming from downstairs. When she arrived in the kitchen, Ida had a platter of bacon and eggs on the table.

"I thought I'd skip breakfast and get an early start," Suzanna said apologetically.

"Skip breakfast? Good gracious, Darla Jean, that's the most important meal of the day." Ida pulled a tray of biscuits from the oven and started plunking them into a basket. "A person can't possibly do a proper job on an empty stomach; it's like trying to get a car to go without gas."

"Well, I guess I could take time for a quick bite."

"There's no hurry; sit down and relax." Ida filled a mug with coffee and handed it to Suzanna. "Rushing through meals is what gives people indigestion. I know, because your granddaddy suffered with it for years. Every time I saw him, he was chewing on one of those antacid tablets. Finally, I laid down the law and told him there'd be no more hurrying dinner, and in no time at all he stopped needing those tablets."

Suzanna pulled a chair out and sat. "I've not been bothered with indigestion."

"That's because you're still young. But start scarfing down meals now, and sooner or later it will catch up with you." Ida set the biscuits on the table, then lowered herself into the chair next to Annie.

"Grandma, are we still gonna make cookies this afternoon?" she asked.

"Yes, dear, but first we'll clean out the closet in your mama's room so she'll have a place for her clothes."

"Don't bother about me," Suzanna said. "I didn't bring that much."

"Didn't you say you had luggage?"

"Just the suitcase I brought back from the bus station."

"Oh. Well, then, we can start in Annie's room. That used to be my sewing room, and the closet is stuffed full of remnants, buttons, bits of trim…"

As Ida rambled on about how she once loved to sew but had gotten away from it over the last few years, Suzanna noticed the way she named things. Annie's room, Darla Jean's closet, the bed in your mama's room. It had such a sound of permanence that she had to remind herself they were leaving in two days, three at the most.

Knowing those few days would fly by all too quickly, Suzanna tried to hurry things along but it was impossible. Following the bacon and eggs, Ida downed several cups of coffee and then insisted Suzanna try a biscuit with her homemade peach jam. With one thing and another, it was after ten when they finally trudged upstairs and began digging through the closet. Before a single shelf had been cleared, Ida began rummaging through a box of scraps, suggesting they were the perfect size for making some doll dresses.

Turning to Annie, she said, "You have a doll, don't you?"

Annie shook her head. "Un-uh, just Bobo."

"Bobo's a dog. I mean a doll that's like a baby or a little girl."

Annie shook her head again.

Squatted down inside the closet, Suzanna pulled a paper bag filled with buttons from the back of the bottom shelf. "Do you have a box for buttons?"

Ignoring Suzanna, Ida focused on Annie. "No doll at all? None?"

"Earl said I'm too big for dolls."

"Earl? Who's Earl?"

Hearing the name, Suzanna cringed. She backed out of the closet and glared at Annie.

"Earl's the reason we left Florida," she said. "I moved in with him after my daddy—"

Hit with the realization that as Darla Jean her daddy was supposed to be William's son Tommy, she stopped smack in the middle of the sentence, buried her face in her hands, and turned away.

"I'm sorry. So sorry. I just can't…"

Her voice was thick and wobbly, filled with the weight of tears that threatened to break free. Without turning to face Ida, she said, "We can't stay here, we've got to—"

Before Suzanna could finish, Ida pulled her into a hug. "You're not going anywhere. Don't you think I already know how terrible Tommy was? He turned his back on his own daddy, and I'll bet he did the same to you. He was as mean a man as ever lived."

"No, you don't understand—"

"I understand more than you might think. But what's done is done. Over with. History. We're never going to talk about this Earl or your daddy again. Not ever. Not you. Not me. As far as I'm concerned, the past is dead and buried."

"But there's more, I'm not—"

"Hush. There's nothing else to talk about. Leave it be. The important thing is that you're here now, and that's all that counts."

Feeling the warmth of Ida's arms, Suzanna knew she wanted to stay. She wanted it for Annie and for herself. It had been years since she'd put her head on someone's shoulder and allowed the tears to come, but she did it now. Shamelessly, the way she'd done when her mama was still alive. As they stood there, one woman comforting another, no words were necessary. The only sound was the soft snuffle of her sobs.

Annie waited for a while then cautiously asked, "Why is Mama crying?"

Ida looked down with a smile. "Because she's happy that you're both going to be staying here with me for a good long time."

"I'm happy too, but I'm not crying."

"Only grown-ups cry when they're happy."

Ida laughed, then Suzanna pushed back the last of her tears and laughed with her.

⚜

That night when Suzanna tucked Annie into bed, she sat beside her and told the biggest lie of her life. A lie she swore was truth.

"You really are Annie Parker," she said. "Duff was Earl's name, and he wanted us to use it while we were living with him."

"But, Mama, he never called you Darla Jean, how come?"

Suzanna forced a thin splintery laugh. "You know how I sometimes call you nicknames like Pumpkin or Sweet Potato?"

Annie nodded.

"Well, Suzanna was Earl's nickname for me."

Making up the story as she went along, Suzanna told of an old guitar Earl had long before Annie was born.

"He didn't know how to play a lot of songs, but he knew this one called Oh Susanna, so he used to play it all the time and sing along. He said I was his Suzanna."

"I never heard—"

"It was before you were born. He sold that guitar when you were just a baby, so you couldn't possibly remember. And now that we're not living with Earl anymore, you're big enough to understand the truth, so I thought you should know."

"Can you sing it for me, Mama?"

Suzanna leaned over, kissed Annie's cheek, and tucked the lightweight blanket around her shoulders. "Okay, just this one time, but then like Grandma said, you're never to talk of it again. Now that we're here I'm going back to using Darla Jean, my real name, and you are Annie Parker, period. No questions asked. Nothing more to discuss. Get it?"

Annie gave a sleepy nod. "Sing the song, Mama."

Before Suzanna finished the first verse, Annie was fast asleep.

That night Suzanna tossed and turned for hours, thinking of how she'd lied to her own child, lied about the very truth of who she was. As despicable as that might be, there'd been no alternative. If she and Annie were to live a life of lies, then Suzanna alone had to carry the burden of guilt.

Annie could never know of it. She would grow up believing she was a true Parker. She would be free to both give and take Ida's love. She could walk tall and be proud of who she was, and that above all else was what Suzanna wanted for her daughter.

A sliver of light was edging its way onto the horizon when Suzanna finally climbed from the bed and knelt beside it.

"Please, God," she prayed. "Let me do this one thing for my daughter. Up until now, Annie's life has been filled with anger and resentment and I have stood aside, unable to make a change. Lord, let me no longer be powerless. Let me give her a grandmother to love and a life unlike the one I knew. I ask nothing for myself, Lord, only that You allow me to do this one thing for my child."

SUZANNA

Becoming Darla Jean

Days turned into weeks, and they never finished cleaning out a single closet. Suzanna pruned the hydrangeas, cut the grass, and painted the back porch while Ida sat at the sewing machine making dresses for Annie's new doll.

At first, Suzanna lived in constant fear of being discovered. She jumped when the telephone rang, peeked from behind the curtains before answering a knock on the door, and looked over her shoulder as she moved through the aisles of Piggly Wiggly. When the fear swelled to the size of a melon and felt as though it would cause her chest to split open, she went in search of something that needed to be done. In time that busyness pushed the fear back. Although it remained a part of her, it ceased to be the whole of who she was.

The change was something she neither saw nor felt. As the days grew longer and the evenings warmer, little pieces of Suzanna began to disappear and were replaced by pieces of Darla Jean. Since there was little to go by, she crafted the image as she went. Hours were spent browsing through the old family album, lingering over the photos of Tommy and Caroline, searching for similarities between them and her parents.

With her daddy, it was the slicked-back hair and the sneer, the right edge of his lip hiked up as if he were about to lay into someone. But Caroline was far more difficult; she had the soft blond curls Suzanna remembered her own mama having, but it had been over fifteen years and the memory of her mama's features had faded. Sometimes she could find the edge of a smile or the sound of her laughter, but that was it. Without realizing it, Suzanna had begun to remake herself into the woman who was Caroline's daughter.

Mornings when they sat at the breakfast table, Ida would tell of the grandfather Suzanna had never known, of how he so often spoke of her, wondering where she was and if she was happy. On a day that was drizzling rain and not well-suited for sitting on the porch or running errands, they stayed at the kitchen table sipping a third cup of coffee.

"Did you know that you're your granddaddy's namesake?" Ida asked.

Suzanna shook her head. "I don't see how."

"Bill's middle name was Gene, spelled with a G, not a J." Ida hesitated a moment, gave a soulful sigh, then added, "It was one of the few nice things Tommy did for his daddy; that was before he found out we were planning to be married."

She went on to tell of how, early on, William had plans to build a playhouse in the back yard and buy a canopied bed so that as soon as his Darling Jean was out of the crib, she'd have her own room at the house.

"Darling Jean, that's what he called you, and every time he did it Tommy got madder than a wet hen. By then he'd grown quite testy with his daddy; if it wasn't one thing, then it was another. Bill had a million lovable qualities, but Tommy apparently didn't inherit a single one of them. Such a shame. If he'd have been more like his daddy, we would have all had a happier life."

Hearing that, Suzanna felt Darla Jean's anger rise up.

"Isn't that the God's honest truth!" she said, echoing Ida's regret.

She never tired of listening to Ida's stories, and it seemed Ida never tired of telling them. Later that day when she told of how William had dearly loved her Bananas Foster, Suzanna suggested they make a batch right then and there.

"Granddaddy would have loved this," she said, sensing the presence of her legendary grandfather as she set the dishes on the table.

Afterward, as they sat licking the last of the buttery rum sauce from their spoons, Ida looked across at Suzanna and Annie.

"This was a wonderful idea," she said and smiled. "Having you girls here is like having a piece of your granddaddy to hold onto."

With each story, each hug, each shared cup of coffee, Suzanna grew fonder of Ida. Late at night, when the house was quiet and everyone else asleep, she would lie awake, reliving the stories of that day, imagining herself growing up in that house, loved and respected, the kind of girl Bobby Doherty would have married. The kind of girl who would never in a thousand years have moved in with a man like Earl Fagan.

In those few short months, a new kind of happiness crept into the house. Rooms that had been darkened for nearly a year suddenly had the windows flung open and were flooded with sunlight, and the stillness that followed William's death was replaced by the sound of barks and giggles as Annie and Scout ran from room to room. Suzanna began singing as she went about her tasks, and instead of fretting about the closets that needed to be emptied out or the baseboard that needed repairs Ida sewed doll clothes. She also made Annie a gingham apron with her initial appliqued on the pocket.

"Now you can help me make cookies," she said, and that's what they did.

Working side by side, the two of them mixed, measured, and baked a fresh batch of cookies every day. At first Suzanna thought such an overabundance of sweets would spoil Annie's appetite, but it never happened. At suppertime, she cleaned her plate. Before long her bony little arms and legs grew plumper, and her cheeks took on a rosy glow.

That summer as Annie ran barefoot across the back yard, ducking in and out of the sprinklers and chasing after Scout, Suzanna sat in the lounge chair listening to Ida's stories and feeling happier than she could have ever imagined possible.

In the first week of September, after Ida set a pot of yellow chrysanthemums on the front porch and a handful of leaves had begun changing color, Annie asked if she could take Scout for his evening walk.

"That would lovely," Ida said, "but put your shoes on first so your feet don't get scraped on the cement."

Annie wrinkled her nose. "Do I have to? They hurt."

"What hurts? Your shoes?"

Annie nodded. "They squish my toes, see?" She pointed to a red spot on her big toe.

Ida laughed. "Well, seeing as how you've grown, I'd say it's time for some new shoes. You'll need them before school starts."

At the mention of school, Suzanna felt a twinge of apprehension slither down her spine, but before she had time to give it much consideration Ida suggested they get Annie registered the next morning.

"We'll stop by the school then drive over to Main Street to shop. She could use a few new dresses and some sturdy shoes." Raising her hand with the palm facing Suzanna, she warned, "Before you say anything, I want you to know this is my treat. A grandmother is entitled to spoil her great-granddaughter if she wants."

Suzanna started to protest, but her heart wasn't in it. She was picturing the birth certificate still stuffed in the side pocket of the suitcase: "Annie Duff" written in the scrawled hand of Dr. Melrose. Duff. She'd hoped to never see the name again, but she'd forgotten about the birth certificate.

Early on, when she was still Suzanna, she'd plotted and schemed, sweeping away any last remaining traces of the name Duff. She'd made Annie a Parker, merged Tommy and her daddy into the same ill-tempered person, and etched the word "grandma" on the inside of her heart, but she'd neglected this one thing.

Now, Suzanna couldn't dismiss the thought of what was to come. No matter how hard she tried to ignore the problem, her thoughts kept jumping back to that first day when Ida told Annie, We're Parkers, all three of us. Family. But Annie wasn't a Parker, and neither was she.

Not a Parker.

Not even a Parker whose name had been changed by marriage. She was a fraud, a phony, a con artist about to be found out. Before she tucked Annie into bed, the happiness she'd felt for weeks was gone. Her heart was heavy as a sack of stones and devoid of hope.

That night Suzanna pulled her suitcase from beneath the bed and took out Annie's birth certificate, hoping against hope that the ink was blurred or the paper too worn to be legible, but neither was true. Sitting at the tiny desk in her room, she held the paper one way and then the other, squinting at it, trying to see if there wasn't some way the name Duff could be mistaken for Parker. Minutes ticked by and as she came to realize the impossibility of it, her eyes filled and streams of tears began to roll down her cheeks. The future she'd tried so hard to believe in was one she had no right to. Tomorrow it would be gone. Vanished, just like all the other hopes and dreams she'd nurtured. Just like Bobby Doherty. She would be forced to leave here, and Annie would suffer the shame of her lies.

A single tear plopped onto the birth certificate, and Suzanna grabbed a tissue to blot it away. As she did so, the first F in Duff smudged; it was just the tiniest bit, barely noticeable, but enough to brighten her hopes. Searching through the desk, she found two blue ink ballpoint pens and one black one, similar to the one Dr. Melrose had used when he wrote Annie's name on the birth certificate.

The clock ticked off one hour, then two, then three as she sat there trying to replicate his handwriting, heavy in some areas, lighter in others, letters not fully formed and sliding into one another. She practiced writing Annie Duff over and over again, until she at last had it perfect, then she added a tail onto the back of the D making it appear to be a P. Holding the paper out and scrutinizing it, she felt reasonably satisfied. Moving on, she closed the top of the u and made it look more like a small a, then she moistened the tip of her finger and ever so gently smudged the bottom half of the first f so that it was less readable. After adding a leg to the second f to make it appear more like a k, she finalized the process by sliding an illegible er onto the end of what had been Duff. She repeated this process fourteen times on the scratch pad, then when she deemed it almost believable, she made the same changes to Annie's birth certificate.

In the blank space where there'd been no father's name, she wrote "Earl Duff." If the worst that could happen happened and they challenged the forgery, she would say Dr. Melrose had mistakenly given Annie Earl's last name and then tried to correct it. If they refused to accept the altered birth certificate, Suzanna had no idea what she would do. Leaving here, the thing she'd once thought imminent, now seemed unthinkable.

The pale pink of morning was lighting the sky when she finally crawled into bed.

A short while later, when she sat down at the breakfast table, Ida looked over and asked, "Are you feeling okay?"

Knowing her eyes were rimmed with red, Suzanna gave a weary nod. "I'm just tired. Last night I had trouble falling asleep." In a last-ditch effort to stave off the inevitable, she said, "Perhaps we should hold off on going to register Annie for school. We could do it next—"

"You don't have to come. Go back to bed and get some rest. I can handle this myself."

The thought of Ida trying to defend the forged birth certificate was worse than if she herself had to do it.

"No," she replied glumly. "This is something I need to do myself."

With Suzanna dragging her heels as if she were walking the last mile, it was late morning before they arrived at the school. She suggested it might be faster if Ida waited in the car, but of course, Ida would not hear of it, so the three of them went in together.

The registrar's table was set up in the central hall and in front of it a waiting line.

"Perhaps we should come back later," Suzanna suggested.

Obviously overhearing her words, the woman in front of her turned. "The line moves pretty quickly." A flicker of recognition flitted across her face, then she smiled and said, "Ida? Ida Parker, right?"

Ida nodded and returned the smile. "And you're…"

"Margaret Boden. The Saint Agnus choir, remember?"

"Good gracious, it's been years!" Looking down at the little redheaded girl, Ida asked, "Is this your granddaughter?"

Smiling proudly, Margaret nodded then introduced Becky to the group. "And is this pretty little sweetheart your granddaughter?"

Ida chuckled. "Her mama's my granddaughter; Annie's my great-granddaughter." She went on to introduce Darla Jean, and a full-blown conversation ensued. Moments later they were joined by another mom who said she was still singing in the choir.

By the time they reached the registrar's table, the group of women were crowded together and chattering like a group of magpies. Their laughter grew louder, and the hallway was soon filled with the echo of their voices. When Suzanna finally stepped to the table, she wrote Annie Parker on the registration and listed Ida's address. But with the commotion going on behind her and her nerves already frayed, her writing was almost illegible.

"Do you have a birth certificate?" the volunteer at the registration table asked.

Suzanna nodded, pulled the folded paper from her pocket, and handed it to the woman.

The volunteer checked the date on the birth certificate. Just as she was moving her finger across to where Suzanna had altered the name, a howl came from the back of the line.

"She bit me!" a childish voice wailed.

The volunteer's head snapped up, and she stood to see what was going on.

"Quiet down back there!" she yelled. "I will not stand for such behavior when—"

She was interrupted by an irate mother. "Speed it up, Esther! The kids are getting impatient. They want to get out of here."

Several others joined in, voicing complaints. Standing there with a steely-eyed glare, Esther insisted that unless the crowd quieted down, they would be here all day. When the complaints finally ceased, Esther returned to her seat.

By then Suzanna had snatched the birth certificate and folded it back into her pocket. As she turned to walk away, the flustered Esther called out, "Wait, I need to verify her last name."

Almost in unison, the three women who had been chatting answered, "Parker! She's Ida's great-granddaughter."

With a look of irritation still stuck to her face, the registration clerk gave a nod then waved the next person forward.

As Suzanna hurried from the building, Ida had to hustle to keep up with her.

That afternoon as they strolled along Main Street browsing in one shop and then the other, Suzanna began to believe that for the first time in her life this was something she could hold on to. She and Annie would stay here forever. Next week, after Annie started school, she'd look for a job and find herself a small apartment, not far off in New Jersey, but right here in Cousins, Georgia. This was where they'd build a new life, and Ida Parker would be their prestigious family tree.

EARL

No More Waiting

For almost five months Earl Fagan clung to the belief that Suzanna would return. It seemed a reasonable enough assumption since she'd left most of her clothes hanging in the closet, a bunch of crap in the bathroom, and Annie's tricycle on the back porch.

He didn't care a bean about Annie, because the kid was a nuisance, but Suzanna, that was a different story. He'd fallen for her the first time he'd seen her behind the register at the Snack Shop, her belly rounded out and her breasts twice the size they were now. He'd suspected there was a chance she could be pregnant, but she didn't say anything about it so neither did he.

They got friendly and went out half a dozen times—movies, dinner at the Chinese place, an afternoon at the county fair—then she told him. It was a spur-of-the-moment thing that he hadn't expected. He'd gone into the Snack Shop figuring to get a Ring Ding and a Coca-Cola and there she was, standing at the counter, red-eyed and teary.

"What's wrong?" he asked, and she burst out bawling.

That's when she told him a boy from school had gotten her pregnant then and would soon be going off to college.

"And as if that's not enough," she sobbed, "Daddy said he can't live with the sight of my big belly anymore, and I've got to get out of his house."

"So, do it. Leave. Move out."

Suzanna grabbed a napkin from the counter, blew her nose, then tossed it in the trash can.

"Oh, just like that, move out?" she repeated. "And where I am supposed to go?"

"I got a house off Shady Creek Road. You can come stay with me."

With the cynicism still crackling through her words, she said, "Yeah, sure. And I'm supposed to believe you ain't looking for something in return?"

"I'm not," Earl said indignantly. "I got an extra room I ain't using. You can have it for as long as need be."

Two days later Suzanna moved in with him. She slept in the spare room for the first three months, then a month after Annie was born, she painted the room pink, turned it into a nursery, and started sleeping in Earl's bed.

As far as Earl was concerned, it was good back then. Annie was small enough that she slept most of the time, and Earl had what he'd wanted all along: Suzanna. Their problems didn't start until the kid was about three; that's when Suzanna began harping on him about drinking and cussing.

"How's Annie supposed to grow up respectable when she sees you acting like this?"

She didn't say it just once, she said it over a thousand times. The same thing, again and again, like a stuck record.

When Earl had had enough, he laid into her, punched a hole in the wall, and walked out. From then on he did most of his drinking at Maloney's, but even that wasn't good enough.

Suzanna was always on his back about something. The arguments turned violent and began to happen more frequently. Usually they ended with him passing out or her saying she was going to leave and take Annie with her, but as far as he was concerned those were nothing but empty threats. The truth was she had nowhere to go, no job, and no money. A number of times he'd laughed in her face when she said it, but back then he never dreamed she'd actually follow through.

Now, after five months, he was genuinely worried. Suzanna could be irresponsible about a number of things but never about Annie. Earl believed that if she were coming back, she'd have done so in time to register Annie for school.

Sticking to that thought, he'd tidied up the house, gotten rid of the beer cans and whiskey bottles, and cut back on the drinking. For almost two weeks he'd been painfully close to sober, but now school had started and there was still no sign of Suzanna.

The second week of September he got caught behind a school bus, and as he sat there watching kids scramble on and off thoughts of Suzanna overwhelmed him. That was the day he broke down and cried. He called the bowling alley, said he was too sick to come to work, then bought a half-gallon of whiskey, went home, and drank himself into a stupor.

Three days later, he decided that he was going to find Suzanna and bring her home. He'd do whatever he had to do to keep her. If it meant giving up drinking, he'd do it. If it meant getting married, he was willing to do that too. Despite the never-ending arguments and having to put up with her kid, his life with Suzanna was a lot better than life without her.

Without much to go on finding her was not going to be easy, but Earl believed anything was possible if you set your mind to it. He started by going through the things she'd left at the house; he was looking for a name, address, or telephone number. After two days of emptying out every drawer in the house, checking the pockets of her jeans and jackets, and paging through her books, he tried asking neighbors along the road. He showed the picture he carried in his wallet and asked if they'd seen Suzanna coming or going.

Most shook their head and answered no, but the Widow Hawkins gave a nod and said she'd seen Suzanna at the library.

"That was some time ago," she added. "Not recently."

Figuring this might turn into a lead, Earl dredged up a tear, then with a great deal of display brushed it back.

"Sorry to be so emotional," he said, "but she took my little girl, and I'm trying to find the child."

Widow Hawkins raised an eyebrow. "If you're the girl's daddy, you've got every right to know where she's at!"

"True as that may be," Earl said morosely, "I haven't been able to find her."

"Suzanna's daddy used to work with my Chester; far as I know he still lives over on River Road. Have you checked with him?"

Earl shook his head. "I doubt she'd go back there. They parted on pretty bad terms to hear her tell of it."

A look of doubt tugged at Widow Hawkins' face. "Family's family. A spat's not nearly enough to stop a girl from going home to her daddy."

Earl thought about it for a second, then grinned. "You just might be right."

With a look indicating she was pretty pleased with her own suggestion, she added, "His place is way down on the eastern end of River. T. P. Duff it says on the mailbox."

That same afternoon, Earl drove across town and went in search of the mailbox with T. P. Duff stenciled on it. Three times he drove past the dilapidated two-story house before he caught sight of the faded name on the mailbox. He pulled into the rutted drive that led to a garage behind the house, parked the car, and got out.

After he rang the doorbell three times, he heard the shuffle of footsteps inside. He waited a minute and, when no one opened the door, rang the bell for a fourth time.

"Knock it off!" yelled a voice from inside.

Leaning toward the door so he'd be heard, Earl hollered, "I'm looking for Mr. Duff!"

Seconds later, the door jerked open. With his hair smashed to one side like he might have been sleeping, the man eyed Earl suspiciously. "I'm Tom Duff; what business you got with me?"

"I'm looking for your daughter—"

"I got no daughter."

As Duff stepped back and tried to close the door, Earl stuck out his foot and stopped it. "I'm talking about Suzanna; she's your daughter, ain't she?"

"No more she's not."

Trying to sound sympathetic, Earl said, "Look, man, I understand the crap she gave you; it was the same with me. But I still gotta find her."

"Why? She owe you money?"

"Some, but that ain't it. Look, I got a bottle of Jack Daniels in the car; how's about I get it, then you and me can have a drink and maybe hash this thing out?"

Duff wavered a moment then said, "Get the bottle if you want, but if this is about Suzanna thinking she's gonna come back home, you're wasting your time."

"Don't worry; it's nothing like that."

Earl scampered back to the car, reached under the seat, grabbed the bottle, and followed Duff into the house. They sat at the kitchen table across from one another and spent the afternoon downing one drink after another.

For the most part, Duff had no answers to give Earl. He apparently hadn't seen or heard from Suzanna since she walked out eight years earlier.

"What about friends?" Earl asked. "She have anybody she was close to? Girlfriends she might've gotten in touch with later on?"

"A few girls used to come around once in a while. Can't say I remember their names."

"What about the guy she was going out with, he ever come around?"

"All the time, but I ain't remembering his name neither. He was in her class, a big deal football player. For sure I'd recognize his name if I heard it. Maybe if you had a picture—"

The mention of a picture gave Earl an idea. "What about a yearbook? Suzanna graduated that year, didn't she? Did she get one of those yearbooks with all the pictures in—"

Duff was already shaking his head. "She was two months from graduation when she left here big as a house. I can't say if she ever graduated or got one of them yearbooks. Damn shame. You raise a kid up for eighteen years, you got a right to expect…" His voice trailed off as he poured himself another drink.

"Did Suzanna leave anything behind? Stuff she maybe stored in the attic?"

"Nothing's stored. A few weeks after she left I figured she wasn't coming back, so I gathered up her stuff and set it out with the trash."

"Too bad." Earl sat there for a minute then came up with another idea. "I might be able to get one of them books. Say I do, you reckon you could pick out the kid Suzanna used to go out with? The one who's Annie's daddy?"

"Annie, huh? That's what she named the kid?"

Earl nodded. "The girl's seven years old and supposed to be in school, but Suzanna took off. Now, I'm thinking maybe she's back with that guy. The one who's Annie's daddy. So if you could point him out, then…"

"I could pick him out all right," Duff said, "but you're wasting your time. He ain't gonna help none with the kid. Way back when, he told Suzanna he'd get her money enough if she wanted to get rid of it, but if she had that baby she was on her own."

He drained the glass. "The boy ain't the one to blame. He was looking to make something of his self before he got tied down with a family. Suzanna, she's the one. She wouldn't listen to reason. She wanted the baby, and that's all there was to it."

Segueing into a tale of how his daughter's life could have been different, he continued on, but by then Earl was no longer listening. He was thinking about how he could get his hands on a yearbook and wondering if Suzanna had indeed left him to be with the kid who was Annie's daddy.

He could still remember how she'd cried hysterically when that kid left for college. She'd shed all those tears over the football player but not a single one for him. Earl was the one who'd taken her in, given her a home, provided for her and the kid all these years, and this was the thanks he got? Her leaving without so much as a goodbye? He deserved better. Yeah, they argued from time to time, and he probably said some things he shouldn't have, but that was no reason for her to run off. They could've talked it over, worked it out.

As he thought back to that last fight, Earl could hear himself telling her that if she wanted a new life, she should find Annie's daddy and have him give it to her. She must've known he didn't mean it. She'd driven him nuts with her harping, and he was pissed off. You piss a man off, he's bound to say things he don't mean. That ain't cause enough for leaving.

If Suzanna thought she could just take off and give Mr. Football a chance to play the daddy card now that he was done with college, she had another think coming. Earl wasn't going to stand still for it. He'd been the one who was there when she needed somebody, and he wasn't about to step aside now.

He'd never really wanted kids, but he'd put up with Annie for Suzanna's sake. Mr. Football wasn't willing to do it, but Earl was. If Suzanna couldn't see that was the true measure of love, then he'd have to find a way to open her eyes and make certain she saw it.

Whatever he had to do, he'd do it. He was not going to lose out to Mr. Football. No way. No how.

SUZANNA

The Decision

Once Annie was successfully registered for school, Suzanna found moments when she could almost believe they actually were Parkers. No one—not the shopkeepers, not the doctor who gave Annie her vaccination, not even the school registrar—raised an eyebrow when Ida Parker said Annie was her great-granddaughter. True, there was always a chance Darla Jean would show up, but it had been 25 years since her family moved away. The likelihood of her returning now seemed so remote that Suzanna could sometimes push it to the back of her mind and pretend it didn't exist.

With each passing day, the pieces of Darla Jean that had settled inside of her grew stronger. She began thinking of William not only as Ida's deceased husband but as the kind-hearted granddaddy who'd waited for her return. She'd see Annie chasing Scout across the backyard or traipsing up and down the wide staircase and picture what her Darla Jean childhood would have been like. Instead of living with a daddy who could barely tolerate the sight of her, she should have been here, sleeping in the canopied bed Granddaddy had promised.

For the first time in years, Suzanna felt happy about who she was. It was the same sense of contentment that came with being Bobby Doherty's girl, the feeling of being a person who was well-liked and respected. She no longer saw herself as simply a survivor; she was now a respectable mom and treasured granddaughter. Like a snake, she'd shed her skin and been born anew. The tarnished reputation that dogged her steps for years had been left behind in Sun Grove and was all but forgotten.

That September, Annie started school. For two weeks, she'd been chattering away about how excited she was, but when the morning finally arrived she was strangely quiet. She turned her nose up at Ida's banana pancakes and claimed her stomach was hurting.

"Maybe it's just butterflies about starting school," Suzanna suggested.

"It's not," Annie said. Then she sat there looking glum and staring down at the uneaten pancakes until it was almost time to leave.

Before they left the house, Suzanna pinned a note inside Annie's sweater. "This is Grandma Ida's address and telephone number so if there is any kind an emergency—which I'm sure there won't be—you can ask a grown-up to call here."

With a look of concern tugging at the corners of her mouth, she asked, "Does this paper say I'm Annie Parker?"

"Of course, it does. I told you—"

"Does it say Darla Jean is my mama?"

"Yes, it does. Remember I told you only Earl called me Suzanna, but the truth—"

With that worried look still stuck to her face, she said, "I know, Mama. I know."

Hand in hand they walked the five blocks to the school, and once the building came into sight Annie's steps slowed significantly. Again she complained her tummy hurt.

"I think I'm too sick to go to school."

"You're not sick. You're just feeling anxious because this is something you've never done before. You'll be fine. It's a chance to meet new friends and have lots of fun."

Annie looked up, her eyes glistening with the threat of tears. "Mama, will you still be here when I come out of school?"

Suzanna squatted down and pulled Annie into her arms. "Of course, I will. I'm your mama. I'll always be here for you. Forever and ev—"

"But what if Earl comes and says you should be Suzanna again?"

Annie's fear wrapped itself around Suzanna's heart and squeezed it so tight she could barely breathe.

"I'll never be Suzanna again, and I'll never, ever leave you, Annie. I'm your mama, and that's more important than being Suzanna or Darla Jean or anything else in the world. I will always, always, always be here for you. I swear I will."

"Is a swear the same as a promise?"

"It's better than a promise. You can't ever take back something you swear you'll do."

A barely perceptible smile curled Annie's lips as they walked down the corridor to the classroom. At the door, Suzanna kissed her daughter's cheek and turned to leave.

"Don't forget you sweared," Annie called after her.

Suzanna turned, smiled, then mouthed the words, I won't forget.

By the time she left the building, Suzanna was no longer smiling. She was thinking back on the fear she'd seen in her child's face. It was not just imagined, it was real. Annie was afraid she'd be abandoned, forgotten, left behind as Earl had been. Suzanna thought leaving would prove a woman could strike out on her own, make it alone, not depend on anybody. But apparently Annie saw it differently. She was frightened that she too could be abandoned.

The weight of that thought settled in Suzanna's chest like a stone, and her steps slowed. Inching one foot in front of the other as she moved along, she thought back to how she'd had that very same fear when her mama was taken away to the hospital. For months on end, she'd barely slept. At night, she'd listened for the sound of the door closing or her daddy's car pulling out of the drive. When the long afternoons stretched into evening, she'd wander from room to room, checking that her mama's dresses were still hanging in the closet and her daddy's ashtray on the table beside his chair. Night after night, she went to bed worrying that the next morning would be the one when she'd wake and find the ashtray gone or the closets emptied out.

Annie deserved better than that.

She was still a child; a child who needed the security of a loving family and a home to call her own. That was something she'd not had with Earl. Suzanna thought about it for a moment and could not recall even one time when he'd lifted Annie into his arms and told her how very special she was.

As she thought back on those turbulent years, tears filled Suzanna's eyes. Although she'd loved Annie from the moment she'd first felt movement inside her belly, she'd not shown it as a mother should. Moving in with Earl was a mistake. She'd done it not for Annie but because it made life easier for her.

Her second mistake was not offering Bobby Doherty the chance to know the beautiful child they'd created together. Back then she'd reasoned that he didn't care about Annie, but the truth was that her pride prevented her from asking. Was living this lie, pretending to be Darla Jean, going to be her third mistake? Was she doing it for herself, or this time was she doing it for Annie?

Suzanna thought back to that first night when she'd stayed at Ida's because it was a convenience, a cozy bed instead of a park bench. Something that made life easier for her; it was the same reason she'd moved in with Earl. That thought churned in her stomach until the bitterness of it rose into her throat and remained there.

She stopped, stood for several minutes then turned and walked back toward the school. A single question circled through her mind over and over again. What was better for Annie? To stay meant forever living with the risk of exposure. To leave meant losing the grandma Annie had already come to love.

When she reached the school, she glanced down at her watch: 9:15.

She could go in, get her daughter, and make it to the bus station in time to catch the 10:30 Greyhound to New Jersey. Annie's class wouldn't be dismissed until noon; by then it would be too late. She was the child's mama; she could claim a family emergency and say her daughter was needed at home. She hesitated a moment and thought about Annie's reaction.

But, Mama, you said we really are Parkers, so why do we have to leave Grandma?

Suzanna sat on a bench opposite the school playground and tried to think it through. It seemed as if there were two voices battling inside her head. One asked, Why put yourself at risk? The other argued, For once in your life, do what's right for Annie.

Had all those years of living with her father made her like him? Selfish, thinking only of himself; was she really any different? She'd hated him for not being what a parent should be. Was she destined to make the same mistake?

The sun climbed higher in the sky, and the minutes ticked by as the voices argued first one side and then the other. Then a single thought settled in her mind. To admit the lie meant forever losing Annie's trust. Knowing that was a truth she couldn't change, she made a decision.

She would be Darla Jean; not simply pretend but force herself to believe it right down to the core of her being. She would think like Darla Jean, act like Darla Jean, and be the kind of mother Darla Jean would have been. It wasn't enough to simply love Annie; she had to protect her and to do that she had to give her soul over to becoming Darla Jean. As of this day, Suzanna Duff would cease to exist. The memory of whatever came before would be wiped away. There would be no more Bobby Doherty, no more Earl, no more memories of her father. Annie would be first and foremost in every decision she made. She had made any number of mistakes in her life, but this time she would get it right. Annie would never live the life she'd lived; she would see to it. Annie would now and forever be Darla Jean's daughter.

And if the day ever came when Suzanna's identity was challenged, she would stand bare-faced and swear it was what she'd always believed.

Moments after she'd made her decision, a bell rang and the double doors of the school swung open. Annie came running out hand in hand with another little girl and broke into a smile when she saw Suzanna waiting. As they headed home, she bubbled over with stories telling of her new best friend and the wonderful time they'd had.

Walking together, the tiny hand held securely in hers, Suzanna prayed that for once in her life she'd made the right decision.

IDA

Opening a Door

Ida sat at the kitchen window picking at the loose thread on her sweater and watching as Darla Jean pushed Annie higher and higher in the swing. The swing was old, the wooden seat splintered in places, but no one had ever thought to take it down, much less replace it. The swing was like the rooms on the third floor, there but not something of concern.

A few months ago she'd been certain of what she wanted, but now she was not at all sure. There had been too many changes in her life, and she questioned whether she was ready for yet another one.

When she'd first come to this house, she and Bill used every room. He read his newspaper in the library, she spent mornings in the sewing room, they'd breakfasted in the alcove, and enjoyed an evening cocktail in the den. The kitchen was filled with the yeasty smell of fresh-baked bread, and there was always company coming or going—out-of-town friends, neighbors stopping by. Why, there were even weekends when they'd push the parlor furniture aside and dance to the tunes of Tony Bennett or Perry Como.

All that stopped when Bill got sick. There was sometimes an evening when he felt up to a cocktail in the den or a few hours of television in the living room, but even that disappeared after a while. He was confined to his bed, and Ida seldom left his side. Other than an occasional trip to the kitchen to warm soup or fix a peanut butter sandwich, she lived in the bedroom. But it was a big house and, with taking care of Bill, more work than she could handle; so, one by one, the other rooms were closed off. After nearly two years of living in just one room, Ida had come to believe she didn't need a house, especially one as big as this. She was actually looking forward to moving into a small apartment. A one-bedroom, perhaps, with an efficiency kitchen.

Now things had changed. Scout and Annie raced across the back yard, up and down the stairs, played hide and seek in the dusty library, and banged in and out of the front door a dozen times a day. Scraps of material and patterns were scattered about in the sewing room, and if Darla Jean should decide to start having gentlemen callers she would need a decent place to entertain them. The more Ida thought about it, the more she realized that selling the house might not be such a good idea after all. Yes, there was the problem of expenses, but if she were extra prudent she'd be able to hang onto it for at least another year or two.

Ida was still waffling about what to do or not do when Suzanna suggested they start readying the house for the market.

"Not this week," Ida said. "We've got too many things to do."

Suzanna looked at her with a raised eyebrow. "What things?"

"Tomorrow is a big sale at the Sew & Sew Shop, and I'm supposed to make cookies for the Thursday children's hour at the library." When Suzanna stood there looking unimpressed, Ida added that she'd also promised to finish the sweater she was knitting for Annie's new doll.

"Surely the doll's sweater can wait," Suzanna said.

"Not really." Reaching into her knitting basket, Ida pulled out a ball of blue yarn and began click-clacking her needles. "A promise is a promise, and I certainly wouldn't want to disappoint Annie."

"I find it hard to believe you're putting this project off just because Annie needs a sweater for her doll. There's something else troubling you."

Ida's needles slowed, and she gave a weighted sigh.

"Perhaps," she mumbled, not looking up.

Suzanna crossed the room, squatted down beside Ida's chair, and gave her hand an affectionate squeeze. "I think I know what's wrong."

Eyeing the well-intentioned expression, Ida asked, "How can you know what's wrong when I'm not all that sure myself?"

"Because I know how much you loved Granddaddy. You're afraid if you sell the house, you'll be leaving all those sweet memories behind and—"

"That's not the only thing troubling me."

"Oh? Well, then, what—"

"I'm beginning to think my selling the house isn't really what Bill wanted."

"But you said—"

"I know what I said," Ida replied crisply. "But things have changed. After Bill passed away, I had only myself to consider. Now I've got a family to think about."

Suzanna's mouth dropped open. "Family? Do you mean Annie and—"

"Of course I do. You're family. Your granddaddy would want you living here in his house. He always said, 'Darla Jean will come back, and when she does, we'll have her room ready and waiting for her.' You know, I've told you that."

"Yes, but you also told me the house was too big and you couldn't afford to—"

"Money problems have a way of working themselves out. Bill always said a person needs to focus on the things that are important and not take chances with something they can't afford to lose."

"Exactly," Suzanna said with an affirmative nod. "So why risk your financial security by holding onto a house that's—"

Ida smiled and shook her head. "Darla Jean, don't you understand that you and Annie are the things I can't afford to lose? We're family, and I know your granddaddy would want us to stay together."

"Selling the house doesn't mean we'll be separated. I plan to find a job right here in town, then get an apartment. Wherever you live, Annie and I will come to visit two or three times a week."

Ida gasped. "Visit? Visiting is for strangers, not family."

At a loss for words, Suzanna sputtered, "I didn't intend…"

Ida reached down and patted her cheek. "I know you mean well, but you and Annie need to stay here. This is where you'll get to know your granddaddy, where you'll discover the heritage he left behind. Darla Jean, your granddaddy may be gone from this earth, but I assure you, his spirit is still right here in this house. As long as we stay, he'll be watching over us."

Suzanna said nothing for several moments. Then she blinked back a tear and looked up at Ida. "I want to stay, truly I do. Living here, I'm happier than I've been in a long time." She hesitated, her lip quivering. "But the truth is you can't afford this house, and I can't allow Annie and me to become a financial burden."

Ida opened her mouth to speak, but Suzanna shook her head. "No, let me finish. You claim Granddaddy would want you to take care of me, but I think he'd also want me to take care of you." She went on to say that she'd stay but only if Ida allowed her to get a job and pay an equal share of the household expenses.

For a long while they went back and forth, speculating on precisely what the late William Parker's intentions would have been. Suzanna argued that sharing expenses made sense since she had planned to get a job anyway and would much prefer paying rent to Ida as opposed to a stranger.

With her arms folded tight across her chest, Ida just sat there shaking her head side to side.

"We're family," she said emphatically. "Family does not pay rent to one another. If you've got extra money, then start saving for Annie's college education."

With both of them apparently wanting the same thing but neither of them giving an inch, it seemed to be a stalemate until Ida finally came up with what she called a suitable solution.

"I'm not in favor of strangers tromping through the house, but I guess it would make sense to open up the third floor and rent out the rooms."

"What third floor?" Suzanna asked.

"The door at the end of the upstairs hallway opens into a staircase. We've got two fair size rooms up there and a small bath."

With the look of disbelief clinging to her face, Suzanna said, "Bedrooms?"

Ida nodded. "Of course they're bedrooms. Bill and I fixed them up thinking your parents would sooner or later be back for a visit, but they never came. So eventually, we just closed the door and forgot about them. I didn't see any sense in cleaning rooms that no one was using."

Still looking a bit stunned, Suzanna agreed it was a good plan.

"As long as I do most of the work getting the rooms ready," she added.

SUZANNA

The Third Floor

The following Monday, Suzanna again suggested they get started on the cleaning project, and this time Ida agreed. After Annie left for school with Lois Corky, who was now her best friend, the two women trudged up the staircase to see what did or didn't need to be done. When they reached the landing, Ida turned right and pushed open the door.

"This room's the largest," she said and flipped the light switch. Nothing happened.

"Hmm. Could be the bulb's burnt out."

Easing past Ida, Suzanna saw shadows of furniture but little else. "We're going to need some light. It's too dark to work in here, and…" She stopped, sneezed three times in quick succession, then finished her sentence. "It smells kind of musty."

"No wonder; this room's been closed up for almost twenty years." Moving gingerly, Ida made her way across the room, pushed the drapes to one side, and raised the shade.

Sunlight flooded the room, a cloud of dust mites swirled through the air, and Suzanna sneezed again. She reached into her pocket for a tissue, then looked up and gasped. Sitting against the far wall was the most amazing bed she'd ever seen.

The ceiling was slanted on that side of the room, and the top arch of the bed rose to the precise point where the wall met the ceiling. It was a dark wood, dulled by layers of dust, but its beauty was still shining through. The crest of the arch was an intricately carved cluster of roses, and beneath that a trailing vine reached out to the far edge of the headboard.

Almost as if the bed were calling to her, Suzanna crossed the room and plopped down atop the flowered spread. A poof of dust rose into the air, and she began sneezing again.

"God bless you," Ida said. "It's that coverlet. We need to get rid of it. It's full of dust and beyond saving."

Tracing her finger along the edge of a flower, Suzanna looked up with a grin. "No, it's not. We can air it out and—"

Ida laughed. "That coverlet's almost as old as I am. I had it before Bill and I were married. And the bed's older still; it belonged to my mama before me.

Suzanna's grin grew broader. This wasn't just any bed; this was a bed with a heritage. A heritage that belonged to Darla Jean Parker. A plan flitted across her mind then doubled back and settled in. Not just now, but before the day was out she would ask Ida about it. No, not Ida. Grandma Ida.

Ida turned back toward the landing. "Let's check the other room. Then we'll strip the beds, take the drapes down, and start cleaning."

She led the way across the short hallway to a second door.

"Now this room's going to need a lot of work," she said, fumbling for the light switch. "Definitely a new bed and fresh wallpaper..." She snapped the switch, and the overhead brightened the room. "This is the room Bill intended for you, but then, well, you know what happened."

Suzanna stood there, her eyes wide and her throat too choked to speak. In the center of the room was the canopy bed Ida had told her about. The organdy covering now drooped on one side, dusty and yellowed with age, but seemed no less beautiful. Her eyes scanned the room trying to take hold of every detail: the ballerina lamp on the nightstand, a partially-finished doll house in the corner, the small rocking chair. The love that had gone into creating this room was obvious. It was still here.

"Your granddaddy built that dollhouse for you." Ida circled the bed and lifted the canopy ruffle back into place. "He started it before your christening and worked on it for a long while, even after Tommy left town. When he didn't hear from Tommy for all that time, he finally realized we were not likely to see you for a good long while. He gave up working on the dollhouse, carried it up here, and set it in the corner. The next time we see

Darla Jean, she might be too old for dolls,' he said. That day he closed the door to the third floor, and I didn't open it again until now." Pausing a moment, she gave a lingering sigh, then added, "Losing you just about broke your granddaddy's heart."

As Ida went on, saying how after so many years she'd forgotten about the dollhouse, Suzanna thought of her own childhood and then of Annie's; both soiled by anger and sadness, nowhere was there a memory to compare to the childhood Darla Jean had left behind. Her eyes filled with tears; then she turned and allowed her head to fall onto Ida's comforting shoulder.

Wrapping her arms around Suzanna, Ida made the shushing sound a mother makes to a fussy baby. When the tears subsided, she held her at arm's length and said, "Your granddaddy wouldn't want you crying your heart out like this. He thought this would be a place of happiness, not tears."

"I know," Suzanna said and started sniffling again.

"Well, then, why on earth are you carrying on this way?"

"Because seeing all this makes me realize how much I missed, how empty my life and Annie's life has been."

"Well, if it makes you that sad, I'll have the junk man come and cart it all away, kit and caboodle. You won't ever have to see it again."

"You can't do that!" Suzanna exclaimed. "We'll give Annie this room; it's what Granddaddy would have wanted."

"Allow a seven-year-old child to sleep up here with a stranger in the next room?"

"We can rent the second-floor bedrooms instead, and I'll take the other room up here. It'll be kind of like being where Granddaddy wanted me to be, and I'll get to sleep in the bed that belonged to your mama."

"Why would you want to do that? The downstairs rooms are much nicer. The furniture's newer. They're bigger and airier."

Suzanna sniffed back the last of her tears. "I know, but there's a part of Granddaddy that's still in this room, and I want Annie to have the chance to know what a wonderful man he was." She hesitated a moment then smiled ever so slightly. "This may sound silly, but that bed and the things in here make me feel as if I can reach out and take hold of the past. It's like I haven't lost anything; it's been right here waiting for me. Being able to live with the things that meant so much to you and Granddaddy kind of makes up for all I missed out on."

Ida's eyes filled with water, but she held back the tears and began bustling around the room gathering the things she claimed needed washing.

That same day they threw the third-floor windows wide open, took the curtains down, and allowed the scent of the wisteria in the back yard to roll through the long-forgotten rooms.

As Suzanna rubbed lemon oil into the curves and crevices of the ornate bed, she allowed her mind to run free with thoughts of Ida as a young woman and, even further back, Ida's mama, a young bride slipping out of her corset and gown and climbing into this bed to begin life as a wife and mother. When the headboard gleamed with a shine that reflected the smile on Suzanna's face, she knew this truly was the beginning of a new life for her and Annie.

She may not have been born Darla Jean Parker, but she now was and she would not allow anything to change that. Nothing. Not the past, present, or future. And certainly not any lingering thoughts of her daddy or Bobby Doherty.

CHANGING TIMES

The Rental

Once Suzanna and Annie were settled in the attic rooms, the two women began readying the second floor for renters. The closets were emptied out, the furniture polished to a shine, and a stack of freshly-laundered towels placed on each dresser.

On Thursday afternoon, with the house now in pristine condition, they sat together at the kitchen table and composed an ad to run in the classified section of The Town Crier. After almost two hours of going back and forth over what was the most appealing description, they discovered the cost of the ad was based on word count and shortened it considerably. In the end, the ad simply offered two large comfortable guest rooms for rent at reasonable rates. Although they eliminated the part about an oak-lined street and charming ambiance, the ad did state that the rooms overlooked a garden and the house was within walking distance of town. At Ida's insistence, it also indicated, "Female Preferred."

"We'll be sharing the hall bath," she'd said, "and a woman can never be too careful, especially with a child in the house."

That Sunday there was only one telephone call, and it was not an inquiry about the rooms. When Suzanna picked up the telephone, Pastor Higgins asked if Ida was ill since he'd missed seeing her at Sunday services. After that there was nothing. Not a single call.

"Weekends might not be the best for rentals," Suzanna suggested. "Perhaps we should try the weekday edition."

Ida agreed, and on Monday morning she telephoned the newspaper and told them to run the ad for the remainder of the week. She also tweaked a few things they thought might help. Instead of reasonable rates, the second ad gave a firm price of $17 a week and added free parking and telephone.

The next three days seemed to linger on forever, and by Thursday, when they had not received even one inquiry, Suzanna began to worry.

"Perhaps we're going at this wrong," she said. "Newcomers might not be reading the newspaper. We need to pin a notice on the bulletin board at Piggly Wiggly and the bus station. Those are places where it's sure to be seen."

Ida frowned. "Piggy Wiggly is okay, but the bus station? Who knows what kind of transients that will bring?"

Looking Ida square in the face, Suzanna raised an eyebrow.

"Annie and I came through that bus station," she said. "Cousins is a relatively small town; there's only a handful of people stopping here anyway. Relatives mostly or someone coming for a job."

When Suzanna reminded Ida that if they didn't rent the rooms it would be difficult to hold onto the house, she finally agreed.

That afternoon Suzanna donned the one sundress she had, took the hand-lettered signs, walked to town, and thumb-tacked them to the bulletin boards. At Piggly Wiggly, she also stopped in to see the manager and asked if they had a position available.

"I'll take anything," she said. "Cashier, packer—"

"Sorry." He shook his head. "There's nothing right now."

"Oh." Disappointment stretched across the full width of her face.

"Maybe in December," he offered. "There's a chance Debbi Hicks, our bakery clerk, might be retiring. If you're still interested, stop back then."

Suzanna promised to do that, then walked out with her feet dragging and her shoulders slumped. As she passed the First Federal Savings building, she thought about applying for a job, but that thought disappeared almost as quickly as it came. She couldn't even get a job at Piggly Wiggly. Without references and a work history, she wouldn't have a prayer at the bank. Even if she'd used her own name, what job experience did she have? Being a clerk at the Snack Shop was not much of a qualification. On top of which, she'd dropped out of high school just weeks before she was to graduate.

Walking home, Suzanna moved one foot in front of the other almost mechanically. At first their plan had seemed perfect, but now things weren't looking quite so good. Finding a renter was more difficult than they'd anticipated, and she was beginning to fear that landing a job would pose an even greater challenge. With the attic rooms now opened up, she no longer wanted to consider the thought of leaving. She wanted to remain in that house as much as Ida did. Moving meant letting go of the memories she'd found tucked into the corners of those third-floor rooms, and worse yet was the thought of Annie not having the canopy bed that Granddaddy had intended for her. She simply couldn't bear that. If they didn't rent the rooms, it would be up to her to find a way to keep the house. Ida was too old to work, and somebody had to be there when Annie came from school.

There was no getting around it; Suzanna had to find a job. Lost in thought, she walked so slowly that at times it seemed as though she had come to a standstill. She was looking down at her feet when an image flashed through her memory. Her daddy, his face drawn into an angry scowl, his arm raised, his finger pointing to the door as he told her to go and stay gone. She'd moved in with Earl because she had nowhere else to go. It was different now. She had a home with someone who loved her. Who loved Annie. After all those years of hardship, she couldn't let this slip away. She had to find a way to make it work. She owed it to herself. Even more importantly, she owed it to Annie.

A renewed sense of determination rose in her, and she quickened her step. She would not be defeated; there were plenty of other jobs. She could clean houses, take tickets at the movies, or find a shop willing to try her as a sales clerk. She'd be bold about it, admit up front that she had no experience then offer to work the first week for free to prove she could do the job. A prospective employer would surely see the value in that.

By the time she arrived home Suzanna was bubbling over with ideas, but Ida nixed them all. With her face set in a stony expression that obviously meant business, she told Suzanna, "You've gotten yourself in a tizzy for no reason. I have absolutely no doubt that we'll find renters for those rooms, and besides, the idea of cleaning people's houses for a living is preposterous. There's no money in that. You're a smart girl with charm and personality…"

She cast a critical eye toward Suzanna's sundress then continued, "You'll find yourself a good job but not dressed like that. You need a proper outfit. A suit maybe or a tailored dress."

"I can't afford—"

With the frown lines deepening across her forehead, Ida replied, "Darla Jean, I didn't say you should buy anything. Next week, the LoCicero Shop is having their annual sale, and I'll be taking you in so that Miss Dixie can outfit you properly."

"But, Grandma, you can't afford—"

"Hush! I do not want to hear another word about what I can or cannot afford. I may not be wealthy, but your grandfather certainly did not leave me destitute. It may be a stretch to keep this big house, but we have more than enough to live comfortably."

Having said her piece, Ida headed back toward the kitchen.

Suzanna followed in her footsteps. "I didn't mean—"

Ida stopped and turned. "I know you didn't, but you've got to stop worrying and trust me." As the anger faded from her face, it was replaced by a sly grin. "I may be up in years, but I've still got all my marbles. While you were gone, I made a few phone calls."

"To who?"

"People who can get the word out about us having rooms for rent. Bill had quite a few friends in town, and those friends were more than happy to help. Bo Cascio, the office manager at the tool and die company, said they've got a new receptionist starting next week, and Delbert Stanfield, the loan officer at First Federal, said an insurance agent just rented a storefront on Clover Street."

As it turned out, Ida learned the receptionist would be living with her sister and the insurance agent was a man with a wife, three boys, and a golden retriever. A third week rolled by without any responses. Then one afternoon when Suzanna was outside planting some impatiens in the back yard, the call came.

The young man said he was Gregg Patterson and that he'd been referred by his sister-in-law who was a friend of Pastor Higgins' wife.

"Christine Davis, the English teacher at Barston Junior High is going on maternity leave, and I'll be filling in for her this semester."

With the sound of disappointment threaded through her words, Ida replied, "The room is better suited for a woman."

It was meant to be discouraging but not absolute. Although she'd not told Darla Jean, she too was getting a bit concerned and wanted to hear him out.

"I'm kind of desperate," Gregg Patterson said. "I start work on Monday and still haven't found a place to stay."

"Isn't there a hotel over there in Barston?"

"Closed for renovations, and the rooming house is full up."

Still apprehensive about having a man in the house, Ida asked, "Did your sister-in-law tell you Cousins is a good twenty miles from Barston, and with rush-hour traffic…"

"Yes, she mentioned that, but as I said, I'm desperate."

Ida then wanted to know exactly who his sister-in-law was, how long she'd known Pastor Higgins' wife, if he had additional references, and whether or not he was a smoker. After he'd answered those questions, she bombarded him with a dozen more. Only after she was satisfied with his answers did she say that he could come and look at the room.

As she hung up the telephone, she wondered if she was making a mistake. The thought of having a strange man in the house with two women and a little girl was not only worrisome but downright exhausting.

Feeling the need to be her sharpest when she interviewed him, Ida decided to take a short nap before he arrived. She was sound asleep at 5:30.

Suzanna came in from the yard with clumps of dirt stuck to her knees and a flower petal caught in her hair. As she was removing her muddy sneakers and garden gloves, she heard the bell but figured Ida would answer. Minutes later a heavy knock sounded. She brushed a few leaves from the front of her tee shirt and hurried to the door, expecting it be a neighbor returning one of Ida's casserole dishes or Lois coming over to play with Annie. Instead, it was a man dressed in a chambray shirt with the sleeves rolled up. He had a nice smile and wore glasses; a cluster of dark curls dropped down on his forehead.

"Hi, I'm Gregg Patterson," he said and stuck out his hand.

She returned his handshake without any mention of her name, then stood looking at him inquisitively.

"We spoke earlier, about renting the room…"

"Oh, you must have spoken to Ida." She caught the mistake and quickly corrected herself. "Grandma Ida, that is." As she leaned in a bit closer, she could see his eyes were the same blue as his shirt. "I'm Darla Jean Parker, her granddaughter. Come on in. Grandma might be napping, but wait here and I'll get her for you."

"Please don't, there's no need to wake her. If you could just show me the room, I'll write a check and leave it with you."

Suzanna gave an apologetic half-smile. "I wouldn't feel right doing that. Grandma was pretty insistent about only renting to a woman. I'm surprised she even said you could come to look at—"

"I know," Gregg said. "She explained the situation and gave me a third degree that would make the FBI proud."

When he grinned, his smile had a certain warmth to it. The kind of warmth that made her wish she was wearing some makeup and wasn't quite so scruffy-looking.

"Please excuse my appearance," she said and returned his smile. "I was planting flowers out back. There's a lovely garden and both rooms overlook it…" As she spoke she reached back, pulled the rubber band off of her ponytail, and shook her hair loose. "A good-size closet and driveway parking if you need it."

"I can park on the street if need be. During the week, I'll be using the car every day to drive back and forth to Barston." He went on to explain that he'd be working at the junior high school as a substitute for the English teacher who was taking a maternity leave.

"Oh, so you'll only be staying for a few months?"

"No, a full year. Mrs. Davis is taking an extended leave. And," he added hesitantly, "I'm kind of hoping something permanent opens up in the meantime. My brother, Philipp, and his wife live in Barston, and since that's all that's left of our family I'd like to settle down somewhere nearby. Phil offered to let me stay with them, but I don't want to intrude on their privacy."

They chatted for a few minutes more. Then Suzanna asked if he'd like to join her in a cup of coffee and wait for Grandma Ida. "I'm sure she'll be down in a few—"

"I'd love to," he cut in and smiled again.

Ida opened one eye and peered at the clock.

"Good grief! It's after six!"

Hurriedly climbing out of the bed, she slipped her shoes on, smoothed her hair, and started downstairs. Halfway down she heard the sound of a man's voice, followed by a peal of laughter coming from the kitchen. When she rounded the dining room and stepped into the kitchen, Annie jumped out of her chair and ran over.

"Grandma! Guess what?" Without allowing Ida time to answer, she spat it out. "Mister Patterson is gonna live with us, and he knows how to make puzzles!"

"Maybe live with you," he said correcting her. "If your grandma is willing to have me."

"Yes," Ida nodded, "and that's yet to be decided."

"I do hope you'll allow me to rent the room, Mrs. Parker," he said. "I'm quiet, clean, and pretty much keep to myself, so I assure you I'll be no bother." He went on to explain that his parents were killed in an automobile accident two years ago, which left only him and his younger brother, Philipp. "Phil and Ginger are expecting a baby in December, and I'd like to be there for them. That's why I left Villanova."

"Villanova University?"

He nodded. "I was an assistant professor at the school of engineering."

With a look of suspicion tugging at her eyebrow, Ida asked, "Why would you leave Pennsylvania and a job like that to be a substitute teacher in a small-town junior high school?"

"Family," he said and smiled. "Like many people, I never really thought about how much those relationships mean. Then I lost my parents, and it was devastating. Without Mom's Sunday dinners and Dad sitting beside me to watch a football game, I felt such emptiness. I realized no amount of prestige or money takes the place of family. So I sold my house, put my stuff in storage, and took this job so I'd be here when my brother's first child was born."

His words settled in Ida's heart as gently as a feather falling to the ground, and she knew what her answer would be. The influence of such a man would be good for Annie and possibly even for Darla Jean.

That thought was still floating across her mind when Gregg asked if her could see the room.

Looking across at Suzanna, Ida gave a wave and said, "Darla Jean, take

Mister Patterson upstairs and show him the blue room. It's bigger and has a nice size desk in there."

Suzanna and Gregg disappeared up the stairs then returned in a matter of minutes.

"It's a lovely room," he said. "I'd be delighted to live here."

"Then live here you shall," Ida replied.

As he sat there writing a check for the first month's rent, Ida invited him to stay for dinner. Not surprisingly, he said yes.

EARL

Searching for Suzanna

Once Earl got it in his head that Suzanna was most likely with the guy who was Annie's daddy, nothing was going to dissuade him. The Monday after his meeting with Tom Duff he drove over to the high school, determined to find a copy of her high school yearbook. It was after ten when he arrived, and school was already in session.

He came through the door and wandered along the hallway, occasionally peeking into a classroom window then moving on. He figured they'd have copies of the 1952 yearbook at the principal's office and if not there the school library for sure.

For ten minutes, he walked up one hallway and down the next looking for someone to ask, but other than the people in the classrooms there was no one and no signs pointing the direction to an office or guidance counselor.

"What kind of a dumb ass school is this?" Earl mumbled as he neared the end of the third hallway. "How's a person supposed to find their way around?"

He took a left, circled past an empty gymnasium, spotted a room marked Teacher's Lounge, and pushed the door open without bothering to knock. No one inside. He stood there for a few moments looking around, then started toward the bookcase opposite the sofa. The top section of the unit was shelving, the lower portion cabinets with closed doors. Starting with the middle shelf, which was eye level, he fingered through what was there; mostly novels, Advise and Consent, Hawaii, Anatomy of a Murder. Stacked alongside the books was a bunch of paperbacks. He stretched his neck and browsed the top shelf. More of the same plus a few on psychology and health. On the bottom shelf nothing but stacks of papers.

"Waste of time," he grumbled, then squatted down and pulled the cupboard doors open.

Boxes of stationery, staplers, some coffee cups. He was reaching further back when the bell rang and startled him. Almost instantly, he heard doors swing open and voices echoing through the previously empty hall. He bolted up, hurried out of the room, and latched onto the first kid he saw.

The boy, a head taller than Earl but skinny as a beanstalk, turned with an angry glare. "Who the hell—"

Earl let go of the kid's arm and held his hands up palms out.

"Sorry," he said quickly. "I ain't looking for trouble, just the principal's office."

Before he got his answer, two other boys stopped alongside the kid and eyed Earl suspiciously.

The biggest of the three gave a nod toward Earl then turned toward Beanstalk and asked, "This clown giving you a problem?"

Beanstalk shook his head. "He's looking for Mr. Whisenant's office."

The big guy sneered at Earl as if spoiling for a fight. "What business you got here?"

For a split-second Earl considered giving the wise-ass kid a knee, just to prove he was somebody not to mess with, but he let go of the thought before it was fully formed. He wanted the yearbook more than he wanted to teach this kid a lesson. He couldn't afford to be thrown out of the building before he got what he came for.

Ignoring the kid's attitude, he said, "I'm looking for a copy of the yearbook from when I graduated."

The big kid elbowed Beanstalk and guffawed, "They had printing presses back then?"

"Knock it off." Beanstalk turned back to Earl, motioned toward the side door then said, "Go through there, take the first hallway on the right. It's at the far end."

Earl was in no mood for niceties; he turned and walked off without a word.

As the door swung closed behind him, he heard the big kid yell, "Yer welcome."

The muscle in the back of Earl's neck twitched.

"Screw you," he grumbled and kept walking. The kid didn't know how lucky he was. If circumstances were different, he'd teach the idiot a thing or two, but right now he was more interested in getting what he came for.

As he walked through the door marked Administrative Offices, Earl tried to hide the annoyance he was feeling. Pulling his face into a reasonably pleasant expression, he approached the front desk and asked, "Is this Mr. Whisenant's office?"

The woman behind the desk looked up. "Yes, it is, but I'm afraid he's tied up right now. Can I help you with something?"

"I need a copy of the yearbook from seven years ago." He hesitated a second, then, remembering Annie was already seven, corrected himself. "Make that eight years ago."

"My goodness, that would be 1952, or did you want '53? It really doesn't matter, because I doubt we have any that far back."

Trying to sound affable, which wasn't all that easy since he was already in a foul mood, Earl softened his voice. "Would you take a look? It's kind of important. Sort of like a gift I promised her."

She smiled and gave a knowing nod. "The year your daughter graduated, right?"

The pissed-off expression slid right back onto Earl's face.

"Wife," he snapped. Suzanna wasn't his wife or daughter, but to get that yearbook he had to say something.

The woman's face blushed crimson. "Oh. Of course. Why, you're much too young. I wasn't thinking… I hope you don't think I meant—"

"You wanna go check on that book?" Earl cut in, his patience growing thinner by the second.

Scurrying off like a frightened rabbit, the woman disappeared into the back office and was gone several minutes.

As he waited, Earl paced back and forth across the room. He didn't like being here anymore than he did when he'd quit coming 20 years earlier. Just being in the building gave him the willies, made him feel like a loser. Having to back down to some smart-ass kid was like running a buzz saw up his back, and the thought of this old crow suggesting Suzanna might be his daughter made his skin crawl. He felt a rash rising up on his neck and was on the verge of walking out when the woman reappeared.

"I'm sorry to be gone so long," she said. "I called over to the school library to ask if they had any, but unfortunately they don't. Mr. Whisenant has eight copies from 1958 and three from '59, but that's it. Nothing older."

"You know where I can get one?"

"Not really," she said apologetically. "You might try the county library. I can't say for sure whether or not they keep the yearbooks, but it's worth checking."

Anxious to get out of there, Earl gave a nod of thanks and was gone. As he made his way back to the door, he kept an eye open for the big kid but the hallways were now as empty as they'd been earlier.

By the time Earl made it to the library, he was feeling a bit discouraged and starting to wonder if maybe there wasn't some other way to find Suzanna. He walked up to the desk and asked if they kept copies of the Sun Grove High School yearbooks.

"We have archive copies," the librarian said.

Earl's face brightened. "Do you have 1952 or '53?"

"Yes. All the way back to 1942."

Figuring that if he didn't find Mr. Football in one book, he'd surely be the other, Earl asked to borrow both the '52 and '53 books.

The librarian gave a tolerant smile. "As I said, they're archive copies. We don't lend archived reference books. You can read them here, but they can't leave the library."

"What kind of dumb rule is that? Isn't the whole idea of a library to lend books?"

With her eyes fixed in an unflinching glare, she repeated, "Not reference books."

It was obvious to Earl that he was not going to get around this woman and her no-borrowing-reference-books rule, and it was almost as obvious that looking through the books on his own was not going to be of much help. The whole idea had been to get Suzanna's dad to point out the guy she was dating; then he'd have something to go on.

A feeling of frustration started picking at him, and his stomach churned. "Look, this is kind of an emergency. If I can't borrow the books, then at least let me buy them."

"We do not sell our reference books," she replied crisply.

"I'm not gonna keep the damn books. Think of it this way: you sell them to me today, I show them to the guy who's supposed to point out somebody, then tomorrow I give them back. You keep the money. Everybody wins. No harm, no foul, right?"

"Wrong. I will repeat this one last time. Reference books do not leave the library. Not for you, not for anyone."

"You ever thought of sometimes making an exception?"

"No, I have not. If you wish to look at our archived books, I will take you back to that section. If you do not, then leave. But if I see you trying to sneak one of those books out of here, I will call security."

Given no alternative, Earl begrudgingly said he'd go ahead and look at the yearbooks. He followed the librarian back to the archive room and sat at the table as he waited for her to give them to him.

Once the books were in front of him, he started leafing through the pages of the 1952 book. He was looking for something but had no clue what it might be. Twelve pages in, he came across a picture of Suzanna. Younger, her face a bit fuller, her smile even more beautiful than he remembered.

As he sat looking at her, the ache inside of him grew more fierce. It hurt as nothing before had ever hurt. More than the knee that had once been shattered, more than the time his daddy had taken a baseball bat to him, more even than the mama who'd walked off and left him with that very same daddy. He'd survived all those things, but he didn't think he could survive losing Suzanna.

Page by page he went through the book, scanning the faces, looking for something, anything, that might give him an idea of who he was looking for. He found it on page 34. It was a picture of a pep rally, and there in the background was Suzanna, gazing starry-eyed into the face of a blond kid wearing a Panthers football jersey with the number 23 on it.

He flipped back to page 21 and found the picture of the football team. There he was, standing smack in the center of the lineup. Same face, same smart-ass grin.

Earl moved to the bottom of the page and read through the names and positions. Sure enough, the kid was number 23. Robert James Doherty, nickname Bobby. Running Back.

He flipped further back to the alphabetical listing of students and found what he was looking for: Bobby Doherty, Class President, Varsity Football, Debate Team.

He moved on in search of something more, but there were only bits and pieces. A snapshot of Bobby standing at a podium, a few words about how his aspiration was to be a lawyer, and another picture with Suzanna. In the second picture, she had that same enraptured look as in the pep rally photo.

Not once had she looked at Earl that way. Not once. That thought was bitter as gall and all but impossible to swallow.

Earl closed the book, pushed back in his chair, and sat there thinking, first weighing the probability of Suzanna still loving Mr. Football and then wondering if he could make her realize what a mistake she was making. He thought about how he would promise to change, volunteer to adopt Annie, give up drinking, and correct the dozens of other things she'd complained about. If he did that, would she smile at him the way she'd smiled at Bobby Doherty? Earl was willing to chance it. But first, he had to find Suzanna.

Before he left the library, Earl had a plan to find Bobby Doherty. There were only so many law firms in Sun Grove, and if he wasn't working in town it was probably somewhere nearby. More determined than he'd ever been about anything, Earl made up his mind to leave no stone unturned until he found what he was looking for. If Mr. Football wanted his kid he could have her, but the only way Earl was giving up Suzanna was over his dead body.

SUZANNA

Getting to Know You

Gregg Patterson moved in the next day, and right from the start it was apparent that Ida had taken a liking to him. Before the week was out, she invited him to join them for dinner on three different occasions. Twice, he accepted. The third time they were sitting at the breakfast table, and he said he had plans with his brother.

"After work I'm going to pick up a pizza, then Phil and I will work on the nursery. We want to get the painting done while Ginger's visiting her mom."

The mention of family brought a smile to Ida's face. "It's nice that Ginger has her mom living nearby."

"Actually, she doesn't. Ginger's from Florida, and her mom is still there."

Annie gave a gapping tooth grin and said, "We lived in Florida too."

Gregg looked over at Suzanna and smiled. "Well, then, you need to meet Ginger. Perhaps one evening—"

"We weren't there long," Suzanna cut in, "a few years maybe. My family moved around a lot."

"It's the opposite for me. My parents lived in the same house from the day I was born until the day I left home."

"That's so nice."

"Yes, it was," he said, sounding a bit nostalgic. "But I was young and too foolish to appreciate it. I wanted excitement. The year I graduated, Phil

82

and I set off on a cross-country trip in my old Plymouth. We made it as far as Florida; then the car fell apart."

Ida laughed. "Fell apart?"

He joined in the laughter. "Yes, literally. It was a junker to begin with, so we left it on the side of the road, walked into town, and started looking for a job. That summer was when Phil met Ginger."

Talk of Florida was something Suzanna wanted no part of.

"You'll have to excuse me," she said. "I've got to get Annie off to school."

As she started up the stairs, she heard the lighthearted sound of their conversation continuing. Gregg was telling of how both he and his brother had worked as waiters that summer.

In the weeks that followed, Gregg settled into the Parker house as if he were a member of the family. Once or twice a week he had dinner with them, and when something was squeaky, loose, or broken, he was on it before anyone even realized it needed fixing. The high-ceilinged staircase light that had been dim for ages now had a bright new bulb, and the wobbly rail on the back porch stood straight and steady. He parked his car on the street, left the driveway clear for Suzanna to pull Ida's car in or out, and seldom left the house without asking if someone needed something from the store.

"Are you running low on milk?" he'd say or ask if he should pick up a fresh loaf of bread.

After he'd put an end to the annoying drip of the kitchen faucet, Ida said, "I don't know how we ever got along without you." Then she glanced over at Suzanna with a sly wink.

Although Suzanna said nothing, the many charms of Gregg Patterson were not wasted on her. She'd noticed. On evenings when he'd ask if they'd mind him joining them to watch television, she'd answer, "Of course not," and scoot over to make room for him on the sofa.

Not only did she not mind, she looked forward to those nights. Gregg was company, the likes of which she'd not known since Bobby Doherty. He was smart, fun to be with, and interesting, especially when he spoke of the years he'd taught at Villanova. As he told of how in the early spring, when the campus turned green, the students who had rushed from building to building all winter began napping under the shade of the oaks, she laughed and found herself wishing she too could have been there.

On just such an evening, after they'd had dinner and settled in front of the television to watch The Price is Right, a loud clatter came from outside. There had been thunder and rain all evening, but this was more like metal smashing against metal.

"What in the world…?" Suzanna jumped up and hurried to the door.

Gregg and Ida were right behind. Halfway across the porch, all three of them stopped short and watched as Homer Portnick climbed out of his big black Buick and stood looking at the rear end of his car, which was now embedded in the side of Gregg's Oldsmobile. As they stepped down from the porch, a clap of thunder sounded and the rain started up again.

"No need for all of us to get wet," Gregg said. "There's nothing you can do; go back inside, and let me take care of this."

Ida tugged Suzanna onto the porch; then they turned back to watch.

Portnick, an elderly man with stooped shoulders and a hangdog expression, gave a weary sigh.

"I suppose that's your car," he said.

Gregg nodded. "Afraid so."

"I didn't expect it to be parked there." Before he could say anything more, a sudden gust of wind took Portnick's hat and sent it tumbling down the street.

"Figures," he mumbled and shook his head. "That was my lucky hat."

"Want me to try and catch it?" Gregg asked.

Portnick shook his head. "Too late. Whatever luck it had must've ran out, otherwise I wouldn't be here." He stood there looking as pitiful as possible, then said, "I'm real sorry about your car."

"What happened?"

"Can't say for sure. I was all set to back out of my garage; looked and saw the way was clear, then I heard that noise, and my car was smacked into yours. I don't see so good at night, and what with the rain and all…"

"Accidents happen. I'm sure your insurance will cover it."

Portnick eyed the two women standing on the porch, then nervously leaned in and said, "See, that's a problem. There is no insurance."

"No insurance? Why—"

"Don't worry, I've got money enough to have your car fixed, and I'll pay."

"But why don't you have insurance? Everyone has—"

"Not everyone," Portnick said solemnly. "You get old, and they make you take a new driving test. Mess up on those questions, and they won't give you a license."

"You don't have a license either?"

Portnick shook his head. "That's why I'm hoping you won't see a need to report this to the police."

Gregg stood there for a moment, fingering his chin and looking at the crumpled condition of his car.

"Okay," he finally said. "I won't report the accident based on two conditions."

"Anything."

"First off, you do have to pay to have my car fixed, and secondly, you have to agree to go back and get that driver's license."

"What if I still don't pass?"

"Oh, you'll pass this time." Gregg looked up and grinned at Ida. "Mrs. Parker and I will coach you until you can answer those questions without thinking twice."

Portnick beamed. "That's a fair enough deal."

"One more thing," Gregg added. "There's no more driving until you get your license and some insurance."

Gregg came inside, called for a tow truck, then got behind the wheel of Portnick's Buick and pulled it into the garage. Although Gregg's car had a good-size dent in the door, Portnick's had a pencil thin scratch on the fender.

After the tow truck hauled the Olds away, Ida brought out a bottle of brandy that had belonged to William and poured everyone a drink. As the three of them sat around the kitchen table discussing how they'd have to keep an eye on Homer Portnick, Gregg mentioned that he'd arrange for a rental car tomorrow.

"You'll do nothing of the sort," Ida said. "Darla Jean will drive you back and forth until your car's been repaired."

He glanced over at Suzanna and smiled. "If you're sure it's no trouble."

Suzanna was sure. Very sure.

With the long drive back and forth to Barston, Suzanna and Gregg found time to talk in a way they hadn't done before. Each morning after she dropped him off at the school, she'd return home and find herself counting the hours until it was time to go back.

For a reason that she couldn't put her finger on, she felt comfortable with Gregg. The kind of comfortable she'd felt with her mama. He listened without judging; he encouraged her to talk but never pried. He told her about his childhood, a girl he'd once been engaged to, and the loneliness he'd felt after his parents were gone.

When the conversation fell to her, Suzanna skipped around, telling bits and pieces of her life but nothing in its entirety. She spoke of Bobby Doherty in the broadest strokes, saying only that she'd fallen in love with a football player, ended up pregnant, and been left behind when he headed off to college. Earl she said almost nothing about, only that it was a bad relationship and a mistake she'd never repeat.

With the trace of a smile edging the corner of his mouth, Gregg asked, "Does that mean you'll never take a chance on love again?"

Suzanna hesitated a moment as the thought of Bobby Doherty drifted across her mind.

"Probably not," she answered, knowing that there could be no one else. Not as long as Bobby still had a stronghold on her heart.

IDA

William's Will

That week brought a landslide of changes to the Parker household. It began the day after the accident when Ida received a letter from the bank. Opening the envelope, she found a copy of Bill's mortgage on the house. The first page was stamped CANCELLED. Ida's heart clenched in her chest as she dropped into the chair. Fearing the worst, she unfolded the letter.

It was a form letter stating the cancellation document for the mortgage on the Parkers' house was enclosed, and it had been a pleasure doing business with them. It was signed Marilyn Walker Smyth, Mortgage Counselor.

Stunned, Ida sat with her heart fluttering and her breath coming in thin little stops and starts. Right now, she was managing; getting by on a shoestring maybe, but getting by nonetheless. She'd be in better shape once the second room was rented, but even then she wouldn't have nearly enough cash for the remainder of the mortgage. The bank wasn't going to settle for what savings she had left, and if she did give it all to them she'd be wiped out. Completely. There wouldn't be a dime left for electricity, telephone, or even food.

She thought back to five years ago when William had taken out a mortgage and assured her it was the best possible interest rate. At the time, he'd labored over every little detail, making sure every T was crossed and every I dotted. The house was in both names so she'd assumed the mortgage would remain in place after Bill's death, but apparently the bank had other ideas. Now she was stuck with the responsibility of paying the mortgage off or trying to get another one.

She knew nothing about mortgages and had barely listened when Bill rattled off comparisons and asked her opinion. She didn't have an opinion and without giving it a second thought had said, "Do whatever you think best." Now she regretted those words. She should have listened, paid more attention; then she'd know how to fix this.

As a feeling of helplessness settled over her, she leaned forward, dropped her face into her palms, and began to sob.

"Dear God, Bill," she cried. "What do I do?"

For a brief moment, she felt the weight of a hand on her shoulder. Then she heard the familiar voice say, "Stop feeling sorry for yourself, and do as I'd do."

Startled, she lifted her head and turned to look, but no one was there. "Bill?"

There was no answer; only the tick of the mantel clock.

He'd been there, she was certain of it. She'd recognized his voice, felt the reassurance of his hand. But do as he'd do was something she didn't understand. She puzzled over it for several minutes then remembered Delbert Stanfield, the loan officer at First Federal. He was a vice president, more than likely Ms. Smyth's boss. He was also Bill's friend, a man Bill trusted.

As that thought took root and grew, anger overcame Ida's feeling of helplessness. She stood, stiffened her shoulders, and headed for the kitchen telephone. Before Delbert finished his hello, she lit into him.

"I'm sorely disappointed in you, Delbert. Bill was a loyal customer and a friend. After he gave you all that business, you pulling an underhanded trick like this is almost unthinkable!"

"Ida?" Delbert sputtered. "What on earth is wrong?"

"Wrong?" she snapped. "I'll tell you what's wrong. The bank cancelled the mortgage on our house, that's what's wrong! Now, what am I supposed to do when—"

"Wait a minute," Delbert said, interrupting Ida's tirade. "You don't have to do anything right now. At the end of the year, the city will send you a bill for next year's property taxes."

"And what about getting another mortgage? You're the only bank in—"

"The house is paid off. You don't need a mortgage."

Ida hesitated a moment, allowing what he'd said to settle in her head.

"Paid off?" she finally asked. "But how…"

"Bill had a home life insurance policy—"

"I know he had life insurance. The company sent me a check, but it's not enough—"

"That check was for the insurance policy where you were the beneficiary. This one is different; this was a home life policy. On this one, the bank is the beneficiary, not you. The policy pays off the mortgage when something happens to the homeowner." Delbert paused, then asked, "Didn't Bill tell you about it?"

Ida thought back on the hundreds of thousands of conversations they'd had. They'd talked about anything and everything. They'd struggled through the Great Depression together, watched presidents come and go, shared the anguish of losing their grandchild. She remembered all those moments, but she couldn't recall that conversation.

With words made heavy by the memories, her answer came in little more than a whisper. "I don't remember."

After she'd hung up the telephone, Ida returned to the chair and sat there thinking. Her first impulse was to share the good news the minute Darla Jean got back from Barston, but after mulling it over she began to wonder whether it was wise to do so.

She thought back on the dreadful days before Darla Jean returned. The house was silent, the mood somber, and the days lingering on for hours longer than they should have. She'd tried to shorten those dreary days by going to bed before the sun started its journey toward the horizon, but it was a wasted effort.

The nights were no better than the days. The tiniest noise startled her awake; then she'd lie there feeling the emptiness Bill had left behind. Some nights she carried a book to bed thinking she'd read, but that too was useless. No matter how many times she read or reread the words, she failed to catch the drift of the story.

The day of the memorial service, Darla Jean had been on her way to New Jersey. It was only after Ida asked for help that she changed her mind and stayed. Opening up the third floor, renting the room to Gregg—all done for the same reason. Because I needed them. Now, things would be different. With the house paid off and Bill's insurance money in the bank, she was financially stable. She didn't need help to clear away the clutter or a boarder who'd pay rent, but needing and wanting were two different things.

The truth was she wanted Darla Jean to stay. She wanted Gregg to stay. She'd seen the spark flickering between them and could imagine them one day married, living here in this house. Annie would grow up here, and there would be more babies. This house was never intended for one lonely old woman; it needed children. It needed the patter of footsteps on the staircase, the warmth of laughter echoing through the rooms, and the sighs of lovemaking whispered in the dark of night. If Darla Jean stayed, there was the promise of all those things, but if she decided to leave…

Ida shivered at the thought. It was not something she was willing to risk. It would be better for her to say nothing and make the necessary arrangements just as Bill had done. When she joined Bill in the hereafter, Darla Jean would inherit the house and all that was left. But for now, she had to leave things exactly as they were.

Later that afternoon when they went grocery shopping at Piggly Wiggly, Ida plunked a standing rib roast into the shopping cart.

Suzanna raised an eyebrow and asked, "Isn't that a bit extravagant?"

"It's a special occasion," Ida said with a smile. "When Gregg gets his car back, I'm thinking we'll have a lovely dinner party and invite Homer Portnick to join us."

"Nice," Suzanna said, "but a meatloaf would be just as good and more affordable."

Ida struggled to hold back a grin as she moved on to selecting some fresh tomatoes.

SUZANNA

Fear of Ginger

Although the daily trips back and forth to Barston meant two hours of driving every day, Suzanna didn't mind. In fact, she enjoyed it. In the morning, she rose earlier, took time to apply lipstick, then twist her hair into a clip with a few carefully placed tendrils falling loose. On that first morning, she'd blushed when Gregg commented on how pretty she looked; then on the return drive back to Cousins, she'd stopped at the drugstore and bought mascara. That evening she wore her sundress when she picked him up.

Oddly enough, the commute back and forth felt rather like a date. They shot flirty smiles at one another, chatted easily, and laughed at things that were only vaguely humorous. Although she was reluctant to admit it, even to herself, Suzanna started counting the hours until she would pick him up again just moments after she'd dropped him off. That was until the third day. That afternoon Gregg telephoned and asked if she could pick him up at his brother's house.

Before he finished telling about the porch set he and Phil were assembling, her thoughts flashed back to the morning she'd heard him talking about the sister-in-law from Florida. Going to her house was definitely was not something Suzanna wanted to do.

Several seconds of silence ticked by; then she sputtered something about not knowing where Phil's house was and being terrible with directions.

"Oh, you won't have any trouble finding the place," Gregg said. "It's on the same road as the school. Just keep going for another three miles, make a right on Verbena, and it's two houses in."

"Three miles, huh?" she stalled, trying to think of an out.

After a lengthy silence, Gregg asked, "Darla Jean, are you still there?"

"Um, yeah. I'm still here."

"Well, it's okay, isn't it? You picking me up at my brother's?"

There was no out. She couldn't say no, because Ida would ask why. Feigning a sudden illness wasn't going to work either since it was almost time to leave. With an edgy tremor in her voice, she answered, "Sure, it is. I was just jotting down the directions."

"Okay then, I'll see you at about five," he said and hung up.

When Suzanna set the receiver back in its cradle, her heart was racing. She took several deep breaths and tried to gather her thoughts.

Why Florida? Why now, when everything was so perfect?

She reasoned that the chance of Ginger being from Sun Grove were a million to one. Florida was a big state. Sun Grove was a small town, a nothing place. Not the sort of town where frat boys would spend a summer. She was on the verge of buying into that thought. Then she remembered: Gregg and his brother hadn't planned on visiting. Their car broke down. They were stranded.

Sun Grove was a place where a person could easily enough get stranded. Suzanna had felt that way for most of her life. Maybe the same was true of Ginger. Wasn't it possible that she married Gregg's brother to escape Sun Grove?

Possible, perhaps, but she's not the one telling the lie.

For the remainder of the afternoon, Suzanna ran through scenarios of what she would do if Ginger did recognize her. She considered turning it off with a laugh, claiming Suzanna Duff had to be a look-alike. Supposedly everyone had a twin somewhere. Or she could say she'd suffered a bout of amnesia and only recently remembered her true identity. New schemes popped into her head one after another, each of them more foolish than the one before and none of them believable. The sorry truth was that if Ginger recognized her, the life Suzanna had built here was as good as gone.

If this were only about her she could live with it, but she was not the only one involved. It would break Ida's heart to discover she was not Darla Jean. All the trust, the hopes and dreams, would be gone in a flash. And

Annie… Suzanna couldn't even bear to think of how it would affect Annie. She'd have to be dragged off kicking and screaming, torn from the arms of the only grandmother she'd ever known. It would be worse than it was before they came to Cousins. Back then, she and Annie were united against a common enemy: Earl. If they had to leave here, Annie would see her as the enemy.

Suzanna closed her eyes and pictured Annie standing side by side with Ida, their faces knotted with anguish, their eyes angry and accusing. Her lies, harmless as they might have seemed, would destroy the people she loved most.

With her heart heavy as a sack of stones, Suzanna climbed into the car and started for Barston. She took the back roads and drove so slowly that the cars behind her began honking their horns. Wrapped in worry, she paid no attention and continued at a snail's pace. When the line of traffic passed Becker's Farm, old man Becker removed his hat and stood with his head bowed as he would for a funeral procession.

When she spotted the school, her eyes filled with tears. She imagined Gregg, wearing his tweed jacket, carrying his satchel briefcase, smiling as she drove up. That was yesterday. Today he might look at her the way he'd looked at Homer Portnick, his expression somber, his eyes unflinching as he asked why.

She turned right on Verbena and pulled alongside the curb. She was late. Hopefully he'd hurry out, jump in the car, and they'd be off. Gone before there was a need for introductions or questions.

The door to the house swung open before she'd turned the ignition off. An obviously pregnant woman stepped out, gave a wave, and started toward the car.

Ginger.

She was younger than Suzanna expected. Her hair was cut short and tucked behind her ears, her skin a pale ivory, her face freckled and without makeup. As she neared the car, there was no flicker of familiarity, just a warm, friendly smile.

Suzanna sat with both hands plastered to the steering wheel and made no effort to move. Ginger reached out, grabbed the handle, and pulled the door open.

"You must be Darla Jean," she said. "Gregg told us you were coming." She leaned in, gave Suzanna a one-arm hug, then kissed her cheek.

"I'm supposed to pick Gregg up here."

"I know, but the guys are still working out back. Come on inside, I've made some sandwiches and a pitcher of lemonade."

Suzanna shook her head. "I'd better not. My grandmother's expecting me back and—"

"Don't worry, Gregg called her."

"Called Grandma Ida?"

"Uh-huh. He explained that putting the porch set together was taking longer than they'd expected and asked if she'd mind you staying for dinner."

Angling her legs to the side, Suzanna tentatively stepped out of the car. "Grandma was okay with that?"

"Absolutely," Ginger replied. "She said to stay as long as you like, and she'll make sure Annie brushes her teeth before she goes to bed."

Apparently not sensing Suzanna's resistance, Ginger took hold of her arm and tugged her toward the house.

"I have been absolutely dying to meet you," she said. "Gregg has been talking my ear off about you and that darling little girl of yours. He told me that you're from Florida, and I said, well, now, if that isn't a coincidence..."

Suzanna's back was stiff as a ramrod as she moved one foot in front of the other. Her chest felt as though it was caving in on itself, and there was no way to escape. Her breath caught in her throat, and she felt a trickle of perspiration roll down her back.

When she heard the sound of Gregg's laughter coming from the back yard, desperation took hold of her, and she said, "Please let's not talk about Florida. I hated it there. All that heat and humidity..."

Ginger stopped, turned to Suzanna with a wide-eyed expression, then laughed out loud.

"You can't imagine how glad I am to finally meet someone who agrees with me. For the past three years all I've heard is what a paradise it must be. Not for me. If I sit in the sun for a half hour, I'm blistered. Why, if it wasn't for having Mama there, I'd never go back."

Suzanna released a long slow breath and smiled.

As it turned out, Ginger was from Miami and she'd never even heard of Sun Grove.

"Is that on the east or west coast?" she'd asked.

"Neither," Suzanna replied. "It's in the middle of nowhere."

For the remainder of the evening, that was the last mention of Florida.

After a quick tour of the house, they sat in lawn chairs under a shady oak. Then once the men finished assembling the outdoor furniture, they gathered around the redwood table with one leg that was still a bit shaky. Gregg folded a piece of cardboard and wedged it beneath the wobbly leg.

"We'll look at fixing that tomorrow," he said, then eased himself into the chair alongside of Suzanna.

The hours flew by as they sat and talked. The last rays of sunlight disappeared in a burst of pink and red; then the sky darkened and stars twinkled overhead. The things Suzanna had worried about never came to pass. There were no questions, no red flags, just friendship and conversation. She told about living with Ida and discovering the love of a grandfather she'd never known, then pulled back and let the others do most of the talking.

The men spoke about the repairs yet to be done on the house, and Phil repeatedly thanked Gregg for his help. Ginger was full of chatter about the baby due in December and the job she had just resigned.

"Cavalier's Couture," she said. "It's a darling little shop. I loved it there and I couldn't ask for a nicer boss than Colette Cavalier, but since this is our first baby I wanted to stay at home with her—"

"Or him," Phil interjected with a laugh.

Ginger nodded sheepishly. "Or him. At least for the first few years."

"You won't regret it," Suzanna said, then went on to tell how she'd spent the first seven years with Annie and was glad to have done so.

"I'm not saying every day is a picnic, but being there for your child's first word, first step, first day of school, well, those are things money can't buy."

She didn't mention Earl or how he'd refused to let her get a job.

You've got no car and no way to get around, he'd said, and that was the end of that. If she wanted to be with Annie, she'd have to settle for the few bucks he occasionally left on the kitchen table.

Brushing aside the memory of Earl, she moved on. "Now that Annie's in school, I'm going to start looking for a job."

"Why don't you talk to Colette Cavalier? She needs a sales assistant to replace me."

Suzanna chuckled. "Maybe so, but I doubt I have the qualifications. I have no retail experience, zero fashion sense, and practically live in jeans."

"Makes no difference. Colette lets you wear what you want outside of work. In the shop, she has you wear outfits from her collection. You're a sales clerk but also kind of a model. She says customers are more likely to buy when they see someone wearing the clothes."

"Really?" Suzanna leaned in and asked a number of questions about the duties involved, the type of customers, and whether or not experience was a requirement. Thinking back to her days at the Snack Shop, she said, "I've got a little bit of sales experience but not much."

"I wouldn't worry about it. Colette trains people to do things her way. If she likes you and thinks you'll be good with people, that's what counts."

"It sounds like a dream job."

"It was," Ginger said wistfully. She leaned back and proudly patted her belly. "But I've got a much more important one coming up in December."

They both laughed. Ginger offered to give Colette a call and put in a good word if Darla Jean were interested.

"Oh, I'm interested," Suzanna replied. "Very interested."

The conversation moved on, and Ginger began talking about a new restaurant that had recently opened up in downtown Barston. "They have steaks that are out of this world."

"Instead of telling them about the place, why don't we take my brother and Darla Jean there for dinner this Saturday?" Phil said, looking over at Ginger and giving a wink. "Our treat, to thank Gregg for all the work he's been doing."

"A fabulous idea!" Ginger said.

Gregg turned to Suzanna. "Well, are you okay with Saturday night?"

She hesitated for a second, not because she had something else to do, but because it had been so long, so very long, since someone had asked her out, that she'd all but forgotten how good it felt. She looked up, let her eyes meet his, then nodded.

"Sounds wonderful."

⌒◯✼◯⌒

Later that night, as Suzanna lay in bed waiting for sleep to come, she thought back on the evening and all the promise that lay ahead. She hadn't come to Cousins intending to live a lie but it had happened, and now that lie was turning into reality. She could almost believe her past was truly buried and forgotten. She'd left no evidence behind, taken a few dollars and nothing else. There was no trail for Earl to follow. She closed her eyes for a moment, picturing Earl and the dingy little house on Shady Creek Road, but this time they appeared at a distance, further away than she remembered, surrounded by dark pines and shadows that obscured the ugliness of what she'd known.

She breathed a sigh and relaxed into the pillow, assuring herself that Suzanna Duff was actually disappearing. She was a woman who had simply rolled away like a lost marble. Gone. Completely and forever. Replaced by Darla Jean, a woman with a grandmother who loved her, a grandfather who'd pined for her return, a family history. Soon that same Darla Jean would have a job; a respectable job, one where truckers didn't reach over the counter trying to steal a pack of cigarettes or catch a feel.

The more she thought about it, the more determined Suzanna became. Come what may, she was going to hold on to this new life. If, in the weeks or years ahead, someone stepped forward claiming to be Darla Jean, she would call them an imposter and tell Ida to send them packing. She owed it to Annie. Hell, she owed it to herself.

As she drifted off to sleep, she recalled the look on Gregg's face as he awaited her answer about Saturday night. She pictured the way he seemed to look straight through to the very inside of her heart, and she remembered how at that moment she'd wanted to reach out and touch her finger to the curl that had fallen across his forehead.

SUZANNA

Cavalier's Couture

The following Monday, after Suzanna dropped Gregg off at the school, she drove over to visit Ginger.

"I was in the neighborhood," she said, "and thought I'd stop by."

It was partly true, but the bigger truth was that she couldn't stop thinking about the job at Cavalier's Couture. Suzanna knew she had little to offer in the way of experience and even less awareness of fashion, but with Ginger's endorsement she stood a chance. Not wanting to make it appear as though that were the only reason for her visit, she sat at the kitchen table patiently listening to Ginger's thoughts on decorating and commenting on the pictures torn from baby magazines.

After an hour of chit chat and two cups of overly sweet tea, Suzanna felt settled enough to broach the subject. Even then, she still had butterflies in her stomach and a slightly higher pitch to her voice. Trying to still her nerves, she took another sip of tea, then leaned back in the chair and casually asked, "By the way, have you called Colette Cavalier to find out if she'd be interested in meeting me?"

Ginger slapped her palm to her forehead and laughed. "Good grief, I'd forgotten all about it. Thanks for the reminder." She stood, grabbed the receiver from the wall telephone, and began dialing.

Suzanna felt her heart thump against her chest. "I'm not trying to pressure you into doing this, if you'd rather not."

"No, I'm happy to, and—"

A click sounded, and Ginger suddenly switched to a more sophisticated voice. There was a brief hello, a few words about how she was enjoying her time at home but missed the shop, then she went on to say, "I was devastated by the thought that I might be leaving you in the lurch, so I've found a replacement you will absolutely love. She's tall, attractive, and presents well."

The conversation went back and forth with a few words such as absolutely and without a doubt, then she said, "Yes, she worked in a Florida boutique that went out of business. Unfortunately, no references but I assure you, she's Cavalier's quality."

When Suzanna heard that, her foot began bouncing up and down like a rubber ball. The conversation seemed to drag on forever as she sat there wondering how she was going to fake something she knew nothing about.

When Ginger finally hung up, she looked across with a smile that stretched the full width of her face.

"Colette said to come in tomorrow afternoon. She's anxious to meet you."

Suzanna sucked in a breath. "You told her I had experience?"

With a mischievous grin curling her mouth, Ginger nodded. "So I did. But don't worry, she won't check. She never does. Colette trusts her instinct about people. Right off the bat she can tell whether or not she likes you, and that's what counts."

After such an enthusiastic endorsement, Suzanna walked into Cavalier's Couture expecting a warm welcome, but what she got was a pencil-thin business woman who was taller than she was, had a sharp nose, and an oversized twist of red hair.

Earlier that morning Ida had boosted her confidence and assured her that she was a shoo-in.

"Darla Jean, why on earth would anyone pass up a woman like you?" she'd asked, then gone on to detail how she was beautiful, smart, and talented. As Suzanna started out the door, Ida had kissed her cheek and said, "Don't worry, I'm certain she'll love you."

When Suzanna parked in front of the shop she'd felt pretty sure of herself, but once she saw the icy gray eyes scrutinizing her from top to toe that confidence disappeared. Fearful that beads of perspiration were already rising up on her forehead, she tried to smile as she walked over to the counter, stuck out her hand, and said, "You must be Colette Cavalier. I'm Darla Jean Parker."

"Pleasure," the woman replied as she extended her hand.

She had an accent Suzanna didn't recognize, a nasal sound that made it seem as though she were pushing the words through her nose.

"You are on time, have height, and a narrow waist, all good," she said and gave just the slightest inkling of a smile. "Now tell me about your experience."

Suzanna swallowed hard, and when she started to speak it felt as though her tongue were stuck to the roof of her mouth.

"Well, it's not much to speak of…"

She thought back, trying to remember the key words Ginger had given her, but as she stumbled over the tale about it being a small retail shop with not a lot of traffic, she felt the heat coloring her cheeks. Lying came easy to Suzanna; she could do it and never so much as blink an eye. But after five months of living with Ida, she'd shed too many parts of her former self. She was now more Darla Jean than Suzanna, and the art of lying had been lost.

She stopped mid-sentence and said, "Actually it wasn't a boutique, it was a snack shop. I worked there when I was a teenager. I don't have any fashion expertise, and for the past seven years the only real thing I've done is be a mom to my little girl."

Colette Cavalier's expression softened ever so slightly.

"Honesty is good," she said. "Experience I can teach, but honesty you must have to begin with."

A sense of shame rose up in Suzanna; it came with knowing she was neither a good liar nor an honest person. In trying to bridge the gap between the two, she had somehow fallen into the crack of nothingness in between.

"I'm sorry for wasting your time." She lowered her eyes, tucked her chin to her chest, and turned toward the door.

The sound of Colette's voice stopped her.

"Did Ginger not tell you that I have a keen sense of people? I would have in time known the truth anyway, so let's just move on."

Suzanna lifted her chin and turned back to see Colette pluck two outfits from the rack.

She thrust the clothes into Suzanna's arms, then gave a nod toward the dressing room. "Try these on, and let's see if you present as well as your friend has suggested."

Not quite believing she'd gotten a second chance, Suzanna entered the dressing room and hurriedly stepped out of the jeans she was wearing. She slid the black wool dress over her head, checked her image in the mirror, and gave a gasp. The dress fit as though it had been made for her, and the sparkling rim of gold braid at the neckline seemed to brighten her face. Her shoes were wrong; terribly wrong. She looked down at the flat sandals, hesitated a moment, then kicked them off and walked out of the dressing room in her bare feet.

Colette stood there fingering her chin for a moment then glanced down at Suzanna's feet and smiled. "You must have more fashion sense than you realize; you apparently knew those sandals would ruin the look of the dress."

She asked Suzanna to walk across the room, turn one way and the other, then gave a nod of approval. "Now let me see you in the suit."

After the suit there was another armful of clothes to try on, and for the better part of an hour Colette watched as Suzanna strutted back and forth across the store.

"You're a perfect size 8," she finally said, "I'll give you that. Few people wear clothes as well as you do."

Suzanna heard a hitch of hesitation in her voice and sensed that Colette was looking for someone more sophisticated than herself. Someone with an eye for fashion. Someone who wore the right shoes and already knew the names of designers like Bonnie Cashin and Colette Quant. Someone who had experience. With a sense of urgency rising in her chest, she forced a smile.

"Please at least give me a try," she said. "You won't have to pay me for the first two weeks. That will give me time to learn what I need to know, then afterward, if you don't think I'm right for the job, I'll walk away. No complaints…" Her words trailed off when she could think of nothing more to say.

The apprehension stitched to Colette's face softened, and her voice lost its crispness.

"You remind me of myself when I started in this industry. Hungry for the opportunity, willing to do anything." She smiled, not with a slight upturn of her lip as she had done earlier but a genuine smile, one that was rounded out and full of warmth.

"I was younger than you, only seventeen, and new to this country. Herb Goldman took a chance on me. It was my first job and I didn't know a thing about modeling, but he took me in and taught me the business. If not for Herb, I wouldn't have this shop. Perhaps it's time for me to repay his kindness."

She held out her hand and walked toward Suzanna. "You will have two weeks to prove yourself, and I will pay you a fair wage. In return, you must promise to buy yourself a decent pair of shoes."

❦

Suzanna was not scheduled to start work until the following Monday, and now that Gregg had his car back she had more free time than she wanted, so she spent the remainder of the week trying to keep busy. For the first four days she scuttled up and down the staircase carting the summer furnishings to the attic and bringing down the heavier drapes and warmer blankets. Once that was done, she cleaned the house top to bottom, vacuuming every nook and cranny, sweeping away lost buttons, bits of thread, and a shoelace that once belonged to a sneaker. She polished the furniture to a shine and spritzed the bathroom mirror until it was so crystal clear a person could see beyond themselves.

On Thursday afternoon as she was cleaning the mirror for a third time, she caught sight of her reflection and saw a strange shadow in the blue of her eyes. She bent forward, took a closer look, and discovered it gone. Concerned that it could be the shadow of her past, she decided the house was clean enough. After she'd emptied the pail and tossed the cleaning rags in the laundry basket, she settled at the kitchen table across from Ida and told her about needing new shoes.

"I'm hoping you can see your way clear to lend me a bit of money," she said. "Just until I get my first paycheck. I can pay you back then."

"Sorry, but no," Ida replied, her voice sounding resolute, even though a smile was tugging the corners of her mouth. "I won't lend you the money, but I will take you shopping and buy you shoes."

"You don't have to do that. I can pay you back—"

Ida folded her arms across her chest and gave a stubborn nod. "I know perfectly well what I have to do and don't have to do; this is something I want to do."

"I know you want to, but you need that money to cover expenses and—"

"I've got extra this month; sort of like a windfall that came my way."

"Windfall? What kind of windfall?" Suzanna asked suspiciously.

Ida hemmed and hawed for a few moments then said, "I received an extra check from Social Security. Some kind of bonus."

"Really?" The sound of doubt was still threaded through Suzanna's voice. "Odd, you've not mentioned this so-called bonus before."

Ida folded and then refolded the dish towel she'd been holding. "Oh, didn't I? It must have slipped my mind. Anyway, it's enough for us to have ourselves a nice shopping day tomorrow."

"Well, okay. But I still plan on paying you back."

"We'll see." Ida smiled, folded the dish towel one last time, slid it into the drawer, then left the kitchen.

The next morning as soon as Annie was out the door and on her way to school, they left for Barston. With the sweltering heat of September now gone, the morning was cool enough for Suzanna to wear her jeans and the sweater she'd borrowed from Ida. At 9:30, when the watchman unlocked the front door of Major's Department Store, they were waiting at the entrance.

Their first stop was the second-floor shoe department. After trying on several pairs of pointy-toed flats and a number of high-heeled pumps, she decided on a pair of stilettos made of a leather that was as soft and smooth as a calf's underbelly. Suzanna slid them onto her feet, then stood and walked across carpet to test her balance. After several trips back and forth, she smiled and gave a nod.

Ida waved the salesman over. "We'll take these and the pointy-toed flats."

"Not both," Suzanna hissed as she hurriedly buckled the strap of her sandal. With one foot still shoeless, she looked up at Ida and shook her head, but by then the clerk had walked off with both pairs of shoes and the charge card.

"I can't afford them both," she said in a desperate-sounding whisper.

"You don't have to afford anything. Those shoes are a gift."

"No, I intend to pay you back just as soon—"

"Your granddaddy told me to never look a gift horse in the mouth, and I'm giving you the same advice. Now, that's the end of it. I won't listen to another word about you paying me anything. As far as I'm concerned, you've already given me ten times what those shoes are worth."

"I haven't given you a dime," Suzanna argued.

"Money's not the only means of paying a person."

"I'm sorry, but I really don't understand—"

"That's because you're not as old as me. When you get to be my age, you can see the value of things a lot more clearly. I believe I'm doing exactly what your granddaddy would want me to do."

The mention of a granddaddy that was not rightfully hers made Suzanna cringe. She bent down, slid her foot into the second sandal, and buckled it ever so slowly, all the while wondering if she could ever make up for the lies she'd told. Ida deserved better. She deserved the truth, but that was the one thing Suzanna could not give her. She had chosen her path, and there was no turning back. The only thing she could do was embrace Ida wholeheartedly, return the love that was given, and pray her treachery was never discovered.

"Get a move on," Ida finally said. "I'm anxious for you to take a look at what they've got in the sportswear department."

As they rode the escalator up to the fifth floor, Suzanna again protested, saying she didn't need anything other than the shoes. "Colette wants me to wear her fashions at work, and the clothes I've got are fine for now."

"For gardening maybe, but not if you're dating."

"I'm not dating."

"Not now, but in time you will be." As they passed a display of sweater sets, Ida stopped and held up a cardigan that was the same shade of blue as Suzanna's eyes. "Now something like this would be perfect for weekends or a dinner date."

"Grandma," Suzanna said with an air of frustration.

"Darla Jean," she replied just as emphatically, "you have got to learn to accept gifts more graciously."

Suzanna quit protesting after that, but she couldn't rid herself of the lump of guilt that had settled halfway between her chest and her stomach. Although she said nothing more, she vowed that every dime of her first paycheck would go directly into Ida's bank account. She'd say she too had had a windfall and claim the money was what was left over. Once she actually had the job at Cavalier's Couture and was working steadily she could think about saving for Annie's college and the things she wanted, but her first priority had to be making sure Ida was paid back. Stealing Darla Jean's identity was bad enough; there was no way Suzanna could justify taking gifts that were intended for her.

Even after she'd made that decision, the guilt remained lodged in her chest. When they sat down to lunch in Lady Anne's Tearoom, the only thing Suzanna could manage was a cup of chamomile tea and a slice of dry toast.

EARL

The Search Begins

Once he had Bobby Doherty's name, Earl thought finding him would be a breeze. He left the library, drove to the gas station, and parked in the back alongside the telephone booth.

The county directory was dangling from a chain inside the booth. Earl flipped it open, turned to D, and began searching for Doherty, Robert or Bob. The Dohertys started with Arthur and stretched on for nearly half a column. In all, there were twenty-three: five in Sun Grove, the remainder scattered across the county. Not one of them a Robert, Bob, or Bobby. With this many Dohertys, Earl felt certain he'd find Mr. Football or a relative who could say where he was. Glancing around to make sure no one was watching, he ripped the page from the book; he'd need the addresses as well as phone numbers.

He pulled a pencil from his pocket and marked a check next to the locals. He'd start there and, if need be, branch out. Twenty-three wasn't all that many. He'd come this far; he wasn't going to stop now.

Earl took a handful of change from his pocket, laid it on the shelf, then dropped a dime into the slot and dialed the number for Charles Doherty, the first of the five locals. As the trill of the ring echoed in his ear, he thought through what he'd say. His plan was to try and sound friendly, casually call the guy by his first name and claim to be a classmate planning a reunion or maybe a football player from the high school team. He was trying to remember the name of that team, but before he could pull his thoughts together a woman answered and her voice took him by surprise.

"Charles?" he said without thinking.

"No, this is not Charles," she said in a snippy sort of way. "Do I sound like Charles?"

"No, No, of course not. I just thought—"

"Well, you thought wrong! Charles isn't here. He hasn't been here for six months. Try his girlfriend's apartment, he's probably living there."

"I'm not really looking for him. I'm actually trying to find Bobby—"

"Is this some kind of sick joke? Did Bobbi Ann put you up to this? I suppose she thinks it's fun to torment his wife for believing a marriage is something sacred, for believing that…"

It was hot as hell in the telephone booth. Earl's nerves were already on edge, and now he could feel the sweat rolling down his back. He allowed her to ramble on for a minute then cut in.

"Look, lady, I got nothing to do with whatever's going on. I'm just trying to find the Bobby Doherty who played football for Sun Grove High back in 1952. Do you know him or not?"

"Not!" she said and banged the receiver down.

"Asshole," Earl grumbled into the dead line.

He waited a moment, trying to hold back the irritation he was feeling. He couldn't afford to sound like he was spoiling for a fight if he wanted to find Bobby. He had to make them believe he was a friend looking to catch up with a classmate. He opened the telephone booth door for a breath of air, then dropped another dime in and dialed the number for the second local, Diane Doherty.

The phone rang twenty-eight times, then Earl hung up and waited for the clink of his dime dropping into the coin return.

With discouragement already feathering the edge of his thoughts, he dialed the number for Frank Doherty, the third local. A man answered on the second ring, and Earl felt his optimism rise. Men were easier to talk with. They could carry on a conversation without becoming unreasonable or flying into hysterics.

"Afternoon, Frank," he said. "I'm looking for a Bobby Doherty; played football back in '52—"

"Who is this?" Frank cut in. "And why are you looking for Bobby?"

The questions coming at him like that shook Earl, but he tried to keep his voice level. "Me and Bobby played football together. I'm in town so I thought I'd look him up, maybe have a few beers, talk about old times."

"Played football where?"

Earl was starting to sweat again. "High school."

"High school, huh? What team?"

Earl hesitated. He'd seen the name of the team in the yearbook, but it was no longer there in his mind. He closed his eyes trying to picture the red and black lettering on the team shirts, and that's when Frank spoke again.

"You don't remember me, do you?" he said. This time his voice was a lot sharper and weighted with the sound of suspicion. "I was the team workout coordinator; seems you'd remember that."

Frank hadn't said if you were actually on the team but Earl sensed the thought was there, hanging onto the end of his statement. Realizing the conversation was headed south, he tried to backpedal.

"I broke my leg early on, dropped out, but me and Bobby stayed close. I figured—"

"What'd you say your name was?"

Pinned to the wall as he was, Earl said the only thing that came to mind. "You might not remember me. I'm Suzanna Duff's brother."

"We didn't have a Duff on the team. Ever. What's going on here?"

"Nothing. You've got it all wrong—"

"No, pal, you've the one who's got it wrong. I'm gonna hang up, but if I hear from you again or get word of you bothering any of the players on that team, the cops are gonna get involved."

A click sounded, and the line went dead. Earl knew he'd blown it. He shouldn't have called and left himself wide open to questions. He should have driven by the house, looked around. Suzanna had Annie with her. If she was there, he'd see kid toys on the porch or in the yard. Driving by first to get the lay of land, that would have been smarter; much smarter.

He'd thought knowing Bobby's name would be enough to find him, but it wasn't. He'd need more information; the name of the team, the coaches, other players. He wasn't prepared this time, but next time he would be.

Earl returned to the library three afternoons in a row. He gave a polite nod to the librarian, asked to see the yearbooks for '50, '51, and '52, then sat in the research area going through them page by page. He read the team stats, studied the names of the players, and made a lengthy list of Bobby Doherty's classmates. When his brain grew weary, he turned to the picture of Suzanna and sat touching his finger to her face. He thought back on how happy he'd been when she was with him and silently swore that once she came back he'd never give her cause to leave again.

By the time Earl was ready to resume his search for Bobby, he'd made up his mind to go at it a different way. No more rushing into things. He'd take it slow, scope out the houses, watch who was coming and going, then make his move. Suzanna had already been gone five months, so what difference did another week or two make? In the end he'd have her back, and wasn't that what mattered?

Determined to avoid another go-around like he'd had with Frank Doherty, he mapped out a story that would melt the heart of almost anyone then worked on fine tuning it until it was smooth as silk. Once he found a person who might know something, he wouldn't try to pass himself off as a classmate. Instead he'd say his kid brother was on the debate team with Bobby. People were less likely to remember who was or wasn't a debater; those poor schnooks didn't get the glory of the football players. If asked, he'd say his brother was killed in an automobile accident and claim he was trying to put together a memorial. To make the tragedy seem real, he'd look away, as if holding back tears. An act like that was a sure-fire winner, and people were far less likely to press a grieving brother.

Satisfied with his plan, Earl began staking out the houses of the five Dohertys living in Sun Grove. He drove by each house six or seven times a day: early in the morning, late at night, and evenings when he could find time to slip away from his job at the bowling alley. Twilight was a good time to see without being seen. Often he'd park a few houses down and wait, hoping to catch a glimpse of Bobby, but it never happened.

After three weeks of surveillance, he had nothing and was growing more discouraged by the day. The long hours of being squashed down behind the steering wheel made his eyes weary and his legs cramped, and he began to wonder if finding Suzanna was really worth the trouble. He was reluctant to speak to Frank Doherty again and was ready to consider giving up the search when it dawned on him that Frank wasn't the only Doherty around and there was no reason why he couldn't talk to the others. He had a good story now, solid as a rock. This time it would be different.

The bowling alley was closed on Tuesday, so that morning he showered, dressed in tan slacks and the white shirt Suzanna claimed looked good, then drove over to Pauline Doherty's place. It was a squat little pink house surrounded by overgrown bushes and set back from the street. Judging by what he'd gleaned in his surveillance, the silver-haired woman lived alone, which, as far as he was concerned, was better. The last thing he wanted was another encounter such as he'd had with Frank.

Pulling up to the front of the house, he stepped out of the car, looked around to see if anyone was watching, then hurried up the walkway and rapped on the door.

"Hold on, I'll be with you in a minute," a reedy voice called out.

Earl stood waiting, the sun hot on his back, beads of perspiration rising on his forehead, and his stomach tied in knots. It seemed like forever until he heard the shuffling of footsteps coming toward him.

Pauline opened the door and smiled. "Yes?" She was as pale as a ghost and so thin it looked as though a stiff breeze could blow her away.

"Sorry to bother you," Earl said, "but I'm looking for Bobby Doherty and thought…"

Raising a hand to block the sun, Pauline glanced up. "You don't look well. You all right?"

He gave a nod and swiped at the beads of perspiration. "Just real warm."

"Well, no wonder. Here it is October and still a hundred degrees out there. Come inside; I'll pour us a cool glass of lemonade." She pulled the door back and made way for Earl to enter.

"I can't stay," he said, following her into the kitchen. "I'm trying to find Bobby Doherty, and since you've got the same last name I thought maybe you'd know him and—"

"Bobby? I most certainly do. I've known him for ages. His daddy, Harold, was first cousin to my Elgin." She handed him a glass of lemonade and pulled out a chair. "Sit," she said, then dropped down in the chair on the opposite side of the table. "So how come you're looking for Bobby?"

This time the question did not come as a surprise; Earl was ready. Smooth as molasses sliding off a spoon, he told the story of how he was working on a memorial for his kid brother. Adding one final flourish, he said, "I just know Bobby would want to be there."

Pauline gave a lingering sigh and held her hand to her heart. "That's just about the sweetest thing I've ever heard."

Not wanting to blow it by appearing overanxious, Earl hesitated a second then asked if she could give him Bobby's address.

"I would if I could," she said. "But he moved two years back, and I don't think I've got the new address." She stood, crossed the kitchen, pulled a drawer open, and began rifling through a pile of papers. "I might have saved the envelope from last year's Christmas card, and if so, this is where I would have put it."

The anxiety spread across Earl's chest like an army of red ants. "Bobby move someplace in Florida?"

"Uh-huh. West of here. A town with some tropical-sounding name. You've gotta wonder why anyone would give a town out in the middle of nowhere such a fancy name. From what Bobby said, I think it'd be better if they called it Nowheresville or maybe Lost Lakes…"

Pauline's senseless chatter caused Earl to start sweating again. His shirt was stuck to his back, and he could smell the stink of himself. He was a hair's breadth away from grabbing the drawer and dumping the contents onto the table where he could sort through them when she turned with a grin.

"Found it," she said and waved a red envelope in the air.

No longer worrying about whether or not he seemed overanxious, he snatched the envelope from her hand and eyed the return address. Sure enough, it read Bob Doherty, 1476 Hibiscus Cove, Piney Acres, Florida.

A good thing he hadn't given up, because now he had an actual lead.

SUZANNA

The Start of Something Good

Suzanna's first week at Cavalier's was more than she'd hoped for. Colette introduced her to customers, explained the nuances of various designers, and demonstrated how the right fashion choice could change a woman's appearance.

There were dozens upon dozens of tips. One color to brighten a sallow complexion, another to lessen the ruddiness of weathered cheeks, styles to make a woman seem taller or shorter, styles to make her look younger, enhance an eye color, or compensate for a God-given flaw. Suzanna savored every word and tucked each thought away in the back of her brain. It would all be there when she needed it. By the end of the week, she could glide through the shop as gracefully as Colette and pluck a garment from the rack with a flourish that gave a simple wool dress the significance of a ball gown.

On Saturday Colette handed her a paycheck.

"Darla Jean, you really are a fast learner," she said. "You've done well, and the customers like you."

A tear rose in Suzanna's eye, and she blinked it back.

"I think it's because you believed in me and gave me a chance," she replied. "I'll never be able to thank you enough."

Even though the name she used belonged to someone else, the words came from Suzanna's heart and were as sincere as any she had ever spoken.

Leaving the store her steps were so light, it was as though she were floating. The Darla Jean she'd created was becoming real. She had a job, one that would be there tomorrow, and the next day, and the day after that. It was something Suzanna had prayed for. A stroke of good fortune. Maybe her lies had been forgiven, and this was her chance to start over.

When Suzanna arrived home, everyone was gathered in the living room, the fireplace lit, and the room fragrant with the scent of pine logs. Gregg squatted on the hearth adding pieces of kindling to the fire; Ida and Annie sat together on the sofa, a jigsaw puzzle spread across the coffee table in front of them. The crackle of fall in the air and the promise of this place was as perfect as Suzanna had ever known life to be. She was a million miles away from the heartache and pain of Florida. Earl. Her father. Here, there was none of the shame she'd known. This was the second chance she'd been given.

With a sigh of contentment, she lowered herself into the overstuffed chair and kicked off her stilettos.

"Tired?" Ida asked.

"Yes, but in a good way." Suzanna leaned back, stretched her legs out, and smiled. "Today Colette said I've definitely got the job."

"Wonderful!" Ida grinned. "But I'm not at all surprised." She gave Annie a pat on the behind and said, "Scoot over there and give your mama a hug."

Annie ran over and wrapped her arms around Suzanna's neck. "Was you surprised, Mama?"

"I certainly was," Suzanna said with a laugh. "This afternoon, Colette told me to help Dr. Bergmann's wife select a dress for the country club party and said I'm her new fashion coordinator. When that happened, I had to pinch myself to make sure I wasn't dreaming."

Gregg stood and turned to face her. "Fashion coordinator, huh? That sounds like something to celebrate. How about if I take everyone to dinner?"

Ida shook her head. "Count me out. I've promised to make three trays of cookies for the ladies' club."

"Yes," Annie echoed. "And I promised to help."

Gregg eyed Suzanna with a sheepish grin. "Looks like it's just you and me."

After a moment of hesitation, she said, "I appreciate the offer, but after working all week I should probably spend some time with Grandma and Annie."

"Nonsense," Ida said. "You've worked hard. Now you need to get out and have some fun. Go. We've got all day tomorrow to catch up."

Annie hurried back to the sofa and climbed up beside Ida. "Yes, Mama, go. Grandma said you got to go so—"

"Hold on there, missy," Ida jumped in before she could finish, "don't start tattling on our private conversations." She looked down and made a pretense of zipping her mouth closed.

Annie nodded, then hiked her shoulders and giggled as if the two of them had shared some delicious secret.

Gregg eyed the cast-off stilettos and gave Suzanna a playful smile. "You could change into something comfortable, and we'd keep it low key. There's an Italian place in Barston. They've got a jukebox and some really great food…"

He waited for her answer, his head tilted ever so slightly, his expression hopeful. With a cluster of dark curls pushed back from his forehead and a hint of shyness in his smile, he was as different from Bobby as night from day, and yet she was drawn to him. It was his eyes, a blue darker than hers, but the color hardly mattered. What drew her in was the warmth and sincerity that came from them. Had Suzanna tried to refuse him, she would have been unable, because the truth was she wanted to go.

Glancing over at Ida, she asked, "Are you really sure you don't mind…"

Before she could finish the question, Ida and Annie were both shaking their heads.

The corners of her mouth curved upward as she turned back to Gregg. "Well, then, it's a date." The words were barely out of her mouth when a spot of color rose to her cheeks. "I didn't mean a date date, I just meant it's okay; I can go." She paused, knowing that she had once again used the wrong words. "Actually, it's more than okay," she finally said. "I'd love to have dinner with you."

Gregg's smile broadened. He reached for her hand and tugged her up from the chair. "Go ahead and change. I think we might find a bottle of red wine with your name on it."

On the drive to Barston, they chatted as they had when she'd driven him to work and home again, but this time it was somehow different. The conversation was just as easy, only now there was a hint of intimacy woven through the words. It was something Suzanna couldn't quite put a name to—like a shared secret they'd agreed not to mention.

At the restaurant, they slid into a booth and sat across from one another. Gregg ordered a bottle of chianti, and they pushed the menus aside.

"Give us some time," he told the waitress.

At the end of the table, an oil lamp with a red shade flickered as they chatted about Annie and how just that week she'd learned to roller skate, about the aunts and uncles he'd left behind in Pennsylvania and the new baby that would be there before Christmas. When he asked about her job, she explained how she'd at first felt wobbly on such high heels, then learned to pivot and turn almost as easily as Colette. And how, although frightened to death, she'd helped the mayor's wife select a dress that minimized her more than ample bosom.

"It's amazing what you can do when you have to," she quipped.

With his eyes fixed on her face, he told her that he found everything about her to be amazing.

"You've got a glow that shines from within," he said. "Annie has it also. It's not something you see every day." He hesitated a moment then, reaching across the table, took her hand in his. "The first time we met, I sensed you were somebody special, and I wanted to get to know you."

It had been a long time since anyone said anything that flattering to Suzanna, and she blushed. At a loss for words, she turned it off with a lighthearted comment about how she'd just come in from gardening and was a mess.

"A mess?" He smiled and shook his head. "That's not the way I remember it. Yes, you had dirt on your face and some leaves caught in your hair, but that made you look even more adorable." He went on to say how he'd wanted to ask her out that day. "If your grandma hadn't rented the room to me, I would have found another way to get to know you."

Suzanna took a sip of wine, and the warmth of it settled in her chest. It was a good feeling, one she wanted to embrace. It would be easy to love Gregg; he was a good man, fun to be with, caring, and sincere in his love of family. Suzanna knew there were a million reasons to let herself go and only one reason not to: Bobby Doherty. The memory came without bidding, and it stayed even though she tried to push it away.

Eight years ago, he'd flattered her in much the same way. He'd said she was different than the other high school girls and that he'd never known anyone like her. He claimed she was the sun, the moon and the stars, but those words disappeared just days after she told him she was pregnant. In the end, he'd left her with a broken heart and a memory that refused to be forgotten.

Suzanna took another sip of wine and leaned into the conversation, willing thoughts of him from her mind. Closer up she could see the depth of sensitivity in Gregg's expression. His eyes were not just blue but tinged with shades of grey and green, fringed with lashes that were dark and feathery. When he spoke, she could hear the gentleness of his voice, the soft round tones that were as warm and comforting as a quilt. There was no reason to hold back. This wasn't a repeat of eight years ago. This was a new life, and she was not Suzanna. She was Darla Jean Parker.

The sound of music came from the jukebox in the bar, a mix of oldies and current hits. The Shirelles began singing Will You Still Love Me Tomorrow, and a couple from across the room got up to dance. Gregg smiled and glanced toward the small dance floor.

"Shall we?"

She nodded, then stood and allowed him to lead her across the room. As they stepped onto the dance floor, he took her in his arms and she felt the warmth of his hand on her back as he gently brought her closer to his chest. Her heart skipped a beat, quickened, then slowed to a normal rhythm as she lowered her head onto his shoulder.

They danced to the next three songs; then a fourth record dropped into place, and the bitter memories returned. Wanted. Perry Como singing about a broken romance and how he wanted nothing more than the return of his lover. Suzanna remembered the song only too well. After Bobby had gone off to college, she'd listened to it night after night as she paced the floor with Annie in her arms.

The magic of the moment was gone.

"Let's sit this one out," she said, and they returned to the booth.

It was almost ten by the time they ate dinner and after midnight when they returned home. On the upstairs landing Gregg paused long enough to say he'd had a wonderful time, then he touched his hand to her shoulder, kissed her cheek, and said he hoped they could do it again. For a moment, she thought he was going to take her in his arms and kiss her full on the mouth, passionately, and without reservation. He didn't, and as she climbed the stairs to the third floor, she felt an odd sense of disappointment.

SUZANNA

The Harvest Festival

After that night, Suzanna could tell things had changed. Not right away, but over time. Evenings when they settled in front of the television, Ida sat in the big club chair and Annie squeezed in beside her, leaving her and Gregg to sit beside one another on the sofa. Before long Annie's eyelids inevitably grew heavy, and after Suzanna had carried her off to bed Ida generally disappeared as well.

That's when they'd find themselves alone. She'd move closer, and Gregg would wrap his arm around her shoulder. Once they began talking the evening flew by and when the eleven o'clock news came on, it always seemed too soon.

"The news already?" Gregg would say, and there was little she could do but nod.

"I've got an early day tomorrow," she'd say, then snap off the television and they'd head up the stairs together. At the landing, they'd pause long enough for a hug and a quick kiss, then head off to their respective bedrooms—hers on the third floor, his down at the far end of the hall.

Sometimes they'd slip away for an early dinner date, a movie, or an evening with Phil and Ginger, but on weekends he always came up with something that included Annie. A visit to the pumpkin patch, a hayride, the high school football game, the church bazaar. The three of them would spend the day together, and then later, after she'd tucked Annie into bed, she'd come downstairs and spend the remainder of the evening with Gregg. While the weather was still warm enough, they'd sit on the front porch or stroll hand in hand for a number of blocks then return home and settle in front of the television.

When the Harvest Festival came to Barston, posters went up all over town and Gregg invited everyone to go.

"We'll start early in the morning," he said, "and make a day of it."

Annie's eyes lit up. "Will there be pony rides?"

"Pony rides, a carousel, animal shows, games, and lots more," Gregg said. "I'll bet you've never seen anything so spectacular."

Annie was full of questions and he patiently answered each one, telling how the Ferris wheel was taller than a house, the cotton candy sweeter than sugar, and the lights brighter than a Christmas tree.

The house was filled with an excitement that soon became contagious, and after a fair bit of wheedling even Ida agreed to come along.

On Sunday morning, Annie was up before the sun and came running into Suzanna's room.

"Wake up, Mama," she shouted. "It's time to go to the festival!"

Suzanna opened one sleepy eye and smiled. "It's too early. The festival isn't open yet."

"But it will be soon," Annie argued.

"It doesn't open until ten o'clock." Suzanna pointed to the clock on her nightstand. "It's only five now."

Annie's face fell. "Oh."

She folded the covers back to make way for Annie. "Climb in with me, and we'll talk about all the wonderful things we're going to do today. How's that?"

Annie crawled into the bed and snuggled up to her. As they lay curled together in the pre-dawn light, Suzanna retold the stories Gregg had told of the festival. She'd just finished explaining the games of chance and saying how it just might be possible for him to win her a doll or a stuffed toy when Annie cut in.

"You know, Mama, I think Mister Gregg is ready. Can I ask him to be my daddy?"

Suzanna was dumfounded. Years earlier she'd told Annie that the man who was her father wasn't ready to be a daddy, so he'd run off.

"Don't worry," she'd said then. "I'll love you twice as much as most mamas love their babies to make up for him not being here."

There'd never been any further discussion about it, until now.

"Why on earth would you ask that?" she said. "Gregg is a really good friend, but you know he's not your—"

"Yes, I know," Annie replied. "But he likes me and he does nice things like Lois's daddy, so I think maybe he wants to be…"

"Forget about it. You can't just pick somebody to be your daddy. Relationships are complicated and way beyond your understanding. For now, let's be glad we've got such a good friend." She started to tickle Annie. "And don't you dare mention a silly thing like this to anyone else, or I'll tickle you to death."

That afternoon the four of them walked up and down the festival aisles admiring the multitude of crafts on display, sampling foods, and trying their hand at games of chance. After a half-dozen attempts, Gregg finally sunk three baskets in a row and won the stuffed dog Annie wanted. Before the day was out, she'd been on every ride at the festival, taken three pony rides, petted a mama hog, laughed at the dogs in frilly dresses, and consumed enough hot dogs, pizza, candy apples, ice cream, and soda to last her for a month. When her little legs grew too tired to walk, Gregg lifted her onto his shoulder and carried her back to the car.

At that moment, Suzanna wished she had a camera. The sight of Annie with her arms hooked around Gregg's neck and her head leaned against the back of his was one she would keep in her mind forever. Years from now, when the festival was nothing but a distant memory, she knew she would be able to call this picture to mind and once again see the weary smile on Annie's face and the dangling shoelace that had come untied. She'd remember the plaid of Gregg's shirt and think of how his back was straight and strong as he carried Annie. And there in the background, she'd hear the fading sound of calliope music as they left the festival behind. There would be no forgetting this perfect day.

Later on, after Annie and Ida were both sound asleep, they settled in the living room. It was the time of year when the evenings turned cool and the wind came in gusts, scattering dry leaves across the walkway. Gregg carried an armful of logs in and stacked them in the fireplace. His curls were windblown and his cheeks pink.

"This is a good night for a fire," he said and lit the kindling.

Instead of turning on the television as she usually did, Suzanna took the bottle of brandy from the cupboard and poured them both a drink.

"A perfect end to a perfect day."

She touched her glass to his then, without lowering her eyes, took a sip. The amber liquid was warm in her throat and comforting in her chest. It was the shot of courage she needed.

After months of holding back and worrying that this physical attraction was too much too soon, Suzanna was ready to let go. She wanted to move beyond the quick hugs and goodnight kisses on the landing. She wanted to know if this was a friendship or something more, something that could blossom into the kind of love she'd felt for Bobby. She eased back into the cushions of the sofa and lazily tilted her head back. It was an invitation for him to kiss her, not in the casual way he had before, but full on the mouth.

He smiled then leaned over her, his breath warm on her cheek, his forehead grazing hers. She closed her eyes and felt the gentle brush of his lips against her ear.

"I've wanted to do this since the day we met," he whispered then he brought his mouth to hers, and in that singular moment all her doubts fell away. The kiss was long and sweet, a promise of all that was yet to come.

That night the eleventh hour came and went, but Suzanna made no mention of an early morning and neither did Gregg. As he trailed a line of kisses along her neck and spoke of a future together, she knew every last trace of Suzanna was gone. Although she could not say how or when it happened, Darla Jean Parker had let down her guard and fallen in love with this stranger from Pennsylvania.

EARL

Piney Acres Problems

The day after he'd gotten Bobby Doherty's address from Pauline, Earl called the bowling alley and said he'd need to take a few days off. A family emergency, he claimed. He figured he'd do as he did with Pauline: stake the place out in Piney Acres, watch who was coming and going, and get the lay of the land before making his move.

If Bobby was working a day job, getting Suzanna alone would be a piece of cake. Earl could wait until the guy was out of the house, then show up on the doorstep with a bouquet of flowers. He might even swing by the drugstore and pick up one of those stuffed toys for Annie. Him having something for the kid was sure to squelch any doubts Suzanna had.

Earl tossed a few clothes and a bottle of Seagram's 7 into a duffle bag, then headed for Piney Acres. It was a long, slow, crappy drive, mostly back roads full of potholes. Twice he turned down the wrong road and ended up in a cow pasture.

The second time, he could feel the agitation pressing against his chest. Not good. He wanted to be at his best when he talked to Suzanna. He had to convince her he'd changed. But how was he supposed to do that when this trip was one lousy problem after another?

He didn't always understand Suzanna, and now more so than ever. She hated the boonies, and Sun Grove was a city compared to this area. Okay, they'd gone through a number of rough patches and that last night was something that maybe shouldn't have happened, but her leaving him to come here just didn't make sense. Why, he asked himself. Why?

The question got stuck in his head and started to niggle him. Shortly after the paved road turned to gravel, he came up with an answer that only added to his misery. She's still in love with the guy.

That thought was like a razor blade slicing off a piece of his heart. Trying to rid himself of it, he snapped on the radio and started searching for anything to take his mind off of the painfully obvious answer. He hoped to find a talk show or an oldies station, but all he got was static and crackling. After rotating the dial back and forth a dozen times, he finally caught what sounded like a voice and tried to zero in on that. For a while it was like a chicken squawking. When it cleared, he heard Big Jim saying they were in for two days of rain.

"Great, just great," he grumbled and clicked the radio off.

Minutes later he spotted the sign: Piney Acres, 2 Miles. An arrow pointed to the right.

Piney Acres was a town that seemed to rise up out of nowhere: the streets paved with blacktop, the squat little houses clustered together in some spots and separated by overgrown thickets of scrub pine in others. On almost every corner there was a sign pointing the way to the Piney Acres Clubhouse and Golf Course.

Following the signs, Earl turned onto Long Drive Road and headed for the clubhouse. It seemed as good a spot as any to start. He'd ask a few questions, find out where Hibiscus Cove was located, and maybe, if he got lucky, catch someone who'd seen Suzanna.

After fifteen minutes of following Long Drive Road through the different neighborhoods, Earl's frustration was close to the breaking point. The road went nowhere. It was an endless loop that wound its way through the streets then circled around and brought him right back to where he'd started. At first he'd only suspected it, but when he passed the same yellow and pink house for a third time he was absolutely certain.

He drove another five blocks and saw that same blasted sign on every corner. All of them with an arrow pointing to Long Drive Road.

"What the hell..." he grumbled.

He slowed down, hoping to see a second sign indicating a turn-off or a bend in the road he might have missed, but there was nothing. Shortly after he passed the yellow and pink house for the fourth time, he spotted a street sign for Clubhouse Drive. Figuring that had to be it, he turned in.

Several blocks down, the street dead-ended. A single-story building sat directly across the road. It was as low as the houses he'd passed but nearly a block wide. Above the door was a sign that read Piney Acres Clubhouse. Given the aggravation he'd already gone through, Earl was tempted to pull up to the front door and leave his car smack in front of the "No Parking" sign; he didn't, but only because it would have been like thumbing his nose at the place. Right now, he had to make friends with whoever was inside. It was the only way he could find out what he needed to know.

To get from the parking lot to the entrance, he had to circle the building. Three-quarters of the way around, he heard a distant clap of thunder and quickened his step. In Florida the rain could be on one side of the street and not the other. It came and went in the blink of eye and was not worth worrying about. He hurried on and pushed through the front door.

The lobby had a desk and three leather sofas, all empty. In the center of the floor a stanchion sign read, "Golf Restricted – Cart Path Only – Men's Luncheon Canceled".

Earl wondered if that was good or bad as far as Bobby Doherty was concerned. If he were a golfer, would he have gone off to work instead? Or would he spend the day in bed with Suzanna the way Earl used to do?

Thoughts of how he and Suzanna had enjoyed those days saddened him. Annie, she was the problem. She was still an infant back then, but once she got old enough to talk, everything changed. First it was no swearing, then no walking around the house naked, and no drinking. Annie had taken all the fun out of life, and Suzanna didn't even realize it. Maybe if he reminded her of how much fun they'd had, she might consider leaving the kid with Bobby. That was, if he'd be sucker enough to take her.

The sound of laughter came from the back, and Earl followed it down the hallway. Just beyond the double doors was a room full of tables, most of them occupied by poker-playing foursomes. Earl stood there for several minutes; no one turned, looked up, or bothered to greet him. Tired of waiting, he walked over to the nearest table and said, "Excuse me."

The mustached man closest to him glanced up then looked back to his opponent across the table.

"I think you're bluffing," he said. "I'm gonna raise two cents and call." He tossed two pennies into the pile of coins in the center of the table.

The players on both sides folded, but Mr. Mustache's opponent just sat there studying the cards in his hand.

"Excuse me," Earl repeated, only this time his words had a bite to them. "You mind answering a question?"

No one even glanced up, and that ticked him off no end. There were two things Earl couldn't abide: one was being put down and the other was being ignored. Mr. Mustache was doing both. He had half a mind to upend the table and send the cards flying. Then they'd acknowledge his presence. He'd make damn sure of it.

The vein in Earl's neck throbbed, the muscles in his back tensed, and the inside of his head felt hotter than a furnace. At the moment, nothing would have given him greater pleasure than seeing these assholes get what they deserved, but he had to stay focused. Finding Suzanna was why he was there. He drew a deep breath and turned to the player who had folded.

"I'm looking for Bobby Doherty, you know him?"

The player gave a nod, held up a finger, and mouthed the words One minute.

The furnace inside his head burned hotter still. He gritted his teeth and counted backward from ten, as he'd been told to do. Sometimes it worked, sometimes it didn't. Right now, he was on the edge and sliding fast. Just as he leaned forward and gripped the rim of the table, the opponent tossed his cards down.

"I'm out," he said begrudgingly.

As Mr. Mustache was scooping up the coins, the side player turned back to Earl. "Yes, I know Bobby. You a friend?"

Earl gave a non-committal nod. "Yeah, but it's been a while. I'm tight with his cousin, Pauline. She said I ought to look him up while I'm over here."

The guy looked around scanning the room. "I don't see him here today. Could be he's with a lady friend."

"Oh?" Earl felt his heart quicken. This was it; the wait had been worth it. "So, he's got a lady friend, huh?"

Before he could describe Suzanna or ask if Annie was with her, the player guffawed as if he'd just delivered the punchline of a joke. "Bobby don't have a lady friend, he's got a half dozen. The women love him, but only God knows why."

The idea of this guy taking Suzanna away from him and then cheating on her was mind-blowing. After causing such a ruckus over every little thing he did, why would she tolerate cheating? It was way worse than drinking or using a few obscenities. He was about to describe Suzanna and ask if she was the lady friend when a new thought suddenly crossed his mind.

Maybe she wasn't all that tolerant. Maybe she wanted out but had no place to go. If that were the case she'd be glad to come home, especially once he promised there'd be no more drinking or cussing in front of the kid. A grin curled the corners of his mouth. This was gonna be easier than he thought.

Trying not to tip his hand, he said, "So you figure the best place to catch Bobby is at his place on Hibiscus?"

The card player shrugged. "He comes and goes, but you can give it a shot."

Mr. Mustache dealt another hand then leaned back in his chair and looked up at Earl. "You wanna speed this up, buddy? You're holding up the game."

A flash of heat sizzled across Earl's brain, and he again reached for the table. That's when the opponent, a man with silver hair and cool blue eyes, spoke.

"To get to Hibiscus, go back, take a right onto Long Drive, then a left on Palmetto and a quick right onto Hibiscus. Doherty's house is the second one in."

"Thanks," Earl mumbled, pushing the word through his teeth.

He turned and hurried back down the hallway. It was either that or bust Mr. Mustache in the mouth. The fire inside his head was causing him to perspire, and he could smell the stink of it on his skin. Anger came quicker with Suzanna gone, and it was more uncontrollable. Years ago, he'd been able to hold back and keep it in check but now it was tougher.

He had to believe it was a temporary thing, a mood swing that came with spending too much time alone. Once Suzanna was back, he'd get it under control. He was certain of it. Well, reasonably certain.

Following the directions he'd been given, Earl headed for Hibiscus Cove and found it with no trouble. He parked around the corner on Palmetto with the car partially hidden but still having a clear line of sight to the house. It was after four, and the sky was already growing dusky. Soon the lights would be coming on, and he'd be able to see if someone was inside the house. For now, all he could do was wait and watch.

He sat there mulling over what he'd say to Suzanna, and the minutes ticked by so slowly it felt like hours. The problem with waiting was that it left him with nothing to do but think. It was a lot easier when he could move around. At the bowling alley, he could kill an hour working the counter or burn off steam loading pins into the frame. Here the only thing he could do was wait.

When the waiting became so tedious that Earl thought his head would explode, he pulled out the bottle of Seagram's, took a swig, and relaxed into the comforting burn that slid down his throat. That drink was followed by another and then another. As he watched the dark clouds roll across the sky a rumble of thunder sounded in the distance, and before long raindrops splattered the windshield.

With the rain came a blast of cold air that sent a shiver up Earl's spine. The fall weather was one of the things he hated about Florida. The days hot and sticky, the nights cold and damp. After 45 years he should've been used to it, but he wasn't. With a shirt that was too thin and a belly that was empty, he felt cold and hungry. Earlier he'd had no interest in food, but now his stomach was rumbling. He tried to remember when he'd last eaten. Yesterday? The day before? Grabbing the whiskey bottle, he downed several gulps and again found the warmth of it comforting.

It seemed downright stupid for Suzanna to be so dead set against him having a drink now and again. Especially when it was something that made him feel so good. Whiskey had gotten him through many a bad night. It was something he could count on. With a bottle of whiskey in his hand he felt stronger, more powerful, more certain of himself.

When the lights in the surrounding houses started to come on, he downed another swig and leaned close to the windshield, hoping to see through the rain.

Before long the grays and blues of the sky disappeared, and there was nothing but blackness overhead. Still Doherty's house remained dark. Earl imagined them out to dinner. Laughing, happy, enjoying drinks and a hot meal while he sat here cold and hungry. He took another swig. No matter how long he had to wait, he was determined to see it through. He had something to say, and like it or not Suzanna would have to listen.

After several hours, his eyelids grew heavy. He was drifting on the edge of sleep when the sound of a car startled him. He watched as the black sedan rounded the corner and pulled into Doherty's driveway. A man got out, opened the garage door, then pulled the car into the garage and closed the door behind him. There was a woman in the car, Earl was certain of it, but given the rain and darkness he couldn't say whether or not it was Suzanna. The thought that it might be riled him, and he reached for the bottle again.

Minutes later a light came on in the front of the house then a second one in the back. The one in the back had to be a bedroom. Remembering how it was when Suzanna first came to his bedroom, he climbed from the car, opened the trunk, and took out the tire iron. The likelihood was he wouldn't need it, but better safe than sorry.

Rounding the corner of Palmetto, he crossed Hibiscus, his shirt now soaked by the rain but the fire inside of him raging. From the walkway in front of the house, he could see a bar on the left side of the room. Doherty was standing there, a cocktail shaker in his hand. He looked over his shoulder and hollered something, but it was too far away to hear.

Earl moved closer and caught the sound of her voice, muffled but like what he remembered. Closer up he got a look at Doherty and understood what Suzanna saw in the guy. Dressed in a jacket and tie, he was a sharp dresser, had a nice house, and likely came from money. But all that didn't negate the fact that he was a cheater, which was something she probably didn't know.

Doherty filled two stemmed glasses and carried them toward the right side of the room. When Earl lost sight of him, he made his way through the bougainvillea hedge and stood with his back pushed up against the house. He hesitated a moment to make certain he hadn't been discovered, then turned to peer in the window.

Doherty was gone; so were the glasses. Now that he had a full view of the room, Earl saw the hallway leading to the rear of the house. He was ready to head for that window when he heard Doherty's voice. He stepped back into the shadows and remained motionless.

Doherty called out saying he'd be right in; then there was music, and the light was turned off. Anxious to get a look inside that back window, Earl clamored through the bushes. He was almost clear when the heel of his shoe caught on a root, and he tumbled forward. The tire iron flew out of his hand and clanged against the walkway. The light clicked on a split-second later.

With his heart hammering against his chest, Earl flattened himself against the ground, afraid to move a muscle. The light caught the top of the bushes and fell across the yard but Earl remained face down in the dirt, hidden from sight. A shadow moved inside the house. It stopped for a moment then moved on, and the room went dark again.

Earl waited until he was certain the coast was clear before he scrambled up, grabbed the tire iron, and headed toward the back yard. Once there, he saw where the light was coming from. Two clerestory windows. They were a good six feet wide but less than two feet tall and so high up it was impossible to see into the room. He took a step back, trying to catch a glimpse of the woman from a distance, but the only thing he could see was a slow-moving ceiling fan.

In the light of day, Earl might have had sense enough to walk away, but given the amount of whiskey he'd downed and the raging fire in his head he didn't. Instead he grabbed a trash can, dumped the contents in the yard, then upended the can and climbed atop it. Holding onto the window frame, he pulled himself up to where he could see the entire bedroom. It was empty; no Doherty, no Suzanna.

He heard voices again, only this time they came from outside. He let go of the window frame and tried to scramble down, but the can wobbled and Earl went over, landing flat on his back. Before he could move, he was blinded by a flashlight and heard an officer yelling that he was under arrest.

⟳⟲

Since Earl was found with a tire iron, he was considered armed and dangerous and held in the local lock-up for the next 24 hours. On Friday he stood before the district court judge trying to claim it was all a mistake.

"I wasn't myself," he said. "I been sick with worry over my fiancé who took our daughter and run off with a guy named Bobby Doherty."

The judge looked over at Doherty. "You know anything about this, Mr. Doherty?"

"Absolutely not. I'm not a man who seduces young women with children."

Standing firm on his claim, Earl said, "I know for a fact my Suzanna's with a guy named Bobby Doherty. If he ain't the one, then he knows who else has got the exact same name, and he ought to say who."

With a curious expression, the judge eyed Doherty and asked, "Do you know the party the defendant is referring to?"

"No, sir, your honor," Doherty said. "The only other Bobby Doherty I know is my nephew, and he moved to Atlanta over three years ago. He's a highly respected lawyer with Greene and Garrett and a happily married man. I doubt he'd have an interest in cavorting with this man's so-called fiancé."

A light bulb went off in Earl's head. The lawyer nephew had to be the one he'd been looking for.

"Okay, I made a mistake," he said penitently. "Making a mistake ain't a crime."

"No, it's not," the judge replied. "But voyeurism and trespassing certainly is." He banged the gavel down and said, "Sixty days."

"Sixty days!" Earl yelled. "You gotta be kidding me!"

"I assure you I'm not," the judge said, "and if I hear another outburst, it will be doubled."

"What kind of crackpot sentence is that? A man makes one lousy mistake—"

The judge banged the gavel again. "120 days. Do you want to try for six months?"

Earl shook his head and was led from the courtroom.

IDA

A Family Thanksgiving

Two weeks after the Harvest Festival, Ida had a dream that was so vivid it woke her in the middle of the night. In the dream she sat across the kitchen table from Bill, and he looked as he did in those last few years before the cancer. His hair snow white, his hands gnarled and stiff, but his eyes as clear and blue as they'd been the day she first met him. He stretched his arm across the table and took her hand in his.

"Have you thought this through?" he asked.

She nodded, and he smiled.

"I was so terribly lonely in those early days, the days right after..."

She was unable to say the words, but he understood. It was as it had always been. He knew her thoughts before she gave them voice.

"I'd lost the will to even get out of bed. In the morning I'd wake, see the sun in the sky, then pull the covers over my head and turn my face to the wall. Loneliness is worse than cancer, Bill. Cancer only destroys your body, but loneliness, that eats away at every part of you, even your heart and mind."

"I know," he said tenderly. "I've been watching over you."

"Moving on doesn't mean I've stopped caring. I hope you realize that."

"Of course I do. I never meant for you to be unhappy."

"I was for a long time, but now it's different. The house is like it was when you were here, full of happiness and laughter. The day that girl walked into the Elks Club, I knew something good would come of it." She hesitated a moment then gave way to an easy smile. "You brought them here to be with me, didn't you?"

He shook his head ever so slowly. "No, Ida, I didn't. But perhaps He did."

"He? He who?"

Bill chuckled. "You'll find out in time." He took his hand from hers and leaned back in the chair. "I can't stay, sweetheart, but there's something you should know."

"Don't go! Please. Just a few minutes longer—"

His voice grew thin and far away sounding. "I can't stay, but I'll always be here. Even when you don't see me, know that I'm here, watching over you."

Tears blurred her vision, and when she reached for his arm it was no longer there.

"Bill, wait," she cried. "What were you going to tell me?"

When no answer came, the thudding of her heart made it seem as though her chest were going to explode. It was as if someone were shaking her, tugging her arm, calling her to wake up.

She opened her eyes and sat up. There in the darkness of the bedroom they'd shared for all those years, she could sense his presence.

"You're still here, aren't you?"

There was no answer.

Ida leaned back into the pillows and sat there thinking. A sliver of moonlight fell softly across the floor, and the house was so silent she could hear the sound of her breath rising and falling. Remembering his words, a troublesome thought entered her mind. Perhaps Bill was trying to warn her of something, but what?

He seemed pleased at the thought of Annie and her mom being here, so it had to be something else. Gregg? The thought of such a nice young man being of concern seemed ludicrous; it had to be something else. Ida ran through a litany of things to worry about and summarily dismissed each one.

Then it hit her. Time. That's what Bill was trying to tell her. He was trying to warn her that, like him, she had less time than she thought. If that were the case, she would have to do something soon. With the situation as complicated as it was, she was going to need a plan and even then it would be no easy task. She sat for hours trying to figure out a way to overcome the obstacles, work around the truth of what was, and get to where she needed to be. It would be difficult but not impossible. Bill had done it. He'd planned ahead and arranged for a home insurance policy that paid off the house so she'd wouldn't be left homeless. She now needed to be as creative and clever as he'd been.

The sun was coming up when she finally realized the answer to her problem was smack in front of her nose. Gregg. He was somebody she knew and liked. He was a man with principles, a man who cared about family. Why, he'd left a perfectly good job in Pennsylvania to come here just because his brother's wife was having a baby. A man who'd do a thing like that would definitely be a good daddy for Annie. And since he and Darla Jean already seemed crazy about one another, that would make it all the easier.

That evening when they were gathered around the dinner table, Ida brought up the subject of Thanksgiving.

"I'm planning to make a turkey with all the trimmings," she said. "Cranberry sauce, candied sweet potatoes, everything."

"Sounds wonderful," Gregg said. "I'd hate to miss a meal like that, but since I haven't been with family for the past two years, I thought it would be nice to spend it with Phil and Ginger."

Ida gave a cagey grin. "I agree wholeheartedly. I was thinking maybe they could join us." She went on to say with Ginger expecting a baby in less than a month, she'd likely welcome the chance to let someone else do the cooking.

Gregg gave a nod. "That's probably true. I'll call and ask."

As it turned out, Ginger had her mom driving up from Florida to spend the holiday with them. Without a flicker of hesitation, Ida suggested Ginger's mom come along.

"All the better," she said. "I've already ordered a twenty-six-pound turkey, and I don't want to end up with a refrigerator full of leftovers."

Once it was agreed that Phil, Ginger, and her mom, would all be there for Thanksgiving dinner, Ida counted up the number of people—a total of seven. Since there were eight chairs circling the dining room table, she also invited Homer Portnick.

By the time Thanksgiving Day arrived, the sideboard was loaded with cakes and pies, and there was not an empty spot to be found in the refrigerator.

When everyone gathered at the table, Ida was beaming. It was exactly as she hoped it would be.

"Best turkey I've ever tasted," Gregg said.

Homer Portnick stuck another forkful of stuffing in his mouth and nodded.

Conversations crisscrossed the table, and the sound of happiness was everywhere. Ginger patted her stomach, claiming it felt as though she were having triplets. She then had to reassure her mom such was not the case.

"Dr. Ellsworth said there's only one heartbeat, Mom; I think I've just eaten too much turkey." She gave a sheepish grin and laughed.

Gregg told of how it was beginning to look as though Mrs. Davis would not be returning from her maternity leave.

"I think the school may offer me a permanent position," he said then gave Suzanna a wink. "If that happens, I'll be looking to buy a house and settle down here."

"Buy a house?" Ida said. "When I'm counting on the income from your rent?"

That wasn't true, but she needed him to believe it was. It happened too quickly, and claiming to need the rent was the only thing she could think of at the moment.

"Don't worry, Mrs. Parker. I'd never leave you in the lurch. Anyway, I may not know for sure until next spring. If it does happen, I'd need a year or so to find a place and I'd stay until you've found a renter to take my place."

A year? A year can fly by in almost no time. That's why Bill wanted to warn me.

The look of shock on Ida's face faded, replaced by a forced smile. "Although I'm delighted to hear you'll be a permanent member of our community, I'm selfishly glad that you won't be leaving here for a while." A long while, she thought. Hopefully forever.

Anxious to move on, she turned to talk of the holiday, saying it was a time when everyone should stop and count their blessings. She began to recount hers, and they were all related to Darla Jean and Annie. Once she'd finished, the others at the table joined in, each telling of something they were thankful for.

Edna, Ginger's mom, flashed a radiant smile and said that in two weeks she'd be a grandma for the first time.

"I'm going to sell my place in Florida and move to Barston," she added happily. "That way I'll be nearby and can spend time with my grandchild."

Sitting next to Edna, Homer plopped a third helping of mashed potatoes onto his plate.

"I don't have any children or grandchildren," he said glumly, "but I'm sure enough thankful to have finally passed the Motor Vehicle Department test and have a driving license."

"And I'm thankful you're less likely to back into my car again," Gregg quipped.

Everyone laughed.

Phil and Ginger smiled at one another and spoke as one voice.

"We both come from small families," he said, "so we're overjoyed to have Ginger's mom and Gregg here to share in the excitement of our first child."

Annie rattled off a list of a dozen things, including her new doll, her friend, Lois, Grandma's cookies, her canopy bed, and the fact that they'd left Earl behind.

Suzanna cringed at the mention of Earl, then quickly took over.

"That's enough." She gave Annie a playful pat on the head, then said, "What Annie meant to say is that we are grateful beyond belief to be here, have a family, a place to call home, and a job I can count on."

The big surprise came a few minutes later when she gave them her news. "And on top of everything else I have to be happy about, Colette is featuring me as the lead model in the holiday fashion show at the Barston Country Club."

Ginger's eyes lit up. "That's the biggest event in Barston. Colette usually brings in one or two models from Atlanta to work the holiday show."

"It really is big." Ida nodded. "The proceeds from that affair fund the volunteer fire department, so everyone comes to support it."

"Mama, are you gonna be a star?" Annie asked.

"Not a star, but I will get a nice bonus for working the show, and with Christmas just around the corner the extra money will come in pretty handy."

"Actually, you are going to be a star." Ginger's words had the sound of jealousy sticking to them. "This event draws close to 200 people."

She was in the middle of telling how the spotlight was focused on each model as she walked across the stage then swept through the room gathering oohs and ahhs from onlookers when she gave a sudden squeal and jumped up from the table.

"Good grief, my water just broke!"

Ida grinned. "Well, Edna, it looks like you're going to be a grandma sooner than you thought."

In the flurry of activity that followed, she never noticed the worried look that had settled on Suzanna's brow.

SUZANNA

Foolish Fears

The thought of 200 strangers attending the fashion show was something Suzanna hadn't taken into account. She'd naively imagined it to be a gathering of silver-haired ladies sipping tea, asking if this or that outfit came in a larger size. It was sheer stupidity on her part. She should have known. With Colette ordering a special pair of silver sandals for her to wear with the evening gown and paying her an additional $100 to work the show, how could she not have realized the event was going to be really big?

Up until now she'd played it smart and kept a low profile. She'd wisely avoided any situation where someone might speak up and say she was not who she claimed to be, and it had worked. With Ida squarely behind her, no one had even raised an eyebrow at the thought of her being Darla Jean Parker. They'd all, every last one, taken her at her word and she had foolishly allowed it to lull her into a false sense of security.

Now she was going to risk everything, and for what? A pair of silver sandals? An extra $100? A moment of glory? All of it was meaningless compared to what she had: a home where Annie was happy and thriving, a grandmother who loved her, and quite possibly a future with Gregg.

After a worry-filled night of tossing and turning, Suzanna woke Friday morning with dark shadows beneath her eyes and her stomach twisted in knots. She patted a bit of concealer beneath her eyes, dressed for work, then hurried downstairs to grab a quick cup of coffee.

"No breakfast for me today," she said, then filled a mug and sat at the table.

Ida looked up. "Are you sick?" Setting the platter of scrambled eggs back on the counter, she came across the room and held a hand to Suzanna's forehead. "It doesn't feel like you've got a fever."

"I don't," Suzanna replied, "but I'm worried that agreeing to be a model in Colette's show was a big mistake. I honestly don't think I'm up to it."

"Nonsense, you'll be great. You've got the looks, and she obviously believes you can do it or she wouldn't have asked."

"I'm not good in front of a crowd. And the thought of all those strangers—"

"If that's what has you upset, then you're worrying about nothing. The women who go to the holiday fashion show are the same ones who shop at Cavalier's. The only difference is that for this event, they have their hair done and get gussied up."

"What about newspaper reporters? And out-of-towners?"

"Imogene Cranston, the woman who does the social events column for The Town Crier will be snapping some pictures, but she's the only reporter. A few of the ladies invite a cousin or friend from nearby, and some coerce their husbands into coming along. But they're locals out for an afternoon of fun, not people you have to worry about impressing."

Searching for what would sound like a reasonable explanation, Suzanna said, "It's not that…"

She stopped, her breath caught in her throat. There was no logical way to explain her fears; she was stuck in a lie with no way out. Her voice quavered as she forced the words to come.

"It's the thought of being up there in front of a crowd of strangers."

Ida pulled her into a hug. "Darla Jean, you need to stop thinking of them as strangers. Sure, they'll be dressed up, but underneath the ruffles and feathers they're the same women you've waited on for the past two months."

"You really think so?"

"Yes, I do. If you doubt my word, ask Colette. She'll tell you the same thing."

"But Ginger said—"

"You're not Ginger. She never modeled for the show, and judging from the way she talked about it I'm guessing it was something she really wanted."

"Maybe so, but that doesn't change anything. It's still a big crowd and—"

"It changes everything," Ida said. "Ginger's outside looking in; when you want something you don't have, it appears bigger, better, more impressive, something to stand in awe of. But you're on the inside, so you should be able to see the reality of what it is."

With a puzzled look tugging at her face, Suzanna said, "I don't get it."

"Ginger was standing on the edge of the show, so she saw the gathering as one huge and very impressive crowd. But as you're walking through the room, you'll be able to see those people as they really are: ordinary, everyday individuals. Mothers, daughters, sisters, friends, just women out to have a good time."

In an odd way, Ida's words began to make sense. Suzanna thought back on all the times she'd stood on the outside looking in: the father/daughter dance, graduation day, countless Christmases. The happiness of those events had been beyond her reach and she'd viewed them as bigger than life, so perhaps with the fashion show there really was nothing to fear.

By the time Suzanna left for work, she was feeling a bit better about the situation; not confident, but less intimidated. As the day wore on, Ida's description of the event became more and more plausible. Shortly before noon, she worked up enough courage to ask Colette about the people who attended the fashion show.

Colette was squatted down in front of Suzanna, marking the hem on the hunter green suit Suzanna was to wear in the fashion show.

"Most are already my clients," she mumbled through a mouthful of pins. "And those who are not will be once they see you in this outfit."

Suzanna had learned early on that the women who frequented the shop were to be called clients. The word customer, Colette explained, implied a woman was there for the sole purpose of purchasing something whereas a client could expect personalized service.

"That's one of the reasons they pay more to shop here," she'd added in a whisper.

When she felt a tap on her leg, Suzanna turned as she was supposed to. "Along with the clients, are there newspaper or television reporters there to take pictures?"

Colette gave a throaty laugh. "That would be lovely, but so far it hasn't happened. Perhaps in the future…" She slid the final pin into place and stood. "Finished."

As she stepped out of the skirt, Suzanna asked, "If these women are already clients, then why the fashion show?"

Colette gave a sly grin. "A number of husbands come. They see beautiful clothes on a beautiful woman and tell their wife buy this or that regardless of cost. A successful fashion show can make or break a season."

For over a week, Suzanna asked the same question of every customer: were they planning to attend the fashion show. Without exception, they all answered yes, and little by little she began to believe what Ida said was true. There was nothing to worry about. She would look out into the audience and see table after table of familiar faces. They would be the people she knew. People who'd accepted her as Darla Jean Parker.

⌀⟩⟨⌀

Once Suzanna's fear of exposure was quelled, her confidence began to build. It was a feeling not unlike that she'd had back when she was Bobby's girl. Her step became surer, her back straighter, and her head held just a tad higher. She was no longer the kid with a drunk daddy or the dropout who was pregnant. She was now somebody other people admired and wanted to be. Ida bragged to the neighbors about how Darla Jean was the featured model in this year's fashion show, Gregg seemed more attentive than ever, and Ginger flat out said she was envious.

It happened the day Suzanna drove Ida and Annie over to Barston to see Ginger's new baby, a girl they'd named Elizabeth and were calling Lizzie. Ginger, looking exhausted and still in her bathrobe, handed the crying baby to Suzanna and dropped down on the sofa.

"Lizzie's been fussy ever since Mama left, and I haven't had a full night's sleep since we came home from the hospital."

Suzanna lifted the baby to her shoulder, cradling the tiny head in her hand and swaying from side to side. "Annie was fussy for the first week, but before she was a month old she'd started sleeping through the night."

"Figures," Ginger said with an air of discouragement. "Everything comes easy to you."

Suzanna laughed. "It only seems that way. Nothing could be further from the truth." Before she could say anything more, she spotted the tears welling in Ginger's eyes. Handing the baby off to Ida, she crossed the room, sat next to Ginger, and wrapped her in a hug.

"I know life seems overwhelming right now," she said, "but all this is only temporary. Lizzie's adjusting to her new life, just like you are. In a few weeks, you'll see things differently."

Ginger sniffed back a sob. "I'm not you, Darla Jean. I'm never gonna have the chance to do what you're doing. I'll be changing diapers while you're—"

"Be glad you're not me," Suzanna said, cutting in. Without stopping to measure her words or weed out those that might draw a finger of suspicion, she continued on. "My life was one I can't even talk about. For years I envied women like you, women with a loving husband, a home, and a daddy for their child."

"I'm sure you could've had those things if you wanted—"

"Not as easily as you might think, but I didn't care because I had something far more precious: Annie. Working for Colette doesn't make anyone a better or more important person, but the money I earn enables me to give Annie a better life than I had."

Ginger sat there, her eyes wide and her face solemn. As a heavy silence crept across the room, Ida gave Annie a nod and suggested they get a glass of milk from the kitchen.

"I'm not thirsty," Annie said.

"Yes, you are," Ida replied and gave her a nudge.

When the two women were alone in the room, Suzanna took Ginger's hand in hers and held onto it. "Instead of focusing on what you're going through right now, try counting your blessings. Lizzie is a beautiful baby, and she's the one you should be thinking of. Jobs, glory, friends, even lovers can be gone in the blink of an eye, but Lizzie is yours forever. There's a special bond between mother and child, one that's stronger than you might ever dream possible."

Suzanna hesitated as a single thought passed through her mind; then she spoke again.

"If I had to choose between Annie and this job, I'd choose Annie a thousand times over. The job is only a means to an end, but Annie, well, she's a lifetime of love stretched out in front of me."

She hugged Ginger to her chest, and the sniffles subsided.

"Once you're feeling a bit better, you'll see," she said. "You're going to feel the same way about Lizzie."

"I already do," Ginger said and gave a sheepish grin.

Suzanna stood. "It's late, and we should get going."

As they started toward the kitchen Ginger blurted out another question, one that apparently had been on her mind for a while.

"What happened between you and the guy who was Annie's daddy?"

"That's something I prefer not to talk about," Suzanna said and kept walking.

⟊⟊⟊

That evening after Suzanna listened to Annie's prayers and tucked the blanket around her shoulders, she leaned over for a goodnight kiss.

"Mama, should Aunt Ginger be glad she's not you, because you got me?"

Suzanna felt as though a bowling ball had been dropped into her stomach.

"Lord God, no, Annie. Why, you're the best thing that ever happened to me. You're what gives me a reason to live, a reason to be happy."

"Then why should she be happy to not be you?"

Suzanna gave a long and heavily weighted sigh, then sat on the side of the bed and trailed her fingers along the curve of Annie's shoulder. She thought, given the number of years that had gone by, she might have forgotten about that life, but she hadn't. It was right there, as ugly and raw as it had been the day she last saw him.

"It happened a long time ago, Annie, before you were born..." Suzanna spoke slowly, trying to gauge how much she should or shouldn't tell an impressionable seven-year-old. "My daddy was a terrible person. He drank too much whiskey, was meaner than Earl, and—"

"Was he my daddy too?"

Suzanna smiled and shook her head. "No, he wasn't your daddy. He would have been your grandpa, except..." She paused a moment, realizing that Annie's life had been hard enough. She didn't need to know the whole truth. "Except I ran away from home and never saw him again."

"That's okay, Mama." Annie reached across and placed a small hand on Suzanna's arm. "We still got Grandpa Bill. He loves us and is watching over us all the time."

The corner of Suzanna's mouth curled. "Really?"

Annie nodded. "We can't see him because he's dead, but he can still watch over us." With barely a breath in between, she then asked if her daddy was dead too.

"I doubt it, but I don't know for sure. As I've told you, baby, he left before you were born, and I haven't seen or heard from him since."

"Oh. I was hoping maybe he was dead."

"Why on earth would you hope he was dead?"

"Because then I could get a new daddy."

"Who told you that?"

"Nobody. I figured it out. My friend Debbi said her first daddy got dead in a car accident, and then she got a new one."

"Debbi Hicks, the little girl you walk to school with?"

"Uh-huh."

"Her mother married Albert Hicks, that's why Debbi has—"

"You could marry Mr. Gregg. Grandma said he'd make a fine daddy."

Suzanna gave an exasperated huff. "Annie, why'd you go badgering Grandma about this after I'd told you to forget about having Gregg for a daddy?"

"I wasn't the one. Grandma said it first."

"She did, did she? Well, then, I'll have to have a talk with Grandma and—"

"No, Mama," Annie pleaded. "Don't talk to Grandma. If she finds out I told, she'll be mad and it will spoil everything."

Suzanna couldn't imagine Ida being angry with Annie over anything, but she didn't give in. "Okay, if you don't want me to have a talk with Grandma, then you've got to promise me something in return."

Annie nodded. "Okay."

"Promise me you will forget trying to make Gregg Patterson your daddy. That you will not mention it again, and you will not discuss it with Grandma or anyone else. Most of all Gregg."

"Ever?"

Suzanna gave a stern-faced nod. "Ever."

"But what if—"

"Never. Not under any circumstances."

"Okay," Annie said reluctantly.

Suzanna bent and kissed her forehead. "Now close your eyes and go to sleep. Forget we ever had this discussion."

Just as Suzanna was about to snap off the light, she heard a small voice.

"If I forget this discussion, I might forget the promise too."

"You'd better not," she warned and closed the door.

SUZANNA

The Fashion Show

On the day of the fashion show, Suzanna was awake before dawn. The fear of discovery she'd felt weeks earlier was gone; it had been replaced by a nervousness that caused her heart to flutter when she allowed herself to think of the disasters that might happen.

For weeks Colette had instructed her on how to walk with her head tilted at a lofty angle, how to turn without ever breaking stride, and how to smile as though she were the Mona Lisa. But last night during the country club run-through with all three models, she was the only one who'd made a mistake. On the second turn, she'd gone wide and bumped into a table. Then she missed her cue to open the suit jacket and show the lining.

Colette had glared at her and in a voice reeking of frustration shouted, "Mon dieu, have you also forgotten how to smile?"

At the time Suzanna had been so focused on the movement cues that she had indeed forgotten to smile.

"Sorry," she mumbled and fixed her mouth in the look they'd practiced.

After a lifetime of trying to go unnoticed, stepping out into the limelight was more than intimidating. It was downright frightening.

She'd originally agreed to do it because of the extra money, but now she was certain that had been a gigantic mistake. With the way things were shaping up, she'd be happy to just get through the day without looking like a clumsy ox or making a blunder so outrageous that she'd lose her job. Last night Colette seemed genuinely displeased with the run-through. She'd left without saying good night, good luck, or anything. Today Suzanna would have to do better. Much better.

When she climbed from the bed, the sky was still dark and the house as silent as a stone. With her feet bare and her thin nightshirt replacing the elegant gowns and suits, she began walking back and forth across the room, making the turn as gracefully as any model who'd ever strolled a Paris runway. As she circled the chair and passed by the dresser, she envisioned the huge dining room at the country club. She focused her thoughts on the placement of each table and the designated pathway that ran through the center of the room and could see herself moving past the tables, returning to the back room, and then changing into another outfit.

In time the nightshirt became a chiffon gown, and she extended her arm with her fingers lengthened to trail the gauzy wrap that would cover her shoulders. When she imagined herself in the green suit, she went through the motion of opening the jacket and tilting her head downward to draw attention to the paisley lining. That run-though was perfect. She'd remembered every single move and turned without a flicker of hesitation. Now she was ready; truly ready. Nothing would or could go wrong.

The pale light of morning was on the edge of the horizon when Suzanna pulled on her jeans and hurried downstairs. The fashion show luncheon would start at 12 noon, but she had to be at the country club by 9 a.m. A beautician would be there to do the models' hair and makeup. Colette had gone to great lengths to make sure the show was something that would be talked about for weeks to come, and several times she'd made a point of saying the success of their season depended on it. Hearing the urgency in Colette's voice, Suzanna had twice asked if she would prefer to have a third model replace her. Colette wouldn't hear of it.

"You're perfect for this," she'd said. "You know how to show clothes to their best advantage, and when clients see a familiar face they find it easier to envision themselves wearing that same outfit." She'd gone on to say she expected this show to be her biggest and best ever.

When Suzanna entered the kitchen, Ida smiled.

"Well, today's your big day," she said. She poured a cup of coffee, motioned for Suzanna to sit, then pulled a frying pan from the cupboard. "Eggs or pancakes?"

"No breakfast for me. I'm much too nervous to eat."

"Nonsense. It's going to be a long day. You've got to eat something so you don't pass out from hunger while you're on stage."

Suzanna laughed. "Don't worry. If I pass out it will be from fright, not the lack of food."

Ida came around and hugged her shoulders. "Darla Jean, you worry far too much. You'll do a wonderful job, I'm certain of it. Just relax, be yourself, and remember to smile."

That's when it dawned on Suzanna. Remembering to smile was the one thing she'd forgotten to do in this morning's run-though. Smile. When she added that thought to the others already in her head, the burden seemed as heavy as a sack of stones dropped onto her shoulders.

◦◦◦

Colette was pacing back and forth in front of the building when Suzanna arrived at the country club. She pulled into the parking lot and barely had one foot out of the car before Colette came running over with a frenzied look in her eyes.

"Dieu merci! Prayers are answered. I was praying you would arrive early. Danielle is in the hospital, so you will have to—"

"Hospital? What happened?"

"Automobile accident. Terrible." She held a manicured hand to her temple and shuddered. "Truly terrible, but we will talk of that later. Right now, you need to get ready to cover two of her outfits."

As Suzanna stood there with her mouth open, Colette described the two outfits she would add to the three she was already scheduled to model.

"I can't possibly," Suzanna said with a gasp. "Danielle's trouser and jacket outfit opens the show and comes right before my green suit. There isn't time enough to change."

"Yes, yes, you'll have to move quickly, but the stylist will have everything at the ready so you can simply step out of one ensemble into the next."

"But there are specific moves for that outfit. After the first turn, Danielle takes the blazer off and carries it across her shoulder. I haven't practiced that. Can't Elise—"

"No. The trousers are too long for her. It has to be you."

Suzanna felt her stomach clench. The piece of toast she'd eaten now

147

seemed like a chunk of cement lodged in her chest. She'd thought she was prepared, that nothing could go wrong. She practiced every move, memorized the turns step by step. Now here she was, facing a whole new set of challenges; challenges she was not at all prepared for.

"Elise has so much more experience. She'd be better at—"

"You have the right instincts, you'll do fine." Colette took hold of her arm and started toward the clubhouse. "I've switched the order of appearance, so the only rushed change you'll have is the green suit. After that Elise will…"

As Colette's voice droned on saying how she would open the show with the trouser outfit and close it with the chiffon gown, Suzanna could almost see herself dropping the blazer that Danielle had so gracefully draped over one finger.

At one o'clock the clinking of silverware and the rattle of dishes being carried to and from the dining room stilled, and Colette walked to the podium with a newly-ordered presentation list of fashions. Standing just inside the entranceway, Suzanna waited, listening for her first cue. With her hair done and traces of glitter dusting her cheeks, she had never looked more beautiful nor felt more insecure.

Early on she'd flubbed a few moves, but she'd worked on them, ironed out the problems, and felt reasonably confident. That was until Colette changed everything. Now the sequence was different, and on the first two outfits she had to alter the rehearsed route and take a shortcut back to the dressing room because of the quick change.

Desperately trying to still the thump of her heart as she stood there listening, Suzanna missed the first cue when Colette mentioned a stylish wool pant paired with a classic cashmere blazer that could be worn throughout most of the year.

Glancing toward the entranceway, Colette gave a dramatic wave of her arm, brought her voice up an octave, and announced, "And now, to open today's fashion extravaganza, our very own Darla Jean Parker."

The mention of her name quickly roused Suzanna, and when she stepped from behind the partition the audience offered a polite round of applause. As she crossed the floor, her steps were tentative and her expression apprehensive. She turned on cue, slid the blazer off, and casually tossed it over her shoulder. It wasn't the same one-fingered dangle Danielle used, but the jacket didn't land on the floor. Her movements were reasonably close to the mark, but instead of smiling, her brows were knotted and she looked as though she might pass out any second.

When she began to circle the room, she spotted the table two rows in.

Nine people were crowded together: Ida, several of her friends, Gregg, Phil, Ginger, and, right there in front, Annie with a grin that stretched the full width of her face. She jumped up, started waving, and in a little girl voice that pierced the hush of silence, squealed, "Mama, you look soooo beautiful!"

A ripple of laughter rolled across the room, followed by a round of enthusiastic applause, and Suzanna's look of apprehension dissolved into a smile. Not the stiff Mona Lisa smile she'd practiced but a soft curl of her lips that came without thought.

As she strolled past the tables, she saw a host of familiar faces, people who returned her smile and gave a wink or a nod of recognition. They were townspeople. Clients. Silver-haired ladies with teen-aged granddaughters; wives with husbands. Mothers and daughters. It was exactly as Ida had said.

Suddenly Suzanna realized there was no need for fear or pretense. They didn't expect her to be anybody other than the person she'd become. They liked Darla Jean Parker exactly as she was.

When Suzanna stepped behind the partition, the stylist and her assistant were standing by with everything ready to go. Buttons were opened, zippers zipped, and in the blink of an eye the change she'd feared would be cumbersome was over. As the stylist smoothed the back of the jacket, Suzanna heard Colette at the microphone.

"The exquisitely tailored suit Darla Jean is wearing is the jewel of this year's collection."

That was her cue. She stepped from behind the partition and strolled to the center of the room. When she heard Colette describe the paisley silk accent, she loosened a button and fanned the jacket, displaying the lining just as they'd practiced. As Colette's narrative continued Suzanna moved through the room, stopping in all the predesignated places, turning to follow the rehearsed route, and then circling back toward the dressing area just as Elise stepped into the spotlight.

The remainder of the show went as smoothly as the first two presentations with Suzanna wending her way down the main aisle, circling through the maze of tables, and turning on cue without a single hitch. Each time she passed Ida's group, she gave Annie a wink. Twice she slowed as she strolled by, taking in the look of adoration she could see in Gregg's eyes.

Suzanna closed the show wearing a gown of blue silk. It was the cornflower blue of her eyes with pinpoints of light that shimmered in the fabric as she moved. Never in all her life had she looked or felt more beautiful. Her step was as light as that of a ballerina, and her smile came not from practice but from her heart. It was all here, everything she had ever wished for. As she swept past Ida's table that one last time she saw the look of admiration on Gregg's face, and with a smile that was as intimate as a kiss she allowed her eyes to linger on his face for one sweet moment. Something good was happening, and this time she was ready for it.

⟨⟩

The problem with happiness is that it can sometimes blind a person to the reality of life. Had Suzanna not been dazzled by the brightness of Annie's smile and the look of promise in Gregg's face, she might have noticed the stranger sitting at Sylvia Monroe's table. Maybe she would have recognized him; maybe not. It had been over eight years since she'd seen Bobby Doherty and even longer since she'd seen his younger brother. Eddie was fifteen years old back then, a pimply-faced kid with boyish features and a gangly stance. He looked nothing like he did now, so when Suzanna passed him by without a hint of recognition it was understandable.

To Sylvia Monroe the fellow wasn't a stranger; he was her future son-in-law. Not a young man she was particularly fond of, but she had little say in the matter. Christine had met the lad at the University of Florida and, much to Sylvia's chagrin, moved in with him six months later. To make matters even worse, here it was, two years post-graduation, and they were still living together without any mention of when the wedding might take place.

The situation was something Sylvia was forced to contend with, but the thought of Christine not coming home for the annual fashion show was something she simply could not abide. It was a mother/daughter tradition, one of the few things she could look forward to year after year.

This year they'd had a row over it, and Christine, who could be rather snippy at times, argued that Eddie had no interest in sitting through another fashion show.

"We came last year," she said sharply. "You can't expect us to make the trip every year."

"I most certainly do," Sylvia had replied vehemently. "I don't give a hoot whether or not Eddie Doherty comes, but you're my daughter and I expect you to be here."

In the end Christine did come, and she brought the sullen-faced Eddie with her. He complained throughout the luncheon. The chicken salad was too dry, his chair had a wobbly leg, the waiters were too slow, and a host of other things. But as soon as Darla Jean stepped out wearing that first outfit, something changed. The pissed-off look he was wearing disappeared, and he moved his chair sideways angling for an unobstructed view as she moved through the room showing the outfit.

Sylvia noticed it right away. She disliked Eddie for any number of reasons; his flirtatiousness was at the top of that list. She watched him for a few minutes then gave Christine a smug smile and whispered, "Looks like your boyfriend's got his eye on Darla Jean Parker."

Christine turned with an angry glare.

"Cut it out, Mama," she hissed. "I know you'd love to see me and Eddie break up, but you can just forget it. He's crazy about me and has no interest in that model."

With that contentious smile still curling her lips, Sylvia came back with another dig. "If he's all that crazy about you, then why aren't you married?"

Although it was obvious Christine had heard the comment, she didn't respond; she just sat there looking as puffed up as a bullfrog. Several minutes later, when Darla Jean came out wearing that green suit, she elbowed him and snarled, "Stop looking at the model that way, you're embarrassing me in front of Mama."

"Gimme a break," Eddie grumbled. "This is not what you think. I know her. Bobby had a thing with this girl back in high school, and I believe she's the one."

Christine rolled her eyes. "Yeah, sure. In his dreams maybe."

Eddie shrugged. "We'll see."

SUZANNA

A Christmas to Remember

After the fashion show, Colette raved about Suzanna's performance. With an over-the-top flourish, she waved her arm in the air and declared it, "Magnifique!" She then went on to say as payment for stepping in to fill the void, Suzanna would receive an extra day off and $150 for modeling.

That amount was half again more than what Suzanna had expected. Overjoyed at the thought, she asked if she might take the following Thursday off. It was only two weeks until Christmas, and she knew exactly what she wanted to do.

That evening she invited Ida to join her for a Christmas shopping excursion and lunch at Lady Anne's Tea Room. For what was perhaps the first time in her life, Suzanna could see a bright future ahead. The things that for so long had been nothing more than a dream were now a reality. She had a job, Annie had a home and a grandma who loved her, and her relationship with Gregg was growing sweeter every day.

On the nights when she'd tossed and turned, unable to sleep because of worry about the fashion show, she'd found peace in creating an imaginary Christmas list. She'd pictured a shiny red two-wheeler for Annie, a grown-up bike with training wheels that could come off when she was ready. Also new clothes, dresses for school, and a warm jacket for when the January winds blew coldest. She remembered how she'd seen Gregg making notes on a ruled tablet and decided that he should have a leather portfolio, one with his initials stamped in gold, one that he could be proud to leave lying atop his desk.

It was easy enough to think of gifts for Annie and Gregg, but try as she might she could not come up with the perfect gift for Ida. She thought of a dozen different things: fancy robes, jewelry, perfumes, or bath lotions, but none of them were right. None were special enough for Ida. That's when she'd hit on the idea of going shopping together. As they browsed through the stores, she'd keep a keen eye out, watch what Ida admired, make note of the things she stopped to look at, then return the next day to buy Ida's present.

On Thursday morning Suzanna was up early, excited at the prospect of what the day would bring. She had the $150 Colette had paid her for working the show plus $32 she'd saved from her paychecks. More money than she'd once thought possible, and she was going to spend every last dime to give Annie and Ida the best Christmas ever. This would be the Christmas they'd remember years from now. Long after Annie was married with children of her own, she'd look back and remember the year she'd gotten her first real bicycle.

As soon as the breakfast dishes were cleared and Annie was off to school, Suzanna and Ida left for Barston. On the drive over, Ida asked, "What exactly are we shopping for?"

"Some of this and that," Suzanna answered, then she ran through the list of things she wanted to buy for Annie and Gregg. "I'd also like to buy a gift for Ginger and the baby, so maybe we could browse the Emporium and look for some special gifts."

Ida gave a nod. "Good idea. They've got beautiful things. Why, just last week in their newspaper ad, I saw a fur-trimmed coat that would look darling on Annie."

"I'm getting her a cold weather jacket, so you don't have to bother. Save your money and don't worry about—"

"I'm not the least bit worried about money. I've already told you, I came into a bit of a windfall and—"

Suzanna turned with a look of surprise. "That was way back in September. But on Thanksgiving Day you told Gregg you were counting on the money from his rent."

Obviously flustered, Ida waved her hand toward the windshield. "Watch where you're going, and keep your eyes on the road."

153

Suzanna caught the abrupt change of subject. She'd been lying almost all of her life and could spot a bare-faced lie a hundred feet away.

"That windfall story sounds kind of fishy," she said. "I think there's something you're not telling me."

"Nonsense," Ida said and turned her face to the window. For several minutes, she sat there saying nothing, then without turning back said, "Sometimes you don't tell somebody something because they're better off not knowing it."

"Grandma, if you're in need of money, I've got $182 you can have. We'll make do for Christmas. I'll crochet Annie a new scarf and—"

"Oh, for heaven's sake, Darla Jean, money's not the problem. Bill had two insurance policies. One paid off the mortgage on the house, and the other provided me with a monthly income."

"I don't understand. Didn't you originally tell me you had to sell the house because—"

"Yes, I did tell you that," Ida said begrudgingly. "And back then I thought it was true. I didn't find out about the second policy until later on; then I figured maybe it was best not to mention it."

"Why would you not mention—" Suzanna gave a horrified gasp, then pulled to the side of the road and forced Ida to face her. "Did you honestly think I'd try to swindle you out of your money?"

"Lord God, no, Darla Jean! Why, I'd never in a hundred million years think that!" Ida's voice softened as she stretched her arm across the seat and took Suzanna's hand in hers. "I knew right off you had a kind heart like your granddaddy. Remember the first night, how you told me you were headed to New Jersey and had to move on?"

With her eyes fixed on Ida's face, Suzanna gave a nod.

"Well, I didn't want you to go. Before you came I was just sitting here waiting to die, and Scout was the same way. All he'd do was lie down beside Bill's chair and sleep, but that night he ran all over the place with Annie chasing after him. I heard the way her laughter seemed to spread happiness all over the house and figured it was a sure sign that I was to keep you here.

"Yes, I told you I was having a hard time of it and had to sell the house, but I did it because I knew you'd stay to help me out. Later on, when I found out about that other insurance policy, I was afraid if you knew I didn't need you, you'd start thinking about New Jersey again."

"I was only going to New Jersey because I had nowhere else to go," Suzanna said softly. "Honestly, I was just looking for a way to give Annie a better life."

She switched the engine off then reached across and pulled Ida into her arms. For several moments they sat silently; she felt Ida's heartbeat against hers, and it brought back memories of those last days when her mama had held her in much the same way. Suzanna's eyes filled with tears as she remembered her mama's words.

After I'm gone, if God gives you a new mama to love, treasure the gift. Love her the same as you love me, because love given will bring love in return.

Suzanna sniffed back the sob rising in her throat. "That first night we stayed here, I believed Annie and I would have to go through this life alone. We had nothing. No family, no money, and no future." A tear broke free and rolled down her cheek. "I never dreamed that we'd find someone who would become as dear to us as you are."

"I knew right away," Ida said and squeezed Suzanna's hand.

They talked for several minutes and when Ida said they should vow to never again hide the truth from one another, Suzanna almost choked on the lump in her throat. As she pulled back onto the road, she said a silent prayer asking the Almighty to keep the truth of her identity a secret.

That morning they went from shop to shop, finding lace-collared dresses for Annie, a new hat for Homer Portnick, a leather portfolio for Gregg, bath salts for Ginger, and a My First Christmas shirt for little Lizzie. When they finished going through the Emporium, they stashed their packages in the car and headed for the toy store.

Picking out the shiny new bicycle was easy, but deciding on a doll proved to be a challenge. The sales clerk insisted that most little girls now wanted a Barbie, but Suzanna and Ida both had their doubts.

Ida studied the doll and frowned. "Isn't Barbie a bit grown up for a seven-year-old?"

"Not at all," the clerk assured them. "Little girls like to imagine themselves grown up, and having a Barbie doll makes them feel they are."

Remembering her own childhood, Suzanna was about to argue the point and say that wasn't necessarily a good thing when the clerk stepped away to help a woman in search of a Hot Wheels Camaro. As soon as he disappeared down the aisle, she turned to Ida. "I'm thinking we ought to look for a different doll, a baby or maybe a little girl. I don't like the thought of Annie growing up too fast."

"Neither do I."

They moved down the aisle looking at any number of dolls: little girls with porcelain faces, real hair, eyes that closed, and babies that wet or cried. In the end they selected a Chatty Cathy doll with hair as golden as Annie's and eyes that were almost as blue. When Ida tugged the cord and the doll said, "I love you," Suzanna was sold.

Before they left the store, Ida found an Easy Bake Oven, two books, and a pair of roller skates, all of which she insisted Annie needed to have. As she carted the Easy Bake Oven to the check-out counter, she gave a grin and said, "How can I resist buying this for her when I know how much she enjoys baking cookies?"

Once they'd loaded the bicycle and toys into the car, Suzanna could no longer see out the back window. She glanced at her watch: 2:30. Annie would be home at 3 o'clock.

"I'm afraid our lunch at Lady Anne's will have to wait," she said and gave an apologetic shrug. "We spent too much time in the toy store."

Ida chuckled. "Maybe so, but it was the most fun I've had in ages."

That evening when Ida and Annie settled in front of the television, Suzanna and Gregg went for a walk. As they strolled down Cedar Street toward Mulberry where the coffee shop was, she told him about her day.

"I thought I'd find out what Grandma wants for Christmas, but no such luck."

"What happened?" Gregg asked as he wrapped his arm around her shoulders and tugged her a little closer.

"I suggested we browse through the Emporium and daydream about what we'd buy if we had tons of money. Grandma just laughed and said she already had everything she wanted."

"Maybe that's honestly how she feels."

Suzanna gave a thoughtful nod. "You're probably right, but all the same I was hoping she'd stop to admire something special so I'd have an idea of what to get her for Christmas."

"I take it she didn't."

"Oh, she looked at plenty of things, but they were just trinkets or things for Annie. I swear, she spent a half-hour looking through the Christmas shop at the Emporium."

At the corner of Mulberry, they crossed over, entered the coffee shop, and slid into the back booth.

"When we walked through the ladies' wear section, I pointed out one thing and another: a cashmere sweater, a comfy bathrobe, a silk blouse. She barely gave those things a nod, but when we passed through the Christmas shop she started oohing and aahing over every little thing."

When the waitress came over, Gregg ordered two coffees, then glanced across at Suzanna. "Would you like some pie? Or a piece of cake?"

She shook her head and went right back to the story. "There was this snow globe with a little ice skater, and Grandma played with it for a full five minutes." She continued on telling of how Ida had insisted on buying the Easy Bake Oven for Annie, despite her objections that it was far too much money to be spending on a gift.

A knowing smile lifted the corner of Gregg's mouth. "I know you want to get Ida something special, but perhaps you need to look at this through her eyes."

"Meaning what?"

"She's up in years, she's got a house full of things, a closet full of clothes, and most likely a jewelry box full of pieces that she doesn't bother to wear. Maybe she's got all she needs of those things, and all she really wants is a special Christmas with you and Annie."

"Well, of course, we'll spend Christmas with her, but that's not exactly a gift."

"To her, it probably is. You and Annie are family; having you here makes her happier than any gift ever would." He lifted her hand and dropped a kiss into her palm. "I know, because I feel the same way."

The coffee grew cold as she listened to him tell of the emptiness he'd felt after his parents were gone. Suzanna remembered having that same sense of aloneness after her mama's death. She'd cried herself to sleep for three nights straight, then gone to her daddy looking for comfort. He'd called her a whiny-ass kid and said she'd better learn to suck it up, because nobody wanted to listen to a sob story. That was when she learned to hide her heartache behind a wall of lies.

Sleep was a long time in coming that night. Suzanna tried closing her eyes, but even in the darkness she could see the memory as fresh and raw as it had been all those years ago.

That Christmas had been the worst of her life. She'd wished for a tree and a midnight church service with candles and carols, but her daddy would have none of it. Instead, he'd handed her a ten-dollar bill and said to go buy something for herself. She'd hated him for that, so much so that she'd taken his ten-dollar bill and stuffed it into the poor box at the church. If he didn't have love to give, she didn't want his money. That night she'd not even stayed for the service, just put the money in the box and walked home in the drizzling rain.

It was nearing dawn when Suzanna finally decided what she would get Ida for Christmas. She scribbled a quick note, put it into an envelope, and slid it under Gregg's door.

With a plan now in place, she went back to her room and finally fell asleep.

Friday was their busy day at Cavalier's, but despite a steady flow of customers the hours seemed to drag by.

It was close to five o'clock when the store quieted down and Colette turned to her.

"You seem preoccupied, Darla Jean. Is there something on your mind?"

Suzanna gave a slightly embarrassed nod, then explained her plan.

Colette listened, then shooed her out of the shop with a laugh.

"Go," she said. "You've got a busy evening ahead, and I don't mind closing up."

More than happy to accept the offer, Suzanna darted out of the store and headed back to the Emporium. She spent nearly three hours searching for the things she had in mind, then carried the packages to the car, loaded them into the trunk, and headed home.

Ida had supper ready when Suzanna walked in.

"You're later than usual," she said as she bent and pulled a tray of potatoes from the oven.

"Sorry," Suzanna replied. "The shop was busy today." Seeing Gregg at the table, she glanced over and mouthed, Did you get it?

He gave a wink and nodded.

Annie caught the motion. "Grandma says it's bad manners to tell secrets in front of other people."

"Grandma's right, but I wasn't actually telling secrets. I was just saying something I didn't want you to hear, and when it's this close to Christmas that's permissible."

"Was it about a present for me?"

Suzanna laughed. "You'll find out in due time."

Still curious, Annie continued to pry for a few minutes then eventually gave up. As soon as she could, Suzanna changed the subject.

"What are you planning to do this evening?" she asked.

"Well, I don't know about anyone else," Ida said, "but I'm going to bed early. I've got a bunch of cookies to bake tomorrow and need a good night's rest."

Annie groaned. "No TV?"

"Not tonight. I let you stay up late last night so you could watch The Real McCoys, but tonight you're going to have to get your butt in bed early if you want to help with the cookies."

"I do, I do. But can't we watch just one—"

"No arguments," Suzanna cut in. "Grandma said early to bed, and that's that."

Annie delayed it for as long as she could, but after she and Ida disappeared up the stairs, Suzanna breathed a sigh of relief. "I think that's the last we'll see of them tonight, but we'd better wait fifteen or twenty minutes to be sure."

Gregg grinned. "I think we can manage to kill some time. Why don't you pour us a glass of wine while I get a fire started?"

They sat side by side on the sofa, and a tingle of excitement settled in Suzanna's chest as she spoke of how she knew this was going to be the best Christmas ever for both Ida and Annie. The minutes ticked by and after the house had settled into the quiet sounds of slumber, Gregg pulled on a jacket and went behind the garage to haul in a Frazier fir that was considerably taller than he was.

"Big enough?" he asked.

With a grin that stretched the full width of her face, Suzanna nodded.

While he was setting up the tree, she carried in the packages hidden in the trunk of the car. That afternoon she'd retraced yesterday's walk through the Emporium and gathered up the Christmas ornaments that Ida had so lovingly admired. She'd also bought seven strings of colored lights, two boxes of icicles, and a string of glitter garland. While Gregg was twining the lights through the branches of the tree, she switched on the radio and found a station playing Christmas carols.

As they unpacked the boxes and hung the ornaments, Suzanna was reminded of that last Christmas she'd had with her mama. She was nine years old at the time, tall for her age, but not tall enough to reach the top of the tree. Too weak to stand, her mama sat in the chair, saying what a good job Suzanna was doing. When she went to bed that night, the only thing left to do was place the star atop the tree.

Don't worry about it, her mama said, your daddy can do that when he gets home.

That night he'd come home drunk, knocked the tree over, and cussed up a storm about him having to do everything. That had been the last tree she'd had. Until now.

Standing atop the ladder, Gregg straightened the star and smiled down. "How's that?"

She looked up at him and saw a beautiful future. She would forget all that had happened before. For her and for Annie, there would be now and the years ahead. Annie's life would be different than hers. Annie would have a loving grandmother and a daddy who climbed the ladder and set the star atop the tree.

"It's perfect," she said, her voice quavering with emotion.

BOBBY DOHERTY

Remembering Suzanna

Georgia Tech was battling Penn State when the telephone rang. It was the second quarter, and Galen Hall had just completed a pass for the second Penn State touchdown.

Ticked off because the Yellow Jackets failed to stop Hall, Bobby turned toward the kitchen and yelled, "Get the phone, Brenda, I'm busy!"

The ringing stopped, and he watched Penn State go for the point after. As the ball split the uprights, his wife hollered, "Pick it up, it's your brother!"

He lifted the receiver and grumbled, "I'm watching the Gator Bowl. What do you want?"

"Don't rush me, big brother, I've got a blast from the past, and it's one you're gonna want to hear about."

"Can the crap, Eddie, I want to get back to—"

"Okay, okay. Remember that chick you had a thing for in high school? Well, I saw her in a fashion show, and she's looking pretty damn good."

"In a fashion show? JoJo Pepper?"

"Not her, the other one. Tall, blond hair, long legs, used to wear those cut-off shorts."

"Oh, you mean Suzanna Duff."

"Un-uh. This girl has got a double name, you know, like Sally Mae, Donna Sue, something like that."

"I never dated anyone with a double name."

"Trust me, this chick is not one you'd forget. Even then she was a looker. You guys broke up just before graduation and—"

"That was Suzanna Duff."

"Yeah, well, her name ain't Suzanna Duff anymore. Weekend before last, Christine dragged me to another one her mom's country club fashion show events, and your ex-girlfriend was one of the models."

"Get out! Where?"

"Georgia. Barston. It about 80 miles—"

"I know where Barston is," Bobby snapped. "But I gotta tell you, that doesn't sound like the Suzanna Duff I knew. Yeah, she was beautiful, and sexy as all get out, but…"

He hesitated, searching for the right word or phrase. How could he describe a girl like Suzanna? She had a uniqueness that drew him to her. There were times when he felt that he'd touched the inside of her heart, and other times when such a thing seemed impossible. It was almost like she hid her feelings behind a protective wall, one with a huge crack in it.

"She was always kind of guarded," he finally said. "Kept to herself; sort of a loner. Not someone I can see being comfortable in front of a crowd."

"Well, I'm positive it was her, and she certainly doesn't seem like a loner now. She was the star of the show. She's got this cute little girl who—"

"She's got a kid?" The last conversation he'd had with Suzanna flashed through Bobby's mind. The one where she'd turned him down when he offered to help with money for an abortion. "How old's the girl?"

"How am I supposed to know?" Eddie laughed. "She's a kid; seven, maybe eight."

Bobby felt a ripple of anxiety flutter across his chest. Impossible, he thought. Not after all this time. It was one of those things you hoped for but knew would never happen. Suzanna here in Georgia? Not likely.

"What makes you so sure it was her?"

"It's her," Eddie said and chuckled. "I had a huge crush on that chick when you guys were dating. I may not remember her name, but regardless of what she calls herself I sure as hell remember that body and face."

"Did she say anything about me? Ask what I'm doing or where I'm—"

"We didn't talk. I was going to try and catch her after the show, but Christine was giving me a hard time so I didn't bother."

"Maybe I ought to look her up and say hi for old times' sake. Barston's not that far; a two-hour drive from Atlanta."

"I doubt Brenda will like the idea of you looking up an old flame, and besides, your Suzanna Duff is using a different name so lots of luck in finding her."

Repeating the old adage, "Where there's a will, there's a way," Bobby chuckled. He thought of asking for the date of the show and where it was held, but he didn't. He was a lawyer and quite capable of finding information that wasn't supposed to be found. When he hung up, the thought of a child who might be his was heavy on his mind.

He turned back to the television, but the remainder of the game was little more than a blur. He barely noticed when Joe Auer scored on a 14-yard run in the fourth quarter and brought the Yellow Jackets within striking distance. When the two-point conversion failed, he snapped the television off and sat there remembering that last night with Suzanna.

She never asked for much, but that night she did. She wanted way more than he could give. Marriage was out of the question. Maybe not forever but at least until he'd finished college. What was he supposed to do, blow off a Georgia Tech football scholarship? He'd worked damn hard for it; ran practice after practice until he was so tired he could barely stand. Some games left him feeling like he'd been put through a meat grinder, but he didn't quit and he kept his grades up. He could have skated, slacked off on the studies and still gotten a scholarship, but not to Georgia Tech. It would have been to some rinky-dink school where he'd end up in a job not worth having.

Suzanna could have at least tried to understand that he wanted something better. She could have gotten rid of the baby and waited for him to graduate. If she'd agreed to that, they might have gotten married. In time.

It had been over eight years since he'd last seen or spoken to her. He'd tried to contact her a number of times but to no avail. That last night had been ugly and they'd both said things they didn't mean, hurtful things that were sharp and painful as salt in an open wound. When they parted Suzanna had walked away, her head ducked down, her eyes red and swollen, not once looking back to see if he was still there. He was, but she'd not bothered to look. That night he'd waited on the park bench for two hours thinking she might return, but she didn't.

Afterward he was angry. He had every right to be. He'd tried, really tried, to talk things through, make her see the logic in his thinking, but she wouldn't even discuss it. She said she wasn't going to kill the baby they'd made, and that's all there was to it.

After that night Suzanna came to school for a week or two, but they never spoke. They passed each other in the hallway without a nod or sideways glance. He believed that given enough time they'd work it out, but then she disappeared. One week turned into two, and she didn't show up for school. That's when he went to her house, and her daddy said she was gone.

"Where to?" Bobby asked, but he might as well have been talking to a stone. The old man slammed the door and wouldn't open it again, not even when Bobby stood there calling out Suzanna's name and pounding on the door.

He thought she'd come back for graduation, but she didn't. Twice he'd driven over, parked down the street from her house, and waited, but he never saw her coming or going. That summer he left for Georgia.

Now with her name fresh in his mind, he couldn't stop thinking of how it used to be. When they were alone, Suzanna would let down her guard and give herself to him completely. Afterward, when their passion was spent, they'd curl their bodies together and talk of things yet to come.

He thought back on how she would trace her finger along the line of his palm and say that was a sure indication that they'd have a long and happy life together. Now here she was in Georgia, only 80 miles away. Was it possible that fate had given him the second chance he'd hoped for?

Later that evening as he and Brenda sat across the dinner table from one another, he found himself comparing the two women. He'd met Brenda Garrett at Georgia Tech, and they'd hit it off right away. With her dark hair and green eyes, she was attractive; attractive enough for him to notice her sitting across the lecture hall.

They had everything in common, wanted the same things out of life, enjoyed the same people, liked the same restaurants, and she was certainly no prude when it came to sex. Brenda was like an open book. With her he knew exactly where he stood.

It didn't hurt that her daddy was Jerome Garrett, a founding partner in Greene & Garrett. The summer they got engaged, the firm gave him a clerking internship and then fast-tracked him once he passed the bar.

Bobby understood that who you knew could sometimes be more important than what you knew, and thanks to Brenda he'd been introduced to all the right people.

She'd introduced him to her daddy right off, whereas he'd seen Suzanna's daddy a total of three times and not one of them had been under pleasant circumstances. If he'd stayed in Florida with Suzanna he probably wouldn't have made it through Georgia Tech, never mind law school. And it was a given that he wouldn't have the life he was living now: nice house, fancy car, promising future. Had he stayed, he'd be living in Sun Grove, working construction or trapped in a dead-end job. No doubt, calling it quits with Suzanna was the smartest thing he'd ever done. He'd be a fool to get suckered into a relationship like that again.

His thoughts were interrupted by Brenda's question. Startled, he glanced over at her.

"Sorry," he mumbled, "I missed that."

She laughed. "Actually, I don't think you've heard a word I've said all evening. I was asking if something's wrong. After that phone call from Eddie, you've been—"

"It's nothing. You know how Eddie is, he makes a big to-do over nothing. He was carrying on about Christine dragging him to one of her mom's charity events."

Bobby left it at that and moved on to asking what Brenda had planned for Christmas.

That night they made love, and it was good. It was always good. Satisfying, without any lingering grief or recriminations. Afterward Brenda had turned on her side and fallen asleep, but for Bobby sleep wasn't so easy to come by. He was still thinking about Suzanna Duff.

SUZANNA

The Locket

The night Suzanna and Gregg set up the tree, it was after midnight when they hung the last bit of tinsel and well into the wee hours of morning when they went to bed. She had barely closed her eyes when Annie came running into her room bubbling over with excitement.

"Mama, Mama, wake up! It happened! It really happened!"

With sleep still clinging to her eyelids, Suzanna tried to focus. "Wha…"

"The tree elves came last night!"

Suzanna rubbed the back of her hand across her eyes and sat up. "Who came?"

"The tree elves!" She took hold of Suzanna's arm and urged her from the bed. "You've gotta come and see, Mama. It's so beautiful."

Once she was fully awake, Suzanna understood what Annie was talking about and played along. "Tree elves, you say? And what exactly did they do?"

"They brought a giant Christmas tree! It's up to the ceiling!"

As Annie headed back down the stairs, Suzanna followed along. "I've never before heard of tree elves. Who told you about them?"

"Grandma. She said they only come to houses where there are kids, and they leave a tree with bright lights so that Santa will know where to leave toys."

"Oh, so Grandma told you that, huh?

Annie nodded. "And she knows because when she was a kid the tree elves came every year; then when she got old, they didn't come no more."

As they descended the stairs, the tree came into view. Suzanna stopped and gave a sigh. It looked even more beautiful than it did last night. The look of wonder on Ida's face was proof that Gregg's suggestion had been spot on.

That Sunday was cold and blustery, so no one left the house. Gregg lit a fire in the fireplace, and with the Christmas tree aglow they all gathered in the living room and watched Miracle on 34th Street on television. Annie sat mesmerized by the story, and when it was over she announced to everyone that she was just like 8-year-old Susan in the movie.

"What makes you think you're like Susan?" Gregg asked.

"Because I wished for a grandma and a house and got it," Annie said proudly. She glanced over at Suzanna then looked back to Gregg and grinned. "But there's one more thing Grandma and me are wishing for..."

"That's enough, Annie," Suzanna jumped in, sensing what her daughter was about to say. "Keep the rest of those wishes to yourself."

On Christmas Eve, supper was earlier than usual and twice as festive. Even though it was only the four of them and they ate in the kitchen, Suzanna lit the red candles and set the table with the good china. As she listened to Annie chatter on about Santa, the tree elves, and the baby Jesus coming tonight, her heart swelled with happiness. This was the Christmas she'd wished for as a child. Years ago she'd not gotten her wish, but now experiencing it through the eyes of her child seemed even sweeter.

Afterward they walked to church, Annie out in front urging Ida to hurry along, behind them Suzanna and Gregg, strolling arm in arm. It was as perfect an evening as Suzanna could have possibly wished for. The weather, ideal for December, was crisp, cool, and fragrant with the scent of fresh-cut pine. The spirit of Christmas was everywhere: in the smiles of passersby who greeted them, in the bright red poinsettias lining the walkways, and the houses festooned with wreaths and ribbons of garland. But for Suzanna the most joyous thing of all was the wide smile on Annie's face. Every time they passed a house with a brightly-lit tree, she squealed with the delight of knowing that Santa would be stopping there.

Suzanna looked at Gregg and smiled. "She's so excited, I'm never going to be able to get her to go to bed early tonight."

Gregg laughed. "Probably not. Hopefully we can outlast her, because I'd like to spend some private time with you."

Suzanna leaned her head against his shoulder. "I'd like that also."

When they rounded the corner of Birch Street, the church came into view. The doors were open, the lights shone from within, and the sound of music wafted through the air.

Phil and Ginger had driven over from Barston and were waiting in front of the walkway, Phil with his arm wrapped protectively around Ginger, her with baby Lizzie held close to her chest, and Edna, the proud grandma, looking on. As Ginger folded back the blanket to give everyone a peek at the sleeping baby, the sadness she had shown earlier seemed all but gone. She excitedly spoke of how Lizzie was now cooing, smiling, and sleeping for six hours straight; then she leaned toward Suzanna and whispered, "You were right, Lizzie is the best thing ever."

As the group made their way toward the entrance, Suzanna was surprised to see so many familiar faces—the girl from the drug store, several ladies who shopped at Cavalier's, the paper boy, neighbors from the surrounding streets, Annie's classmates and their families—all of them smiling, waving, and calling out Merry Christmas as if she had lived here her entire life. A warm glow blossomed in Suzanna's heart. She had everything she'd ever wanted. A family, a child to love, and a place to belong. The memory of her father and the ten-dollar bill flashed through her mind, but she quickly pushed it aside. Nothing, absolutely nothing, was going to take this new-found joy from her.

The seven of them filled the pew, with Phil anchoring one end, Gregg the other, and Lizzie sound asleep in Edna's arms. After they'd listened to the pastor read the words that told of the Christ child's birth and watched the children perform a pageant portraying the arrival of the Magi, the ushers handed out candles, the lights were dimmed, and the candles lit one from another. Gregg turned and lit Suzanna's, then she bent and lit Annie's.

"Hold on tight," she whispered, "and be very careful." She then held Annie's hand in hers and steadied it as they lit Ida's candle. The organ music grew softer and then faded to nothing, and in a room lit only by the glow of candles the congregation sang Silent Night.

Just as Suzanna suspected, Annie was too excited to go to bed.

"Please, Mama," she begged, "just ten minutes more."

Of course, ten minutes turned into an hour then Ida gave a loud and extremely sorrowful sounding sigh. "It's a shame Santa won't be able to stop here this year."

Annie looked up wide eyed. "What do you mean he won't stop. The tree elves—"

"Despite the tree, Santa won't stop if the children are awake. Don't you remember that poem about the children all nestled snug in their beds? Well, that's why they were all in their beds."

With a look of apprehension pinching her face, Annie asked, "Is that really true?"

"Absolutely," Suzanna said. "Grandmas don't lie."

Annie hesitated a moment. With a look of doubt still clinging to her face, she said, "I'm not really sleepy, but I'll try." After a lengthy round of goodnight hugs and kisses, she started up the stairs.

Ida stayed for a few minutes longer, then followed Annie to bed.

Once they were certain Annie was asleep, Gregg carried in the cartons and gift boxes that had been hidden in the garage.

"I'll assemble the bicycle while you arrange the other things under the tree," he said.

Suzanna nodded, and they went to work. The boxes of dresses and shoes were wrapped in gold paper and tied with red ribbons, the games and toys taken from the cardboard cartons and placed around the tree. As she arranged the toys and gifts, she could almost hear the squeals of delight that would soon follow. She pictured Annie's eyes glistening with happiness, and it filled her heart to know that for the first time in her young life Annie was experiencing the joy of Christmas. Although it was not something she could unwrap or hold in her hand, Suzanna had come to realize it was the greatest gift of all.

When they'd finished, she poured them each a glass of wine and they sat together on the sofa. For a few moments they spoke about Annie, anticipating how thrilled she was going to be. Then Gregg's voice softened.

He brought his body closer to hers and traced his fingers along the curve of her cheek. "You look beautiful tonight."

With a slight blush coloring her cheeks, she thanked him.

"It's the dress from the show," she said. "Colette told me to keep it."

Gregg smiled and leaned closer still. "It's not the dress that's beautiful, it's you. Everything about you. The sweetness of your smile, the tenderness of your touch, the way you look after Annie, how you care for Ida. There's something about you, Darla Jean, that makes people love you...myself included."

Suzanna started to speak, but he touched his finger to her lips and hushed her.

"I came to Georgia thinking I'd spend some time with my family then move on, but you've changed all that. I've fallen in love with you and with Annie too. I'm hoping that in time you'll feel the same about me."

She tilted her face to his and in a voice filled with emotion whispered, "I already do."

He leaned in, his breath warm against her cheek. With his fingers cradling the back of her neck and his thumb caressing her cheek, he kissed her full on the mouth. His lips were soft and sweet against hers, warmed by passion but filled with promise. She circled her arms around his neck, and he drew her closer still. When Suzanna felt the thump of his heart against hers, the fears and heartaches of the past melted into nothingness. She knew that moment and the memory of that moment would forever be in her heart.

⟡

Suzanna had hoped to sleep until eight on Christmas morning, but it proved impossible. Before dawn she heard Annie's footsteps thundering down the staircase, so she pulled herself from the bed and followed her down. She'd reached the lower landing when she heard Annie cry out.

"The tree elves were right! Santa came!"

Before breakfast Annie had unwrapped every gift, played with every toy, and tried on every new dress, sweater, and coat. When she finally settled into making cookies in her new Easy Bake Oven, Suzanna gave Ida her gifts. She'd worried that they were small by comparison: a special Christmas ornament that read Grandma 1960, the holiday apron she'd admired at the Emporium, and a blue velvet bathrobe. The last gifts were the ones Suzanna and Gregg exchanged.

He handed her the small box wrapped in gold paper, touched his mouth to hers, then said, "I hope this is the beginning of many more Christmases together."

Inside the box was a heart-shaped locket.

"It's beautiful," Suzanna said and returned the kiss he'd given her moments earlier. Before she had him clasp it around her neck, she popped the heart open. Inside were two tiny picture frames. One held a miniature photo of Annie; the other was blank.

"I left that side empty for a reason," Gregg said shyly. "Hopefully, in the not-too-distant future, you'll want to use that spot for a picture of somebody special."

Giving the locket a quick glance, Annie said, "Grandma's special. Mama can put her picture in there."

Everybody laughed but when Gregg smiled at Suzanna, she knew she'd already found her somebody special. She told herself that before next Christmas the locket would have two pictures, and she would wear it around her neck every day for as long as she lived.

BOBBY

Finding Suzanna

Christmas came and went in a blur of activity for Bobby Doherty. There was a dinner at the Garretts' house, a get-together with Brenda's cousins, and the New Year's Eve party at the country club where he downed way too many drinks and ended up stumbling over his own feet. That night Brenda had to drive home, and the next morning she was as frosty as an ice cube.

Before he had one eye open, she plopped a glass of orange juice and two aspirin down on the nightstand alongside the bed.

"You were an absolute embarrassment," she snapped angrily. "I'm just glad Mama and Daddy weren't there to see you fall flat on your face."

"I'm sorry," Bobby said penitently. "I don't know what got into me."

"Too many martinis, that's what got into you!" She yanked the blanket back and told him he had an hour to pull himself together and get dressed.

He groaned. "Gimme a break. I'm not feeling all that great."

"I don't care if your head feels like it will pop off your shoulders, we are not going to miss my parents' black-eyed peas brunch."

"Just this once," he pleaded. "Let's stay home. I can light the fireplace in the den, and we'll cuddle up, maybe watch the Rose Bowl Parade. Wouldn't you like—"

"No! Get dressed. We are leaving here in one hour."

Somehow, he made it through the brunch. He'd nodded and bobbed his head listening to Jerome Garrett talk about how it was unthinkable that an upstart such as John F. Kennedy could defeat the Republican vice president, Richard Nixon. He'd also complimented her mama's black-eyed peas and rice, saying that this year's dish was the best yet. But before the day was out, he'd cast those thoughts aside and slid back into remembering how Suzanna would rub his shoulders or massage his calves after a hard workout. She was soft in ways where Brenda was hard; more sympathetic, more forgiving. There were times in life when a man needed a woman like Brenda and other times when he needed someone like Suzanna.

In the days that followed, the memories of Suzanna became like a drug Bobby couldn't get out of his system. The more he tried to push them from his mind, the more he was drawn back to them. He thought about how they'd made love in the back seat of his daddy's car and how she'd twined her legs around his like an ivy climbing a trellis. Back then he couldn't imagine a life without her, but that was before Brenda.

He and Eddie had spoken just once since that telephone call, and they'd not mentioned Suzanna Duff again, but on the Tuesday after the brunch as soon as Brenda left for the bridge club Bobby called his brother.

After a few minutes of small talk about the bowl games, he got around to what he'd actually called about.

"By the way," he said casually, "did you ever recall Suzanna's new name?"

"Nah, I haven't thought about it."

"Think you could look into it for me? Dig around, check the program maybe?"

"I don't think there was a program, and I'm certainly not asking Christine about it."

Bobby hesitated a moment, not wanting to appear overly anxious, then asked about the name of the country club where the event was held.

"Same as the town," Eddie said, "Barston Country Club. But you're not actually gonna try and find her, are you?"

"Not really," Bobby lied. "Just curious, I guess." He immediately changed the subject, asking when Eddie and Christine might be coming for a visit.

Bobby waited a week before he called information and asked for the telephone number of the Barston Country Club. When the operator asked if he wanted Catering or the Golf Shop, he answered "Catering," then wrote the number on the scratch pad in front of him and hung up.

He folded the note paper and tucked it in the breast pocket of his jacket, still uncertain of what he'd do. A voice in the back of his mind whispered that he was asking for trouble, but he reasoned that he wasn't doing anything wrong. Looking up an old friend wasn't exactly a crime. Even though he was already picturing Suzanna lying naked in his arms, he kept telling himself that he just wanted to say hello, see how she was doing, ask about the kid. He didn't know what he'd do if it was Suzanna and if she told him the child was his, but those were pretty big ifs and that was a bridge he didn't have to cross yet.

Over the course of the afternoon, he read through the Fulmore merger three times then laid it on the credenza behind his desk. His concentration was shot; trying to work when his mind was elsewhere was impossible. He'd be doing himself and the firm a favor if he went ahead and made the call; chances were, it would end up being a big nothing. Maybe a girl who looked a little like Suzanna. Eddie wasn't necessarily a source to be believed.

Once Bobby knew for sure, he could put the issue to bed, forget about finding Suzanna, leave thoughts of her in the past where they belonged, and get back to enjoying life with Brenda. Even though he'd assured himself there was no wrong in what he was doing, he waited until after five, checked to make sure Jerome Garrett was gone for the day, then closed his office door and dialed the number he'd been given.

The telephone rang several times before a woman answered. Her voice sounded young and a bit informal for a country club.

Bobby introduced himself and said he was representing a talent agency who had an interest in one of the models who'd worked the December fashion show at the Barston Country Club. In the deep-throated voice he used when there was a need to impress, he said, "I'm hoping you can give me the young woman's contact information."

"Are you a talent scout? Like for a movie or something?"

"Something like that," Bobby replied, keeping the timbre of his voice consistent. "My understanding is that the young woman we are looking for is a blonde with a double name."

"The model from Atlanta was a brunette, so you must mean Darla Jean Parker."

Bobby jotted the name down as he continued. "This Darla Jean Parker, is she from Atlanta also?"

"No, sir, she's a local. Works here in Barston. I'm not real sure, but I think she lives with her grandma over in Cousins."

"Works in Barston? Would you happen to know where?"

"Yes, sir, I sure enough do. Cavalier's Couture. It's the fancy dress shop over on Main Street."

Bobby thanked her for her help and hung up. He studied the piece of paper for several minutes then picked up the receiver and asked the operator for the number of Cavalier's Couture on Main Street in Barston. As she recited the numbers, he wrote them below Darla Jean Parker's name.

It was beginning to look like every piece of information he got only led to more questions. If this Darla Jean Parker was Suzanna Duff, why had she changed her name? And where did the grandma thing come from? Suzanna always told him she'd never known any of her grandparents. If that story was a lie, had there been any truth in their relationship?

He underlined the name in a heavy-handed stroke, then put a question mark at the bottom of the page and drew a circle around it. He sat there for a long while, tapping his pen against the desk, and trying to make sense of it all. It was close to seven when the telephone rang and shook him from his reverie.

Brenda's voice had a thread of irritation woven through it. "It's after seven. Why are you still at the office?"

Bobby stumbled through an explanation of being buried under a mountain of paperwork and then in a move that came as a surprise even to him, said he'd be going to see a new client later in the week. "It may be for just a day or could turn into an overnight thing."

"Can't you hold off until next Tuesday?" Brenda asked. "That's my bridge club night, and it won't be so lonely if you're away."

A sliver of guilt crawled along Bobby's spine. "Yeah, sure, babe, I can hold off 'til Tuesday."

At that point he was committed. He'd come too far and wasn't about to back off now. Besides, he had to know whether or not this woman was Suzanna. If it was, he had a whole lot of questions that needed to be answered.

He refolded the note paper with Darla Jean Parker's name and Cavalier's telephone number, slid it back into his pocket, then left the office and started for home.

BOBBY DOHERTY

Tuesday, January 10, 1961

Bobby arrived in Barston a few minutes after 11 a.m. He drove down Main Street looking for Cavalier's, and once he spotted it he circled the block to drive by a second time. A cold front had come through the night before, so the few shoppers who were out were bundled in wool caps and parkas. He parked two blocks away then got out and walked past the store.

At first the shop appeared empty. Then he saw her behind the counter, her head tilted as if she might be searching for something on a lower shelf. Her hair hung loose, longer than it was when they were together, falling across her shoulder, hiding part of her face. At first he wasn't sure, so he stood for a moment and watched. As familiar as the figure seemed, there was something different about this woman. Something he couldn't put his finger on.

Moments later she lifted her head as if she'd heard something, then turned and walked toward the back of the store. He watched as she disappeared behind a rack of dresses. Her walk was different than he remembered, her stride longer, her back straighter. Even from the brief glimpse he'd managed to catch, he could tell her chin was held at a loftier angle.

He thought he'd know right off whether or not it was Suzanna, but the sorry truth was he didn't. Bits and pieces of the girl he knew were there, but the woman as a whole was different. He waited, hoping she'd return, but several minutes ticked by and he didn't see her again. The wind gusted, and he felt something smack against his back. He turned quickly and found the street empty. A trash can toppled over; a flyaway newspaper was lifted by the wind and disappeared down the street. Shivering in his suit jacket, Bobby wished he'd thought to bring a top coat or a wool scarf. Remembering that he'd passed a coffee shop a few doors down, he turned and headed back. He'd get warm, then check her out again.

He slid onto a stool at the counter and ordered coffee, black.

The counterman, a pimply-faced kid close to the age he'd been in high school, set the cup in front of him and filled it to the brim. The coffee spilled into the saucer, but the kid didn't care. Of course he didn't. A guy that age didn't give a hoot about the nit-picky things; he was too busy thinking about football and sex. After you grew up, that's when life changed.

Looking at the kid made Bobby feel old. He missed the days when all he needed to be happy was Suzanna and the keys to his daddy's car. Life was good back then. Now he was weighed down with responsibilities: a house, a country club membership, a job where he was constantly on call, and if he wasn't tied up with filings and depositions then he was expected to scout out new clients. He didn't have a choice. Brenda wanted things, the kind of things that cost money. He'd thought he wanted the same things, but now remembering how it was with Suzanna he was starting to wonder if he actually wanted this life or had just been sucked into the appeal of it.

For the past four years he'd believed he had it all, but maybe he was only fooling himself, thinking what other people wanted him to think. Remembering how it was with Suzanna lit a fire inside of him, a fire that wasn't going to be squelched by peeking through a shop window. He had to see her, touch her, feel her in his arms again. He had to know if she still felt the same about him. If she did, well, then, maybe they could work things out. Find a way to be together.

He drained the last of his coffee, paid the check, and left.

He walked back, stood across the street from the shop, and watched the woman he thought to be Suzanna. With his eyes glued to her movements, he failed to see the tall redhead who came from the back. A dark cloud hovered overhead, the wind rattled the barber shop sign, and a roll of thunder sounded in the distance. Moments later the rain began.

To prevent getting soaked, he stepped back and stood in the doorway of the dry cleaners. As he stood there he became colder still, and a feeling of apprehension settled in his stomach. A second boom of thunder sounded, louder than the first and far more menacing.

This wasn't at all the way he'd thought it would be. He'd pictured himself strolling into the shop with his shoulders back and his head high; proud, confident, a man to be reckoned with. He'd imagined Suzanna running to him, her arms open wide, her mouth crushing against his. Instead of it happening as he'd thought, she was going about her business, not seeing him, not even noticing he was there.

Lightning flashed across the sky, and seconds later the lights in the shop flickered. Cold to the bone, Bobby shivered and pulled his jacket collar up around his neck. He thought of his nice warm office, a job that few men his age were fortunate enough to have, a lifestyle that almost anyone would envy. If he were honest with himself, he'd face facts. He'd be a fool to give all that up. For what? A woman who wasn't anything like the girl he'd known? No way.

He moved out of the doorway and crossed the street, heading back to his car, but just then Suzanna stepped to the front window of the shop and looked out. Her face was tilted toward the sky, but he saw precisely what he'd been looking for. It was Suzanna, the same Suzanna he'd loved. As she turned and walked toward the back, he burst through the door of the shop.

The redhead walked over to him. "Good afternoon."

Bobby craned his neck looking for Suzanna, but she'd disappeared behind a rack of dresses.

"Are you looking for something special?" the redhead asked.

"Um. Not really." Bobby turned his jacket collar back down and straightened his shoulders. "I'm an old friend of Darla Jean. I was passing through town and thought I'd stop and say hello."

"How lovely." The redhead extended her hand. "Colette Cavalier."

"Robert Doherty." As they shook hands, he smiled, turning on the charm. "If she can spare a few minutes, I thought maybe we could grab a cup of coffee, catch up…"

Colette glanced up. "Here she is now." She raised her arm and gave a wave. "Darla Jean, someone to see you."

Suzanna walked toward the front of the store then stopped dead in her tracks when he smiled and said, "Hi, Darla Jean."

She gasped. "Bobby. I never—"

He smiled. "I know, it's been a long time. Too long." He walked over put his hands on her shoulders and kissed her cheek. He'd hoped for a warmer response but she stood there like an icicle, her face pale and eyes wide.

Glancing over at Colette and then back to Suzanna, he said, "If your beautiful boss doesn't mind, perhaps we could grab a cup of coffee. We've got tons of catching up to do."

"Go," Colette said. "Take the afternoon off. With this weather, I doubt we'll have many customers coming in, so it will be slow."

Bobby flashed her another smile. "Thanks."

"Yes, thanks, Colette," Suzanna said and gave a tight-lipped smile. She excused herself, disappeared into the back room, and returned wearing her coat.

Bobby hooked his arm through hers, and they left the shop.

⟊⟊⟊

Suzanna felt her heart hammering against her chest as they walked along Main Street. A million questions raced through her mind, and she didn't have the answer to even one. Yes, they needed to talk but not here. Not in a town where people knew her and would start to wonder who the stranger was. She suggested a restaurant out on the highway.

"I'm guessing you don't want people to overhear our conversation." He grinned and opened the door to a big black Lincoln. Once she was seated inside, he circled around and slid behind the wheel. As soon as they'd pulled away from the curb, he glanced over and said, "Looks like you've been keeping a whole lot of secrets, huh, Suzanna?"

He was the same as she remembered, so sure of himself, tossing out a grin that already felt far too intimate. "Why are you here, Bobby? How'd you find me?"

"Suzanna, honey, you make it sound like a bad thing. It's not, I've still got feelings—"

"Really?" Her voice was thick with sarcasm. "After not giving a crap for eight years, now you've decided you've got feelings?"

"That's not fair; I tried to get in touch. I went to your house looking for you, not just once, but a number of times. You know what happened?

Your old man told me you were gone. That's it, just gone. No message, nothing. He wouldn't say where to find you, just get out of his house, that was it. You think it was easy, Suzanna? Not knowing—"

"Stop calling me Suzanna!"

"Yeah, right." He gave her a slant-eyed look of cynicism. "I almost forgot, you've got yourself a new name, and from what I hear a grandma who never before existed. Clue me in, Darla Jean, what exactly are you up to?"

"Not what you think, Bobby. Mrs. Parker mistook me for her granddaughter, and I…" Her voice faltered, and she turned her face toward the window.

"You what? Saw a golden opportunity and decided to cash in on it?"

"Is that really what you think of me?" She didn't turn or look back.

They drove in silence until he pulled into a parking space at the Pig n' Pint. After the engine was switched off, he reached across the seat and touched his hand to the back of her neck.

"Look, Suzanna, I'm not here to hurt you. I came because I've never forgotten that night. I've regretted it a thousand times over, but with not knowing where you were there was nothing I could do about it. I had no way to make things right."

His words were so sincere, his touch so familiar. In an odd way it seemed as though no time had passed since they were last together. They stepped out of the car and Suzanna offered no resistance as they walked into the restaurant, his hand on the small of her back, steering her toward a booth behind the bar.

After the drinks were ordered, they began to talk. Bobby explained how his brother had been at the fashion show.

"You probably didn't recognize Eddie," he said. "He's gained weight and now has a beard."

"I guess we've all changed," Suzanna said wistfully. She looked into his eyes remembering how, over the years, she'd wished for this moment so many times. She'd imagined it a thousand different ways but never quite like this. "I have a good life now, someone I care for, a beautiful little daughter—"

He nodded then reached across the table, taking her hand in his. "Eddie told me. She's our child, isn't she?"

Suzanna hesitated a long time before she answered. She could say no, end it here and now, and hold on to the life she'd built. It was a good life; the life she'd dreamt of having. Telling the truth would complicate things. Once Bobby knew, the others would find out and it would be like opening up Pandora's box. The lies would come tumbling out, one atop the other, destroying everything she'd worked so hard to build. She'd be branded a liar and the people she loved would turn away with a look of disappointment or, worse yet, disgust. She would no longer be Darla Jean Parker, she'd lose the grandmother she'd come to love, and Gregg also, maybe even her job. Once she opened that door, there would be no closing it. The word no lingered on her tongue for several minutes, but it never came out.

This wasn't about her. It was about Annie. Good or bad, she deserved to know her father.

Suzanna gave a weary sigh, one weighted with the knowledge of all she was risking.

"Yes, Annie is our daughter," she said, "but she knows nothing of you or the circumstances of her birth." She continued on, explaining how with no place else to go, she'd moved in with Earl. "He was good to me when I needed somebody to lean on, but he was never good to Annie. He barely tolerated her. Last summer I finally realized he was little more than a carbon copy of my daddy, and I wanted something better for our daughter." She went on to tell of Earl's drinking, the subsequent abusiveness, and how one morning she and Annie left, hitched a ride, and landed in Cousins, Georgia.

As she spoke, a pained look settled on Bobby's face. "I'm sorry, I had no idea…"

"That's not true, Bobby. You knew I was carrying your child, and you turned away. When we passed one another in the hallways, you looked the other way and started laughing it up with your buddies. I wanted to be there for graduation, but I couldn't stand the shame so I stopped going to school. A week later, my daddy told me to get out."

"I'll make it up to you, Suzanna. I've got money now. I can help out."

Suzanna pulled her hand away from his. "Money? Is that what you think this is about?"

"No, of course not. I want to pick up where we left off, Suzanna. We were good together, you know that, don't you?"

"Good together, how? In the back seat of your daddy's car?"

"Of course, there was that, but there was a lot more. We had a connection, like this feeling we were supposed to be together."

"Then why did that great connection end the minute I said we should get married?"

He gave an almost imperceptible shrug. "It wasn't because I didn't love you, but the timing and the circumstances were wrong. We were too young, I had my scholarship—"

"So, what's changed, Bobby? Is this where you tell me you want to start over and make things right?"

Instead of answering her question, he leaned forward, so close that she could feel his breath on her cheek and when he spoke, his voice was as soulful and intimate as a kiss. "We belong together, Suzanna. I know it, and you know it." He smiled, brushed his fingertip across her lips, then nested her chin in his hand.

It was a thing he'd done a thousand times before, and the memories came rushing back. She'd told herself that she'd moved on, forgotten about him, forgotten about the way it once was, but all of a sudden she was no longer sure.

"Things aren't the same, Bobby. We've got a little girl who needs a mama and a daddy. Do you think you're ready to settle down, get married, and be the kind of daddy Annie deserves?"

"I'd like nothing more, but you've got to realize, Suzanna, things like that take time. I've got responsibilities. In a few years I'll make partner in my firm. That's not something—"

She gave a cynical snort. "Not something you can walk away from the way you walked away from me and Annie?"

"I've changed, Suzanna. I'm different now. I know what I want, and I want you. I realize we've got a child to think about, and I've offered to help out financially, but where we go from here is up to you. If you give it a chance, I think you'll see the passion is still there. It won't always be easy, but we'll work it out, find a way to be with each other."

He lowered his eyes and his voice grew softer, threaded with what Suzanna believed to be the sound of regret. "Unless you're willing to try, we'll never know if this was meant to be."

She felt a tiny bit of her resolve slip away. After all, he was Annie's father, and they did have a history together. Everybody made mistakes; she'd made plenty of them herself. There was a very real possibility that Bobby regretted the way things ended, that he had looked for her, and that he actually did want them to be a family. If it was true, didn't she owe it to Annie to at least give it a try?

She raised her face and looked into Bobby's eyes. "Would you like to meet Annie?"

"Of course I would, but not right away. It's too soon. You and I need to spend time together, get back to where we used to be."

A prickle of suspicion suddenly crawled up her spine.

"Back to where we used to be?" she repeated. "Does that mean you getting me into bed, or are you actually interested in being a daddy to Annie?"

"I won't lie to you, Suzanna, it's both. Of course, I want to get to know our daughter, but I also want to hold you in my arms and make love to you. I've never stopped wanting that."

It was late in the afternoon when they left the restaurant and drove back to Barston. Bobby parked his car in the darkened lot behind the shops then leaned across the seat, kissed Suzanna full on the mouth, and pulled her body into his. She didn't resist even though it felt wrong and oddly out of sync with her memories. He was the same but somehow different. When he kissed her a second and third time, something stirred in the pit of her stomach and she began to believe the passion was still there.

It was too soon. Much too soon.

"Not yet," she said, but her words had little conviction and were no louder than a whisper. "I think we should wait until—"

He silenced her, covering her mouth with his. When the kiss ended, he ran his tongue along the side of her throat. With his breath hot in her ear, he whispered, "Don't think, just relax and let it happen."

She forced herself to pull away. "No. Not here and not now. We're not teenagers, and this isn't the back seat of your daddy's car. If we're going to make this work, it's got to be different this time." Before she could say they needed to get to know one another again before they jumped into bed, he cut in.

"You're right." He grinned. "The Ellington Hotel is about 15 miles north of Barston. Next week I'll check in, and you can meet me there at five o'clock. They have a nice cocktail lounge; we'll have dinner, dance, and I'll stay the night."

Pushing aside the apprehension she'd felt earlier, Suzanna agreed to meet at the Ellington the following Tuesday.

"This doesn't mean I'm going up to the room with you," she warned, "but it would be nice to spend the evening together and see how we feel about one another."

"I already know how I feel about you," Bobby said with a twinkle in his eye.

He kissed her one last time. She stepped out of his car and headed over to where she'd parked Ida's. As she watched him drive away, a warning bell sounded in the back of her mind, but instead of recognizing it for what it was, Suzanna imagined it to be the chime of wedding bells.

SUZANNA

Shattered Dreams

When Suzanna arrived home, Gregg was in the living room working on a Cinderella jigsaw puzzle with Annie. He glanced up, smiled, then looked back to the puzzle.

"I came by the shop this afternoon, and Colette said you were gone for the day. Where'd you go?"

Suzanna's heart twisted, skipped a beat, then started up again, only faster. "It was on the spur of the moment. A friend I knew from high school came by and asked me to lunch. The shop was really slow, so Colette suggested I take the afternoon off." Not a lie, but not the full truth. "If I'd known you were available, I would have called you to join us." This time definitely a lie.

"It was a last-minute thing. The school canceled afternoon classes because the furnace conked out, and there was no heat in the building." He gave a nod toward the half-finished puzzle and said, "We're looking for Prince Charming's shoe. Want to join in?"

"Later perhaps. I'm going to see if Ida needs help with dinner, then I'd like to freshen up. This rain makes me feel kind of grungy."

Suzanna popped her head into the kitchen, said hi, then hurried upstairs. Normally she would have welcomed the chance to sit with Gregg and Annie, but now she simply wanted to be alone. Even though she told herself she'd done nothing to feel guilty about, the guilt was there. It soured

185

her stomach and elbowed her heart with questions that had nothing but impossible answers.

Yesterday she thought she knew exactly where her life was headed. She was in love with Gregg, and he felt the same about her. It was practically a given; not the fiery passion she'd known with Bobby, but real and filled with promise. Only now Bobby was back, and with him came the memory of all they had once meant to one another. His words echoed in Suzanna's ears.

I've never stopped loving you.

For years she'd waited, hoped and prayed that he'd come for her, and when he didn't she'd cursed him for leaving her behind, abandoning her and their baby. But now she knew the truth. He'd looked for her at graduation, then gone to her house and searched in vain. He hadn't forgotten. Although eight years had gone by, he'd never stopped loving her, just as she had never stopped loving him. Didn't a love like that deserve a chance?

The image of Gregg carrying Annie on his shoulders at the fair flashed through Suzanna's mind, and she felt a crevice open up in the center of her heart. The two parts of her life were divided; on one side Gregg with his easy smile and patient ways, on the other side Bobby with the undying love he'd carried in his heart all those years. Making a choice was impossible, but not making one was worse. It was unfair to everyone, most of all to Annie. She wanted a daddy and now Suzanna could give her one, but which was the right one?

That evening, dinner was a quiet affair. Annie chattered on about how she'd found the prince's shoe, and Ida talked of how she'd gotten material enough to make new curtains and a matching throw pillow for Annie's room. When Annie said the training wheels on her new bicycle had broked, Gregg laughed and said they weren't broke, they just needed tightening.

"I'll fix it after dinner," he added.

Suzanna knew much of their life revolved around Annie—not just hers, but Ida's and Gregg's also. That would change were she to choose Bobby.

Later that night as she lay in bed trying to sort through her feelings, she found herself comparing the two men. They were different in so many ways, but each of them held a piece of her heart. Gregg was a good man, a man who'd already demonstrated his love for Annie. Right from the start, he'd been open and honest with her; shouldn't she be the same? It wasn't fair to give him half a heart when he deserved so much more. He hadn't yet asked her to marry him, but now she was starting to wonder what her answer would be when he did.

Suzanna tried to picture Bobby fixing Annie's bike, but instead she drifted back to thoughts of how it was when they were together. The memories she'd hidden for all those years were still there. The heat of his mouth covering hers, his hands finding the sweet spots of passion, his eyes savoring her nakedness as he whispered promises of love. What Bobby had said was true; they were good together.

Eight years ago she'd walked away; she'd heard him calling her name but hadn't turned back. She was angry and hurt, too prideful perhaps or stubborn. In the weeks that followed, he'd looked the other way when they passed one another in the hallway, but hadn't she done the same thing? They'd been too young to realize that a love like theirs was a once-in-a-lifetime thing and foolishly allowed it to slip away. Now fate was giving them a second chance, an opportunity to make up for the stupidity of their youth. Only a simpleton would ignore such a stroke of luck.

Gregg was a good man and great with Annie, but it wasn't fair to compare the two men when he'd spent all those months getting to know her and Bobby had never even met his daughter. That was something she'd remedy right away.

When she met Bobby at the Ellington, she'd tell him of her feelings and say she was ready to give their love another chance. She'd insist he meet Annie right away; after all, he was her daddy. There was no longer a reason for waiting, and once Annie realized he was her father she would most likely be as taken with him as she was with Gregg. Suzanna would explain that she couldn't move forward without taking Annie's feelings into consideration. They were a package deal; there was no having one without the other.

When she finally closed her eyes, she could almost see Annie skipping alongside of her birth daddy as he regaled her with stories of how he'd come to find her after eight long years of searching. She was drifting on the edge of sleep when she noticed that from the back Bobby looked strangely like Gregg.

The next morning Suzanna avoided having breakfast with everyone and hurried out, claiming that she'd promised to help Colette rearrange the jewelry showcase. As Gregg said goodbye and kissed her cheek, she felt the sharp-edged fingers of regret take hold of her. Last night she'd planned to tell him about Bobby, not the whole story of who she was, but a sketchy version saying only that Annie's father had come back and was asking for a second chance. Today that no longer seemed possible.

In the darkness of her room with thoughts of Bobby crowding her mind, everything had seemed so much clearer. But this morning as she was starting down the staircase, she heard Annie and Gregg laughing together and her heart seized. The realization that she was as fond of Gregg as Annie was came like a bucket of ice cold water splashed in her face. The truth was he made them both happy; happier than she could ever remember.

She thought about it all that day, and the next day, and the day following, but clarity was impossible to find. It seemed like such an old cliché to say she loved them both equally, yet that was indeed the situation.

By the time the weekend rolled around, Suzanna's heart was twisted into one giant impossible-to-unravel knot of uncertainty. And to make it even worse, the furnace at the school had to undergo major repairs and Gregg was at home all week. Him being there made it almost impossible to sort through her thoughts. She couldn't look at him without seeing all the things that had drawn her to him: the warmth of his eyes and the laughter lines that crinkled the corners, the gentleness of his voice, the dark curl that tumbled onto his forehead no matter how many times he pushed it back.

She'd been attracted to him because he was handsome, but over time she'd come to see he was so much more than handsome. He was beautiful, both on the inside and out. There was no doubt she loved him, yet she still couldn't rid herself of thoughts of Bobby; nor could she deny the fact that he was a part of Annie. Together they had created this beautiful daughter. Wasn't that supposed to be a lifetime bond?

On Saturday, Suzanna remained at the shop longer than usual and arrived home after Ida had cleared the dinner dishes from the table. She'd planned to keep her alone-time with Gregg to a minimum, but when she walked in the door everyone was in the living room and they seemed to be waiting for her.

He gave a boyish grin and said, "I hope you're hungry." He came across the room and brushed her lips with a quick kiss. "I made dinner reservations at Alberto's."

Alberto's, with its intimate atmosphere, cozy booths, and smooth music was sure to mean trouble.

"For tonight?" Suzanna said apprehensively.

He nodded. "It's been a busy week, so I thought an evening out would help you relax and unwind."

"It would, except that I'm kind of beat. Maybe tonight we could have a bite here then watch television with Grandma and Annie."

"You'll do nothing of the sort," Ida said. "I've already cleaned up the kitchen. Besides, Gregg's right, you could use an evening out."

Annie giggled. "You gotta do what Grandma says, Mama, 'cause she's the boss."

A short while later they were ushered toward the back booth at Alberto's, and by no small coincidence it was precisely where they'd sat on their first date. A bottle of wine and two glasses were on the table waiting for them.

"You ordered this?" Suzanna asked.

He smiled and gave her shoulder an affectionate squeeze as she slid into the booth. "Yes, it was the best I could come up with at the last minute. I had planned to take you to Le Bouchon tonight, but with you working late…"

"It couldn't be helped; we've been really busy at the shop." The words of yet another lie felt awkward and heavy in her mouth. Suzanna thought for sure Gregg would notice, but if he did he gave no indication.

He leaned forward, his eyes fixed on her face.

"I understand," he said. "It's just that I've missed our spending time together."

She reluctantly allowed her eyes to meet his. "I've missed being together also." After hesitating a moment, she plunged ahead. "But I'm glad to know you understand, because next Tuesday is going to be a late night."

"You'll be working at the store?"

"Part of the day, but I plan to leave about 3:30." The thought that he might again stop by the store had crossed her mind, so she was prepared for it. "Colette is sending me to Atlanta for a retailing seminar. I have no idea how long it will run, but if it's too late I may stay over and drive back early the next morning."

A tiny bit of the happiness she'd seen in Gregg's eyes disappeared, but his smile remained steady. "Colette seems to be grooming you for bigger and better things."

Jumping on that thought because it was an easy topic of conversation, Suzanna quickly agreed, saying it was a great opportunity. For several minutes she rattled on about the countless things she'd learned working with Colette, how she loved her job, and how the money she earned enabled her to give Annie things she'd once thought impossible.

She was talking about how Annie would be able to go to college, which was something she'd not been able to do, when the waitress came to take their order.

"It's late, and I'm not all that hungry," Suzanna said. "Maybe something light?"

The waitress rattled off the names of a few lighter dishes; then Gregg suggested they share an antipasto.

"Sounds good," she said.

Once the waitress was gone, Suzanna went right back to talking about the job.

After a few minutes, Gregg reached across the table and took her hand in his. "I know how much this job means to you, Darla Jean, but wouldn't you like to stay home and spend more time with Annie?"

His voice was soft and the question filled with compassion, so it caught her off guard.

"Well, sure, but this is only for one night," she replied. "Annie understands that if we want a better future, I've got to work. That's a fact of life whether—"

"It doesn't have to be that way," he cut in. "I love you, Darla Jean, and I'd like nothing better than to see you be a full-time mother. Marry me, and I'll give you the future you want. We'll be a family. I'll be a loving husband to you and a good father to Annie. When she's ready, she'll have an opportunity to go to college, and—"

He stopped speaking when the waitress appeared with the tray of food.

A feeling of panic swelled in Suzanna's chest as she sat silently watching the girl set out plates and silverware. She'd pulled her hand loose from Gregg's; now it felt sticky and wet. It was cool in the restaurant, but beads of perspiration were rising on her forehead and she could feel her heart thudding against her breastbone. She wanted the waitress to stay longer, to be an awkward presence that stopped Gregg from speaking, but such was not to be. In a handful of seconds the girl was gone, taking with her any hope of delaying the question Suzanna wanted to avoid.

Pushing aside the tray of olives, meats, and cheeses, Gregg again reached for her hand.

"I was hoping to make this a momentous occasion, take you someplace romantic and propose in a way that would ultimately be the story we'd tell our children and grandchildren, but the school is pressuring me for an answer about whether or not I'm going to stay. They've offered me a three-year extension, and I have to give them an answer by Monday."

Suzanna's heart beat faster, and her head seemed ready to topple from her shoulders. She'd had a single glass of wine, but it felt as though she'd downed a gallon. A week earlier she'd hoped Gregg would ask this very same question, but now things were different. Bobby was back, and he was Annie's daddy. Her birth daddy. How could she possibly deny him the chance to set things right?

As Gregg held her hand in his, a worried look settled on his brow. Apparently sensing her reluctance to answer, he said, "If you honestly love your job and that's what makes you happy, you can continue to work, but at least you'll have the option of knowing you can stop whenever you want…"

As she listened to him speak of his love for both her and Annie, tears filled Suzanna's eyes and she felt a piece of her heart shatter and break away. In a voice choked with emotion she said, "I love you, Gregg, I honestly do, but I need some time before I can give you my answer."

He blinked in surprise. "I'm not sure I understand what you mean. Time? Time for what?"

"To make certain decisions about my life."

He let go of her hand and pushed back in the seat. "We've been seeing each other for over six months, Darla Jean. We've spent endless hours together, and I assumed you felt the same as I do."

"I do, but…"

"But what? Am I missing something here? Haven't you given me every reason to believe—"

"Yes, I have, and don't think this means I don't love you, because I do. It's just that my life is complicated, and there are things I need to sort out before—"

"What things?" His voice had become testy, and his words had the sound of a gauntlet thrown down on the table. The tenderness and warmth she'd seen in his face earlier were gone, his eyes hooded and his brows pinched tight.

Suzanna dropped her hands into her lap and sat looking down at them. She was at a crossroad with no way to move forward or back. Going forward meant crisscrossing the landmine of lies she'd laid out, and turning back meant she'd have to deal with the bridges she'd burned long ago. Even if she wanted to tell Gregg about Bobby, she couldn't. The risk was too great. He was no fool. Once he knew who Annie's daddy was, it would be easy enough to discover her true identity. He'd find out, then Ida would find out, and the life she'd built here in Cousins would be destroyed. She could live with that; she deserved it. But Annie didn't.

"I'm sorry, but I can't talk about it right now. If you'll just give me some time—"

The expression on his face remained rigid. "Darla Jean, if you are genuinely in love with someone, you don't need time to decide whether or not you want to marry them."

As Suzanna listened to his words, she felt the web of lies closing in on her, tightening, binding her to the past. All along she'd believed she was building a new life, but that was simply a lie she'd told herself. The truth was that Gregg had proposed to Darla Jean Parker, not Suzanna Duff. That's who he loved, the imaginary Darla Jean, not her. Bobby knew who she was and loved her nonetheless. He was Annie's real daddy. He had never forgotten, and he was still in love with Suzanna Duff.

The antipasto sat there, olive oil congealing beneath the chunks of cheese and meat, but neither of them touched anything. Gregg refilled his wine glass twice then said the evening was not at all what he'd expected.

"There's nothing you could have done differently," Suzanna said. "I'm sorry. If you'll just give me a few weeks to sort out the complications in my life, we can—" She was going to say perhaps start over, but he cut in.

"Don't rush," he said sharply. "I think we both need time to think things over." He emptied his wine glass and suggested they leave.

On the drive home, neither of them said a word. Several times Suzanna was tempted to offer some sort of explanation, but when she tried to pull her thoughts together, all she had was a bunch of new lies. Lies that sounded as hollow as a tin drum.

Wait until tomorrow, she told herself. Tomorrow their discussion would be less heated. Then she could talk to him, find a way to work things out. Time; that's all she was asking for. A few weeks, a month maybe. Bobby had held onto to his love for her through years of searching. He'd waited eight long years. If Gregg loved her, shouldn't he be willing to wait a few weeks?

If you love someone, truly love them, you don't give up. You find a way to work things out. Gregg was a sensible man. Surely he'd understand.

SUZANNA

Without a Word

That night Suzanna lay awake for hours on end, trying to make sense of the confusion in her heart. When she pictured Gregg's quick smile, the laugh lines that crinkled the corners of his eyes, and the patient way he made time for Annie's questions, she wanted to run downstairs, pound on his bedroom door, and beg forgiveness. But behind each of those thoughts came other ones. Memories of Bobby. For all those years, she'd held onto his love and carried it with her like one half of a broken coin, always waiting, always hoping, always searching for the other half. Now Bobby was here, asking to put the pieces back together again, make them whole, turn them into a family. Whatever the cost, she couldn't deny him that chance.

Shortly before the first rays of light seeped into the sky, Suzanna decided she would go to Gregg and explain that Annie's daddy was back. She would give no names and say only that he was asking her forgiveness. If Gregg loved her the way Bobby had loved her for all those years, he would understand and be willing to wait. If he refused, then that was proof positive Bobby's love was greater.

It was after ten when Suzanna woke and came downstairs. She expected to see Gregg in the living room with the Sunday paper scattered about or sitting at the kitchen table enjoying a second or third cup of coffee and chatting with Ida. The living room was empty, and Ida was the only one in the kitchen.

Trying not to make her search for Gregg obvious, she asked, "Where is everyone?"

"Annie took Scout for a walk, and Gregg left early this morning."

"Left to go where?"

Ida looked up with a puzzled expression. "His brother's place. Didn't he tell you?"

"Tell me what?"

"He left a note to say he'd be staying with Phil for a few weeks. Apparently they're working on some kind of a project." Ida furrowed her brow. "I'm surprised you didn't know."

Suzanna felt as though a sharp knife had just pierced her heart, but she tried to pretend otherwise.

"Oh, right," she said as if it were something that had simply slipped her mind, "I'd forgotten about that."

"The two of you didn't talk about it last night?"

"Um, I believe he mentioned it, but it was late and I was tired." Suzanna's stomach was churning, but anxious to change the subject she said, "I'm starving. Did you make pancakes this morning?"

"Starving? Didn't you and Gregg have dinner last night?" Ida still had that quizzical look tacked to her face.

"Sort of. It was late, so he ordered an antipasto for us to share." She said nothing about how the antipasto had gone untouched.

Suzanna poured herself a cup of coffee and sat across from Ida. She'd thought this morning she'd find Gregg still angry or perhaps refusing to grant her time to straighten things out, but she never dreamed he'd leave without saying goodbye.

Walking away solved nothing; she'd learned that the hard way. It was what she'd done with Bobby, and look at how that had turned out. Eight years wasted. Eight years of heartache and loneliness because she walked away without looking back.

She had a million personality flaws and stubbornness was definitely one of them, but Gregg wasn't like her. He was logical, patient, tolerant even. He was more likely to listen to reason than make snap decisions the way she did. It made no sense that he'd leave without saying something...unless maybe he'd left another note just for her, and she'd somehow overlooked it.

Leaving her coffee on the table, Suzanna hurried up the stairs and began searching for what she believed could be the lost note. She checked beneath the door, on the hall table, under the bed, and when she found nothing, she lifted and shook the scatter rug that was halfway across the room. Still nothing. No note and no trace of one ever being there.

After exhausting the search, she sat on the side of the bed, shoulders slumped and face buried in her hands. She could almost see Gregg settled in the club chair at his brother's house, chatting with Ginger, a bitter smile tugging at his mouth as he claimed their relationship had been a mistake from the very start.

"I'd expected so much more from her," he'd say, and Ginger would most likely nod in agreement.

For a while Suzanna thought of telephoning him to suggest they talk things through rather than end it this way, but when she tried to pinpoint exactly what it was they could talk through she had nothing. The situation was what it was. Yes, she loved Gregg, but that wasn't enough. Bobby deserved a chance. He was Annie's daddy, and nothing would ever change that.

For two days Suzanna went about life as if she were on auto-pilot. She went to work, helped Ida with the dinner dishes, and listened to Annie's prayers as she tucked her into bed, but her thoughts were always elsewhere. She tried to imagine what she would say to Bobby when they met at the Ellington. Although it was proving impossible to forget Gregg, she'd decided that Bobby was her future. He knew her secrets and loved her anyway; he was in love with the real Suzanna Duff. Gregg had been in love with the fantasy of Darla Jean Parker.

Darla Jean was just that: a fantasy. If she were honest with herself, Suzanna would have to admit she'd known all along it couldn't last. Sure, she'd hoped it would, but there's a world of difference in what you're hoping for and what you can actually hold in your hand. Her daddy had taught her that. Her destiny was decided the first time she let Bobby make love to her. Now it was time for her to give up the fantasy, go to Atlanta, and settle into a life as Mrs. Robert Doherty. It would be a good life, and

Annie would be with her real daddy. In the years to come Suzanna would hopefully forget about Gregg, but the sorry truth was she'd never forget about Ida. That loss would be with her forever.

On Tuesday morning when Suzanna woke, the sky was thick with ominous gray clouds and water was cascading from the eaves. During the night, she had heard Annie coughing and twice she'd climbed from the bed to check on her.

Annie was up and starting to dress when Suzanna came into the room and held a hand to her forehead.

"Uh oh. Feels like you've got a bit of fever."

Annie tugged her second sock on. "I'm fine, Mama."

"You're not fine, and with the weather as nasty as it is I'm not going to chance you coming down with pneumonia."

Despite the protests, Suzanna called the shop, told Colette she would not be in, then tucked Annie back in bed, rubbed her chest with Vicks, double-checked her temperature, and spent most of the morning carrying up trays of warm tea, chicken soup, and orange juice. That afternoon she was debating whether or not to cancel her date with Bobby when Annie's temperature slid back to normal.

By then Ida had started coughing, but she insisted it was nothing.

"A twenty-four-hour bug," she said. "It'll be gone by morning."

With a bit of hesitancy hanging onto her words, Suzanna asked if she felt well enough to take care of Annie for the evening. "I have plans to meet an old friend for dinner at the Ellington. I know it'll be a late night, and with all this rain I thought it might be better if I stay over. Would that be okay with you?"

"Of course I'm well enough. This little bitty cough is nothing to be concerned about. A dose or two of cough medicine, and I'll be fine. Besides, with the way you've been moping around the house the past few days, an evening out might be just what you need."

Suzanna nodded. "Yeah, maybe..." There was a strange glumness attached to the words.

That afternoon she moved Annie into the small sitting room next to Ida's, then settled her in front of the television to watch Queen for a Day and American Bandstand.

"If you stay covered up and mind what Grandma says, I might have a secret surprise for you when I get back."

"What kind of surprise?"

"It wouldn't be a secret or a surprise if I told you, would it? But trust me, it's something you've wanted for a very long time."

"A new Barbie?"

"Much better than a Barbie, but even if you guess it I'm not going to tell you. You'll just have to wait and see."

Suzanna kissed Annie's cheek, then tossed a few necessities into a tote bag, climbed into the car and started for the Ellington.

The rain slowed the drive, and by the time she arrived Bobby was waiting in the bar. He flashed the smile she remembered so well, and it was as if all the years of being apart fell away. He walked over to her, put his hand on her lower back, pulled her close, and brushed a kiss across her lips.

She felt a touch of the passion she'd felt in the early days, but something was different. She'd changed; that was the problem. She'd forgotten how to trust him, how to give herself openly and without reservation. Thoughts of Gregg were still in her head; she would rid herself of them, but it was obviously going to take time.

"Would you like to have dinner here," he asked, "or order up room service?"

"I don't think I'm ready for that," Suzanna said. "It's been a long time—"

"Too long, but don't you want to make up for lost time?" He leaned closer, and she felt his breath, heavy and warm against the side of her throat. "If I seem eager, Suzanna, forgive me. It's because I can't wait to feel you in my arms again."

She'd come here wanting the exact same thing, but now it seemed awkward. Pushing that thought back, she said, "I'm eager too, but first we've got so much to catch up on." She linked her arm through his and smiled. "I want to hear all about your life, and I know you're anxious to hear about Annie." She pulled a snapshot from her purse and handed it to him. "This is Annie. She's got your eyes, Bobby. Isn't she beautiful?"

He gave the picture a quick glance, then slid it into his pocket and smiled. "Well, of course she's beautiful. Look at who she's got for a mama." He lifted Suzanna's hand into his, dropped a kiss in her palm, then turned and gave the maître d' a nod.

Moments later they were seated at a table in the back of the room. Bobby ordered a round of drinks—scotch on the rocks for him, wine for her—and as soon as the drinks were delivered, he told the waiter to go ahead and bring the menus.

Once the waiter was gone, Bobby leaned back in his chair, looked at Suzanna with the grin she remembered, and teasingly said, "So, go ahead, tell me what you've been up to for the past eight years."

She began, not with tales of the heartache she'd suffered, but stories of Annie's childhood, how she'd been quick to learn and had an easy laugh. She spoke of the joy she'd felt at hearing that first word and how Annie had walked before she'd crawled. She was talking about how Annie's hands were so like Bobby's with long fingers and a strong grasp when he cut in.

"And this new name, Darla Jean, is that something you're sticking with?"

A moment or two ticked by before Suzanna answered.

"I'm afraid that would be impossible," she said and gave a sigh of regret. "I'd have to tell Ida the truth, explain that you're Annie's daddy and…"

"Don't do it because of me," Bobby said. "You've got that job to consider, and if you're happy there we'll just keep this a secret for a while and see how things work out."

"There are too many complications…"

The thought of Gregg came without warning, and her words drifted off.

Apparently sensing the change in her mood, Bobby reached across the table and took her hand in his. "Let's not talk about this now. For tonight, let's forget about the problems and complications, just enjoy each other's company, and be as we once were. You remember what that was like, don't you, babe? We had something really special, didn't we?"

She nodded and gave a weak smile. "Yes, we had something very special." Without the slightest bit of resistance, she allowed herself to be taken along as Bobby began to talk about the old days, dredging up stories of the nights they'd made love under the bleachers or behind the thick stand of pines in the park and in the back seat of his daddy's car.

As they ate dinner and drank she listened to him, and when the hour grew late she began to believe the spark of passion was indeed still there. For eight years it had been squelched by the anguish of separation, but it was still there and she could again feel it. When he reached beneath the table and ran his hand along the inside of her thigh, she gave a shiver of delight.

A short while later, when he suggested they go upstairs where they'd have more privacy, she agreed.

"Let me visit the powder room first."

Thinking she'd freshen her lipstick and dab a bit of powder on her nose, Suzanna hurried off to the ladies' room. On the way back, she passed a telephone booth and stopped to call home and check on Annie.

The telephone rang fifteen times before somebody finally picked up the receiver. It was Annie who answered.

"What are you doing up this late? Where's Grandma?" Suzanna asked.

"Grandma got sick and threw up. She's on the sofa."

"Is she awake?"

"Un-uh, her eyes are asleep."

Suzanna imagined Ida unconscious and without anyone to care for her, and a sickening fear swelled in her chest.

"I'm coming home right now" she said. "Until I get there, go into the living room and stay with Grandma. If she gets sick again, go next door and ask Mrs. Murphy to come over and check on her."

Suzanna returned to the table, her face pale and her voice edgy. "I've got to leave. I'm worried that something may have happened to Ida."

As she quickly told of her conversation with Annie, a look of disappointment settled on Bobby's face.

"She's probably just sleeping," he suggested. "Can't you stay for another hour or so?"

"No, I've got to get going now." She turned to go, and he followed her out. As they crossed the lobby she suggested, "If nothing is wrong, I can meet you here Saturday night and plan to stay over."

He hesitated a moment then shook his head. "Saturday's no good. Let's just make it the same time next Tuesday."

With worry about Ida foremost in her thoughts, Suzanna quickly agreed.

When they got to her car, she turned to give him a goodnight kiss and he pulled her to him, his hands grasping her buttocks, his tongue pushing its way into her mouth. She wriggled free of him, snapped, "Not now, Bobby!" then climbed into the car and was off.

SUZANNA

An Eye-Opening Revelation

As Suzanna sailed through a string of yellow stop lights, she could feel her heart racing. Ida was not the type to nap and let Annie roam through the house unsupervised. Something was wrong. Drastically wrong. Luckily the rain had stopped, and the drive home took half the time it had taken to get to the Ellington. She pulled in, left the car in the driveway, and came running through the front door.

Ida was stretched out on the sofa, Annie sitting on the floor in front of the television.

Suzanna hurried over, put her hand to Ida's forehead, then turned to Annie and asked, "Has Grandma thrown up again?"

"Un-uh, she stayed sleeping."

Ida's face was hot to the touch, but it was impossible to tell whether she was unconscious or simply in a deep sleep. Suzanna tried shaking her gently, but there was no response. She felt for a heartbeat then glanced over at Annie and said, "Quick, run upstairs and get me the thermometer."

When she finally caught the thump of Ida's heart, it seemed slow; definitely slower than her own. She lifted Ida's hand into hers and called her name, but there was no response. Nor was there any when she slid the thermometer into Ida's mouth then removed it.

The thermometer stalled halfway between 102 and 103. Wasn't that the danger zone for an older adult?

Suzanna thumbed through the telephone directory then dialed the number for Dr. Bergmann. His wife, Miriam, answered.

"This is Darla Jean; Grandma Ida's sick, and I need Dr. Bergmann to come over right away."

"It's after eleven! Albert's already in his pajamas!"

"I don't care if he comes in his underwear, just get him over here. Grandma's got a temperature of 103, and she's unresponsive."

"I'll tell him, but he's not going to like it."

"He doesn't have to like it, he just has to get over here. Remember when your daughter needed that dress for her party, I worked two days straight to get it done. I wasn't crazy about working late, but I did it!" The crackle and snap of Suzanna's words left no doubt as to her expectations.

When she hung up the phone, Suzanna sat beside Ida and waited. The thought of losing Ida flashed through her head, and tears welled in her eyes. The truth was she loved Ida as much as she'd loved her own mama. She could never leave her. Not for Bobby. Not for anyone.

It seemed like hours passed before Dr. Bergmann rapped on the door. He was wearing trousers and what appeared to be a pajama top. Before he was fully inside, Suzanna rattled off a brief explanation of what happened.

"How long has she been unresponsive?" he asked.

Suzanna looked at Annie. "Honey, do you know when Grandma went to sleep?"

"Un-uh. I already went asleep."

"But you were up when I called—"

"The telephone waked me up, so I comed downstairs to tell Grandma."

Dr. Bergmann took over and followed up with his own questions. He asked what time Annie had gone to bed, then if Ida had seemed sick earlier that evening.

Annie nodded. "She catched my germs and was coughing."

"Did she take any medicine when she was coughing?"

Again, Annie nodded.

"Do you know what medicine she took?"

"Grandpa's medicine in the brown bottle." She led them into the kitchen then stopped and looked at the counter with a puzzled expression. "Grandma told me not to touch it because it was grown-up medicine, and she put it up there."

Suzanna poked around in the cupboards for a few moments then checked the garbage can under the sink. The brown bottle was on top of the other trash.

"That's Grandma's medicine!"

Dr. Bergmann read the label and shook his head. "This is cough medicine alright, but William had cancer and this stuff is loaded with codeine."

Seconds later he was on the phone asking for an ambulance.

"Seventy-four-year-old patient, accidental overdose," he said. "Codeine, acetaminophen."

Suzanna stood aside as they lifted the stretcher into the ambulance then she buttoned a coat over Annie's pajamas, and they jumped in the car to follow the ambulance to the hospital. Ida was placed in a small emergency room cubicle, and Suzanna sat beside her while the nurses bustled in and out to monitor and measure her heart rate, breathing, and state of consciousness.

In time Annie fell asleep with her head on her mama's shoulder, but Suzanna could not sleep. She sat there watching the green light of the monitor as it zigzagged across the screen and counting the droplets that fell from the IV into Ida's vein, each drop carrying the life-nourishing antidote. Hours passed, and the palest hint of a rose-colored dawn was feathering the sky when Ida's eyelashes finally fluttered ever so slightly.

Suzanna moved Annie aside and came to stand beside the bed. She took the limp hand in hers and said, "Grandma Ida, can you hear me? Squeeze my hand if you can hear me."

Several moments ticked by before she felt the arthritic fingers press against hers.

Once Ida's vital signs stabilized, she was moved to a private room. Suzanna fussed over her for a while then said, "I should take Annie home and feed her, but I'll come back later this afternoon."

"No need," Ida replied. "I'm going to get some rest, and you should do the same."

After a few minutes of arguing about it, Suzanna gave in. "Okay then, but if you need anything call me right away. Tomorrow morning I'll be here bright and early to take you home."

Ida grinned. "Now that's a deal I'll happily agree to."

⟨◦⟩

That afternoon Suzanna telephoned the shop and told Colette she was going to need a few weeks off. She explained what had happened and said, "Right now my first priority is taking care of Grandma. Once she's on her feet and feeling good, I should be able to return."

Colette expressed concern over Ida then told Suzanna to take whatever time she needed. "When you're ready to come back, rest assured, your job will be waiting for you."

Later on, after she'd fed Annie and cleaned up the kitchen, Suzanna went from room to room straightening things, folding the comforter, placing it across the arm of the sofa, plumping the throw pillows, and wiping away a layer of nonexistent dust. As she moved through the house, she began to realize how much all of this meant to her. It was so much more than just a house. It was a home, a place where Annie was safe and happy, and Ida wasn't a stranger she could walk away from, she was family. Real family.

What would it hurt if Suzanna held onto the name Darla Jean? Nothing, that's what. Once she and Bobby were married her last name was going to change anyway, so what was the harm? She could explain the situation, ask Bobby to call her Darla Jean from now on. Then she'd introduce him to Ida, and that would be the start of their becoming a family. Atlanta was less than 2 hours away. She and Bobby could split their time, three or four days a week in Atlanta, the remainder here in Cousins. Ida would forever be in her life. At their wedding she'd be given a corsage and sit in the first pew. It would be the way she'd always wanted, and, best of all, Annie would have a grandma and a daddy.

The more Suzanna thought about it, the more convinced she became that it would work. When the excitement of such a prospect swelled in her chest, she couldn't bear the thought of waiting another week to tell Bobby. It was foolish for people in love to go from week to week without seeing one another, without having a chance to talk things over. She grabbed her purse, fished through the side pocket, and found the business card Bobby had given her.

She dialed the long-distance operator, said she was calling Atlanta, and gave the number on the card.

As she waited, she tried to think through what she would say, but it was a jumble of happy thoughts running together. She wanted Bobby to feel good about this, so it couldn't sound like a demand. Instead, she'd make it sound like the best thing ever, maybe start by inviting him to the house to meet Annie and suggest he come for Sunday dinner. She'd whisper something to the effect that for now he had to call her Darla Jean, then hopefully in time that name would roll off his tongue as effortlessly as Suzanna now did.

When she heard the first ring, Suzanna chastised herself for such foolish thinking. Here she was, worrying about something that was nothing. Of course Bobby would be happy about such an invitation. He was Annie's daddy; what daddy wouldn't want to know a sweet daughter like Annie?

A woman's voice interrupted her thoughts. "Greene and Garrett, how may I direct your call?"

"Robert Doherty, please."

Seconds later the ring sounded. She expected him to answer, so the woman's voice startled her. Without thinking she asked, "Is Bobby there?"

"Is this Brenda?" the voice asked.

"Um, no. It's Suzanna. Suzanna Duff."

"Sorry about that," the young woman said and chuckled. "His wife is the only one who calls Mr. Doherty Bobby, so I thought…"

Wife?

Suzanna said nothing and sat there, dumbfounded.

"Mr. Doherty is gone for the day; would you like to leave a message?"

"No, I guess not," Suzanna said and hung up.

⟨∽⟩

That evening, after she'd listened to Annie's prayers and kissed her goodnight, Suzanna went to her own room and sat on the edge of the bed with her face cradled in her hands. The man she'd held in her heart for eight years, the man who was the father of her child, had come back looking for nothing but a good time. He didn't want her, and, worse yet, he didn't want Annie. He was a liar, the very worst kind of liar, one who lied his way into a person's heart. Her heart. She'd let Gregg walk away because of him and she'd been on the verge of leaving Ida, hurting her the way she herself had been hurt.

What was the harm? she'd wondered. Now she knew. Over the years, Suzanna had told a million little lies and not once had she stopped to look back at the damage they might have done. Her shoulders shuddered, and tears fell into her palms. She cried, not because of Bobby, but because of the shame burning inside of her.

She'd been such a fool. She'd told herself that because Bobby was Annie's daddy, she was still in love with him, but that too was a lie. It wasn't Bobby she'd carried in her heart all those years; it was the thought of him being Annie's daddy. Not once had she realized that making love in the backseat of a car didn't make a man a daddy. Years of caring, love, and dependability, that's what made a man a real daddy.

Gregg had offered that, and she'd thrown it away. He was a good man, he loved her and he loved Annie, yet she'd hurt him because she was too cowardly to tell the truth. She'd lied, just the same as Bobby had lied. She'd lied to Gregg and she'd lied to Ida, the two people who loved her.

A sad truth settled in her heart. She was no better than Bobby, and perhaps he was exactly what she deserved. A liar for a liar. She brushed back the tears then went to the window and stood there thinking.

In the shadowy moonlight, she could see the roofline of Mrs. Murphy's house and across the street Homer Portnick's Buick parked in the driveway. She knew the neighbors up and down the street. They waved when they saw her drive by and asked about Annie when they came into the shop. For almost nine months this place had been her home, the only real home she'd known since her mama died. She was only a few years older than Annie then, and that's when she'd begun lying.

Back then she'd lied to cover up the ugliness of her life, but here there was no such need. It was a good life, the kind of life a child like Annie deserved. Suzanna wanted to believe she'd done nothing wrong, that she'd simply tried to make an old woman happy, but the truth came at her like a cannon ball. She'd grown to love Ida and they had become like family, but the reality was that no matter how much she wanted to be Darla Jean Parker she was not.

After coming face to face with the pain of Bobby's lie, she knew she could not continue the charade she was living. Ida deserved better. She deserved to know Suzanna was not the granddaughter she'd prayed for to return. Over the months they'd spent together, they'd come to love one another. The truth was a painful way to test that love, but she had to chance it. Hopefully Ida could find it in her heart to forgive such treachery for Annie's sake.

Suzanna prayed she would.

SUZANNA

Starting Over

Thursday morning Suzanna shooed Annie off to school and moments later left for the hospital. When she arrived, Ida was sitting up in the bed. Her face had regained its color, and the empty breakfast tray was pushed aside.

"Looks like you're feeling better," Suzanna said and smiled.

Ida gave a sheepish grin. "I'm fine now but feeling pretty ashamed about the fuss I caused."

Suzanna knew no amount of shame could equal what she was feeling, but she forced a lighthearted chuckle. "Nonsense, it was a simple mistake. You had no way of knowing."

"Well, I'll certainly be more careful in the future. It makes me shudder to think that something terrible could have happened when poor little Annie was there all by herself."

"I'm the one to blame. I shouldn't have left when you and Annie were sick."

Suzanna's voice trailed off. There was so much she had to say, but now was not the time. Later on tonight, after Annie was sound asleep in the canopy bed, she would tell Ida the truth of her identity and everything would change. For now, she was still Ida's granddaughter, and she would cling to every precious minute for as long as she could.

"I brought clothes for you to wear home." She opened the tote bag, pulled out a blue dress, and slipped it onto a hanger.

"Underwear? And shoes?"

"Yep, I think I've got everything."

Ida smiled. "That doesn't surprise me one little bit. I don't know how I managed to get along without you."

"I hope you always feel that way…" Suzanna might have gone on to say something more, but Dr. Bergmann came in.

He listened to Ida's heart, peered into her eyes, then read through the notations on her chart. "Well, it looks like you're ready to go home," he said. "But before I sign a release, I want you to promise you'll get rid of those old medications. With a child in the house—"

"Don't worry, I'll take care of it today," Ida cut in. "I should have done it a long time ago, but I couldn't bring myself to get rid of anything that belonged to Bill. Not his clothes, not his toothbrush, not even his old medicine bottles. Now with Darla Jean here to help me, it will be a whole lot easier."

With thoughts of what lay ahead heavy on her mind, Suzanna welcomed the chance to stay busy. On the way home from the hospital, she suggested they have lunch and then clean out the medicine cabinet.

"Not just the medicine cabinet," Ida said. "Everything. Including the closet and the drawers. We'll pack up Bill's things and take them over to Goodwill. There are people who could use those clothes, and it's a crime for me to keep them packed away where they're not doing anybody any good."

"Are you sure about this?" Suzanna asked apprehensively.

Ida nodded. "Positive. I know it's what Bill would have wanted."

That afternoon they worked together, going through each drawer, sorting the clothes according to suitability, clearing out shoes that for years had gathered dust on the floor of the closet. On one side of the bed was a pile of things to be thrown away: an old toothbrush, the chipped ashtray, gardening pants with the knees worn through; on the other side, clothes earmarked for Goodwill. Shirts packaged as they'd been when they came from the laundry, trousers with the crease as crisp as ever, a brand new leather wallet, a navy blue blazer with a Rotary Club pin still affixed to the lapel.

Ida held the jacket in her hands for a few moments, then loosened the backing on the pin and removed it.

"Bill was real proud of his work with the Rotary Club," she said. "I believe he'd want me to hold onto this." She slid the pin into her pocket then moved on to a drawer filled with socks and undershirts.

When the bed was covered with things to be given away, Suzanna drove down to the Piggly Wiggly market and brought home a stack of cardboard cartons. One by one they packed and labeled each box: shirts, sweaters, jackets, each garment carefully inspected and neatly folded into place. When they finished, there were 14 cartons stacked along the bedroom wall.

Suzanna grabbed the top box and started toward the door. "I'll get these loaded into the car so we can take them over to Goodwill." She was halfway out the door when she caught the look of sadness that had settled on Ida's face. She hesitated a moment then turned back and said, "That is, unless you'd rather we wait a while."

Ida shook her head. "No, it's better to take them now and get it over with." As she scooped up an armful of the things destined for the trash bin, she mumbled, "Once a person is gone from your life, no amount of wishing will bring them back."

Although the words were not meant for Suzanna, she'd heard them and felt the sorrow hidden inside of them. As she loaded the boxes in the car, she began to wonder about the wisdom of telling Ida the truth. What purpose would it serve? Would it do nothing more than pile sorrow upon sorrow? Hadn't Ida already suffered enough?

By the time she'd dropped off the boxes at the Goodwill store, Suzanna had decided the truth of her identity should remain a secret. Simple as that, she'd convinced herself to stay with her story and continue being Darla Jean.

Suzanna had no qualms with her decision and might have stuck with it were it not for what happened later that night. It was after eight o'clock, and Annie was in bed. She and Ida had settled in front of the television to watch The Real McCoys. Then when the first commercial break came on, Ida looked at her with a melancholy smile.

"Cleaning out those drawers today made me realize something," she said. "Something I probably should have realized long ago."

Unsure of what to expect, Suzanna waited.

"There comes a point in life when you have to accept that your days on earth are numbered, and it's time to start letting go of things. Today I saw the wisdom of that, and I've made a decision—"

"What do you mean your days are numbered? Dr. Bergmann said you were fine. The other night's episode was nothing more than a reaction to that cough medicine. There's no need—"

"There's nothing wrong with me now, Darla Jean, but who knows what will happen a year from now, two years from now, or ten years from now. The thing is to be prepared, and that's why I've decided to go ahead and give you this house."

"You decided to do what?" Suzanna sputtered.

"To go ahead and give you this house. Of course, I'd continue to live with you and Annie, but I'd have peace of mind knowing the house will be yours when I'm gone and there will be no questions asked."

Suzanna stood and snapped off the television. "No. Absolutely not. I can't allow you to even consider such a thing. Why, such talk is downright foolish. It's—"

"It's realistic, that's what it is. I'm not going to live forever, Darla Jean, and you're the only family I've got. When I die, everything I own will go to you anyway. All I'm suggesting is that I go ahead and give you the house now. That way, I can rest easy knowing you'll have a forever place to call your own."

Suzanna felt as though the air had been sucked out of the room. Each breath she drew felt like a sledgehammer slammed up against her chest. Until now she'd not taken anything of value from Ida; room and board, yes, but not anything she could lay claim to.

This would change everything. This would make her a thief. No, worse than a thief, a predator who took advantage of an old woman's love. It was wrong, so very wrong. She needed time to think, but there was no time.

She paced back and forth for a few moments then stopped and said, "I can't let you do this, Grandma Ida. I just can't."

"What do you mean you can't let me do it? Why not?"

"Because I'm not really family. I'm not who you think I am." Suzanna turned away, ashamed to let her eyes meet Ida's. "I'm not Darla Jean."

She waited, thinking Ida would say something, but when there was only silence she stood looking up at the ceiling and told her story. She spoke of how on the day of William's memorial service she'd come to the

Elks Club hoping she and Annie could get a free meal, and how when Ida had mistaken her for Darla Jean she'd been too embarrassed to say otherwise.

"I planned to leave right away, catch the next bus to New Jersey, but you were so kind to us, and we had nowhere else to go…" A sob filled her throat, and she choked on her words.

The shame of it was greater than Suzanna had ever known, and in that moment she wanted to disappear, vanish from Ida's sight. "I know what I've done is unforgivable, but I never thought it would come to this. I thought if Annie and I lived here, I could help out and—"

A withered hand touched her shoulder, and she turned to face Ida. "I'm sorry, Ida. I'm so very, very sorry. The last thing in the world I would want is to hurt you—"

"Then hush crying." Ida wrapped her arms around Suzanna and tilted her face so that their eyes met. "You're not telling me anything I didn't already know."

"Didn't you hear what I said? I'm not really your granddaughter. I am not Darla Jean."

The corner of Ida's mouth curled, and her expression softened into a smile. "I know that. I've known it for a long time, but I was happy having you here and didn't see any reason to give up that happiness—"

"You knew? When? How?"

Ida grinned ever so slightly. "A week or so after you came, but by then I'd already fallen in love with Annie and couldn't bear the thought of you leaving."

"But how? Did I say something? Do something?"

"No, it was your eyes. You've got the same blue eyes Bill had. That's why I originally thought you were Darla Jean. Then later on I got to thinking about it and remembered that baby didn't have blue eyes. She had brown eyes like her mama."

"But you never said—"

"Why would I? For the first time in a long while, there was some happiness in this house. You and Annie gave me a reason to live again, and I loved it."

"But you knew I wasn't really family."

"There's all kinds of families, Darla Jean. Some people are born into belonging to one another, and that's their family. But there's another kind of family, one created by people who love each other and are willing to hold onto what they've found. We're that kind of family."

Suzanna stood there with tears streaming down her face. "But you don't even know my real name."

"I don't need to. I'd love you just the same regardless of what you call yourself. I love you because of the kind of person you are, not because of your name." She reached up and wiped the tears from Suzanna's cheek. "Now stop that crying. There's nothing to cry about."

Suzanna's breath hitched, and she sniffed back another sob. "I'm trying."

That evening they sat side by side on the sofa and talked until the wee hours of the morning. Suzanna told everything there was to tell: how her daddy had thrown her out of the house, how she'd moved in with Earl, and how she'd finally left to make a better life for Annie. After a fairly long silence, she also told how Bobby had come back into her life looking for nothing more than a good time.

"He's a married man who doesn't love me or Annie," she said solemnly.

"Do you love him?" Ida asked.

Suzanna thought for a long while before she answered. "I did, but that was a long time ago. When he came back, I thought he wanted us to be a family. I thought he cared about being Annie's daddy. He doesn't, and the likelihood is he never will." She gave a heavily weighted sigh, then said. "It's such a shame, because Gregg would have been a great daddy."

"Does Gregg know about this?"

"Not really." Suzanna went on to tell how he'd proposed that Saturday night and she'd answered saying that she needed time to think. "He said if a person is truly in love, they don't need to think about whether or not they want to marry you."

"He's right," Ida said. "When it's true love, you find a way to overcome the obstacles. You don't just give in to them."

"I know that now, but it's too late. Gregg's gone, and I doubt he's ever coming back unless it's just to clear out his things."

"If you don't give up feeling sorry for yourself and do something about it, you're probably right."

Suzanna looked at Ida with a puzzled expression. "I doubt there's much I can do. He left without saying goodbye, didn't bother to leave a note, and hasn't called since then. I'd say he's pretty much made up his mind that he's through with me."

"Hogwash. Gregg may be angry, but my bet is he still loves you."

Suzanna shook her head dubiously. "Don't you think if that were the case, he would have called?"

"Not necessarily. A man's got pride. You're the one who turned him down, so if you want him back you're going to have to be the one to reach out and make it happen."

That crumbled look of doubt was still stuck to Suzanna's face.

They went back and forth for nearly an hour. Ida told of the challenges she and William had faced and how they'd struggled to overcome them. After she told of how they'd both cried when Tommy left town with his wife and baby, she gave a wistful smile.

"If we'd given up on trying to work things out, just think of all the happiness we'd have missed out on."

That night when Suzanna climbed into bed, she said a prayer. She thanked God for bringing her here and for giving her a second chance to make her life count. It was a prayer of gratitude and she'd not planned to ask for anything more, but at the tail end of her prayer, she said, "And, Lord, if you're not already tired of helping me out, please show me a way to make Gregg love me again."

SUZANNA

Saying Goodbye to the Past

That night Suzanna found sleep hard to come by. She kept thinking through the advice Ida had given her, wondering if indeed there was a chance Gregg would be forgiving. It was a lot to ask. She'd told him almost as many lies as she'd told Ida, and to make matters worse she'd let him walk away thinking her answer meant she didn't love him. She wanted to believe he'd be as forgiving as Ida, but she couldn't help thinking how Ida had less to forgive. She'd known all along Suzanna was not her missing granddaughter.

On Friday morning, when they gathered at the breakfast table, Suzanna poured herself a cup of coffee, then sat there stirring it for a full minute.

Ida looked across with a raised eyebrow. "The cream in that coffee will turn to butter if you keep stirring it."

"Oh, right." Suzanna absently set the spoon aside. "I guess I was thinking of other things."

"What things?" Annie asked.

Aware of how Annie felt about Gregg, Suzanna did not want her to know what happened. "Nothing you need to know about. Finish your breakfast, or you'll be late for school."

"How come you don't got to hurry?" With her face crinkled into a smug grin, she added, "Won't you be late for working?"

"Not that it's any of your business, smarty pants," Suzanna said, laughing, "but I'm taking some time off to help Grandma until she's feeling better."

"I'm feeling just fine," Ida said.

Annie looked at Suzanna. "Grandma said—"

"I heard what Grandma said." Before Suzanna could add anything more, the doorbell rang, and Annie hurried off to join Lori for the walk to school.

That afternoon, Suzanna sat at the desk in her room and began composing a letter to Gregg. On the first page she told him that she'd made a lot of mistakes in her life and not answering yes when he asked her to marry him was one of the biggest. She continued on to say she no longer needed time to think; she knew she loved him fully and completely. On the second page she wrote about missing him and hoping he'd give her another chance. She signed her name, then read the letter back and ripped it into shreds. It was like an empty promise, without truth or emotion, and it said nothing of the lies she'd told.

The second letter told about Bobby and explained how she'd felt obligated to give him another chance, but that too was discarded. Both the third and fourth letters with their scratched-out words and tearstained smudges were also crumpled and thrown into the waste basket. In time, she began to doubt that mere words could convey the anguish and regret she felt.

Pushing back from the desk, she went to the window and stood watching as a lone sparrow hopped across the lawn. The bird was a brownish hue, barely visible in the dry grass as he moved about hidden from the watchful eyes of the hawk or owl. Hadn't she done much the same thing? The only difference was that her disguise was a string of lies.

She watched as the sparrow plucked something from the ground, ate it, then took flight and landed in the high branches of an oak. After a few moments, he chirped; not a song, just a trio of notes. He did it twice again then fell silent and remained so.

She too had remained silent. Had she explained that Annie was, and had to be, her primary concern, maybe Gregg would have listened and understood. Instead they'd parted ways with nothing but a wordless anger between them.

Turning away from the window, Suzanna returned to the desk and began to write. She poured out all the things she'd hidden for so long, filling the pages with line after line that recounted her deceptions and told of the shame she felt. She explained the confusion in her heart the night he'd asked her to marry him and of her discovery that Bobby was a married man. On the ninth page she wrote that she'd loved Gregg then and loved him still, and if he would have her and Annie she would spend forever proving her love. When there was nothing left to say, she signed her name and folded the letter into an envelope.

She sat the envelope on her desk and left it there. The mailman had already come and gone. It was too late to do anything today. She would have to wait until tomorrow to mail the letter.

Saturday and Sunday came and went, but the letter remained on her desk. Twice she picked it up, held it in her hand wondering about the wisdom of her words, and both times she'd walked off leaving the letter behind. Somehow a string of words scrawled across a piece of paper seemed terribly inadequate; there was no back and forth, no exchange of thoughts or chance to correct a misconception. How would she ever know if she'd said too much or too little? In the back of her mind a nasty little voice whispered that once he realized the letter was from her, he might toss it in the trash bin unopened or, worse yet, read it and decide that someone like her wasn't worthy of his time. If that were the case, knowing would be worse than not knowing.

After two days of watching Suzanna worry about Gregg and walk around the house like a lost soul, Ida insisted she go back to work.

"I don't need anyone looking after me," she said. "But you need to get back to work and keep busy. Fretting over whether or not he's going to call will not change anything. If you want Gregg badly enough, go talk to him."

Suzanna shook her head. "That's not as easy as it sounds. By now he's probably told Ginger and Phil, and I'd be mortified to face them."

"Piffle," Ida said and gave a wave of her hand. "With a new baby in the house, I'm sure they've got far more important things to think about."

Suzanna knew there was merit in what Ida said, but Phil and Ginger weren't her biggest fear. She was far more worried that Gregg would turn her away, which was something she couldn't bear the thought of.

Monday Suzanna went back to work. She spent the day creating a display for the new collection of sweaters, answering calls, and waiting on customers. A dozen or more times, she thought about Gregg but didn't wallow in her misery as she had over the weekend. It was near closing time when Miriam Bergmann telephoned to say she'd be in on Tuesday and would need a gown for the country club spring dance.

At times Miriam could be a test of a person's patience, but after she'd gotten Dr. Bergmann up in the middle of the night Suzanna owed her. Tuesday afternoon, Miriam arrived later than expected, then tried on a dozen different dresses before she decided on two, both of which needed extensive alterations. Suzanna remained at the shop until well after eight, marking the seams that had be released to allow for Miriam's ample bosom and pinning up hems that were inches too long. When she arrived home, she warmed the dinner Ida had set on the back of the stove, then went to bed. She closed her eyes and drifted off to sleep without ever remembering it was the day she'd planned to meet Bobby at the Ellington. Had she thought of it, she wouldn't have gone anyway, but she might have been a bit more prepared for what happened the next morning.

The shop opened at ten, but Suzanna arrived shortly after nine-thirty. She parked the car in back of the store, but before she could circle the building to unlock the front door someone grabbed her arm from behind.

"Where the hell were you?" Bobby said and whirled her around to face him. "You were supposed to meet me at the Ellington last night! I waited in the bar until one o'clock in the morning." The muscle in his jawbone twitched, and he tightened his grip on her arm. "You know how stupid I felt, sitting there like some dumb bozo who'd been stood up?"

"Why didn't you give Brenda a call? Maybe she could have joined you?"

The mention of his wife startled Bobby and caused him to pull back. "What the hell—"

"You having a wife kind of complicates things, doesn't it?"

"What'd you do, check up on me?"

"No, when I called the office, your secretary mistook me for your wife."

"Oh, shit. What'd you tell her?"

"I said I was your mistress, and we were planning to shack up at the Ellington."

"Good god, Suzanna, why'd you—"

For the first time, she saw the truth of who he was and felt nothing but disgust.

"Don't worry," she said, "I didn't blow your cover. I told her I'd call back and hung up."

"I'm sorry that happened, babe, but it's not what you think. Brenda—"

"I don't want to hear it, Bobby. We're through. It's over."

"You could at least gimme a chance to explain."

"Save your breath. I'm done. I don't want to see you or hear from you again."

He smiled and opened his arms to her. "Suzanna, sweetie, you can't be serious, not after all we've meant to each other."

She stepped back, widening the distance between them.

"I'm as serious as I have ever been about anything," she said icily. "You're a liar and a cheat!"

His eyes narrowed, and his jaw twitched. "That's rich, you calling me a liar when you're the one pretending to be some old lady's granddaughter. Rethink this hard-ass attitude of yours, Suzanna, or I might have to tell her who you really are."

"She already knows. When I realized the harm a lie can do, I told her myself."

"Bullshit. You expect me to believe—"

"I don't care whether you believe me or not. I told her the truth because I couldn't keep lying to someone I love."

"Is that so?" he said cynically. "Well, how about I stop by the house and see for myself?"

"Go ahead, and say hello to your daughter while you're there. She's a beautiful little girl, Bobby, one you can be proud of."

He hesitated a moment then asked, "So, if I come over to meet our kid, then we can spend some time together?"

"Absolutely not. You're a married man, and I'm not the least bit interested in having some illicit, back-alley affair with you."

"If you think that's all I want, you're wrong, Suzanna. We had something really good together, and if this works out I might be willing to leave Brenda."

"Forget it, Bobby. Do what you want about your wife, but don't make it because of me."

"Not because of you? Why else would I do it?"

"Same old Bobby." Suzanna shook her head and turned away.

Again, he grabbed her arm. "Wait. Didn't you hear what I said?"

She stopped, stood there for a second, then turned back. "Yes, I heard what you said, and I honestly don't care. There was a time when I would have walked through hell for you, and, in fact, I did. That was a lifetime ago. Since then I've come to realize that some relationships are worth saving. This one is not, and it never was."

Suzanna walked away and left Bobby standing there. Seconds later tires squealed, and the big black Lincoln peeled out of the parking lot. She knew then she would never again see Bobby, and that was okay.

SUZANNA

Finding Courage

The confrontation with Bobby had in a strange way empowered Suzanna. For the first time in all the years she could remember, she'd stood up for herself. She'd not lied or tried to bypass the problem but faced it head on, and it felt good.

That night, after she'd closed the door to her room, she pulled her letter to Gregg from the envelope and read it over. The things she wrote were true enough, but there was something missing and Suzanna thought she knew what it was. She remembered what she'd told Bobby, and now more than ever could see the clarity of it. Some relationships were indeed worth saving; the one with him was not, but this one certainly was.

She slid the letter back into the envelope and placed it in the drawer. In a few days she might send it, but for now she had another plan. That night as the moon rose higher in the sky, she thought about exactly what she would do and how she'd handle it.

The next morning Suzanna left the house before the sun had cleared the horizon and arrived at the shop hours before it was to open. She sat at the sewing machine and finished all of Miriam Bergmann's alterations, then pressed and packed the garments so they were ready for pick up. Once that was done, she tagged the sheath dresses that had come in on Monday, sorted them by size, and hung them on the racks. When Colette arrived at ten, she was setting up a new window display.

"My goodness," Colette exclaimed. "It looks like you've been busy."

Suzanna gave a sheepish grin. "Just trying to make up for the days I was out. I thought if everything was caught up, you wouldn't mind my leaving at three o'clock."

"I wouldn't have minded even if you hadn't done all this work," Colette said. "Do you and Ida have plans?"

Suzanna shook her head. "I made a mistake in judgment and hurt someone that I love. This afternoon I'm going to try and make it right."

Colette lifted an eyebrow as her lips curled into a smile. "Ah, yes, and does this have anything to do with that handsome young man who came here looking for you?"

"In a way it does. He was the mistake."

Ten minutes before Suzanna planned to leave, Miriam Bergmann came into the shop and said she'd changed her mind about the blue dress and decided she only wanted the gray one for the country club's function.

Suzanna grimaced. "The alterations are finished. The dresses are ready for pick up. I can't take a return on something that's been altered."

"Finished? Already? You said Friday."

"Yes, but since you were anxious about it, I went ahead and did them so you'd have time for another fitting."

"Whatever," she said and flicked her fingers in the air. "I only want the gray dress. A tuck here and there doesn't devalue the other garment, and for a loyal customer I'm certain you can make an exception."

One word led to another and as the altercation swung back and forth, the clock ticked on. Suzanna nervously eyed her watch, then at 3:15 gave up trying to satisfy Miriam Bergmann and called Colette from the back room.

Moments later, she was in the car and on her way to the school. The time was tight and Gregg sometimes left early, but hopefully she'd make it. When she rounded the corner of Beecham Street, a line of cars was already pulling out of the parking lot. Moving toward the entrance, she eyed the line; Gregg's Oldsmobile was not there. He was already gone or still inside.

She circled the building, pulled into the visitor's lot, and hurried back to the area designated as faculty parking. At first glance, she didn't see the Olds, and her heart fell. Trying to remain hopeful, she walked toward the back of the lot and found it behind a red pickup. He was still inside.

She glanced at her watch—3:40. He was sure to be coming out any minute. She waited. Four o'clock came and went, then four-thirty. A few stragglers left the building, got into their cars and drove off, but still no sign of Gregg.

It was after five, the sky already starting to darken, when she finally decided to leave. Coming here had obviously been a mistake. He could have left with someone else, or perhaps he'd seen her waiting and had no interest in talking. With her shoulders slumped and her eyes turned to the ground, she started toward the visitor's lot. She was several yards away when she heard his footsteps. He was moving toward the car, looking straight ahead, not at her.

"Gregg," she called. Waving her arm, she hurried toward him.

"Darla Jean? What are you doing here?"

Suzanna caught the sound of surprise in his voice, but it was impossible to know whether or not he was glad to see her.

"I've been waiting for you," she said. "I was hoping we could talk. Maybe go someplace, have coffee…"

The sky was darker now and the lot growing shadowy, but she saw him grimace.

"I don't think going for coffee is a good idea, Darla Jean. If you've something to say, we can talk here."

His words were like a slap in the face, one she probably deserved but didn't expect. In a desperate attempt to pull her thoughts together, she lowered her eyes.

"I'm sorry. Truly sorry. I would give anything if we could go back in time and relive that evening, do it over with a different ending, but that's impossible. The only thing I can do now is explain why I acted as I did."

He dipped his chin ever so slightly, an indication for her to continue.

She started by saying she was not actually Ida's granddaughter, then went on to explain how such a lie had come about. "I never meant any harm. I thought Annie and I would stay a day and then be on our way, but that wasn't what happened."

"Does Ida know this?" he asked.

Suzanna nodded. "She does now."

She went on to tell how after almost eight years, Annie's father had found her and wanted to get back together again.

"I saw him a few times then realized he was nothing more than a memory I'd foolishly held onto. I never loved him the way I love you, but at the moment I thought it might be the best for Annie. He knew the truth of who I was, and it meant there'd be no more lying." She gave a weighted sigh, one drawn up from the very depth of her soul. "Living a life of lies is a very difficult thing; you're constantly looking over your shoulder, and you go from one day to the next wondering who's around the corner and when the truth will catch up to you."

"So you lied about everything?"

"Not everything." She hesitated a moment, waited until his eyes met hers, then spoke. "I never lied about loving you. That was true then, and it's true now."

He turned his head, looked away and said nothing.

Suzanna had come this far, and she wasn't ready to give up now. She inched closer and touched his arm. "I'm hoping that you can find it in your heart to forgive me."

"I wish it were that easy," he said and brushed her hand away. "But it's not. That night you had a choice to make, but instead of believing in our future you chose to take a chance on the past—a past that didn't include me. I was devastated, Darla Jean." His voice grew colder, more distant, and he asked, "Or should I call you Suzanna?"

She heard the underlying bitterness in his words but tried to move past it. "Grandma Ida suggested I might use the name Darla Sue. She saw it as a blending of the two. How would you feel about something like that?"

He gave a shrug and stood there looking like a man who was bone tired. "This name or that, I guess it really doesn't matter. If you'd been honest with me that night, we might've worked things out together, but you didn't trust me then and I'm not certain I can trust you now." He pulled his keys from his pocket and dangled them from his finger. "Having a child together is a tie that binds a man and woman together forever. He'll always be Annie's dad, and I'll always be wondering if and when you might decide to go back to him."

He leaned forward and unlocked the car door. "I wish I could be more understanding, but after all that's happened, I'm not certain we can ever find our way back to where we were." He opened the door then turned back. "I need time to think about it, Darla Jean. I need time to decide whether our relationship is worth saving."

As she watched him climb into the car and drive off, the tears she'd been holding back started.

"It is worth saving," she whispered tearfully. "It really is."

Thursday night Suzanna did not sleep a wink. She lay awake staring at the ceiling, wondering if she'd said too much or too little. Over and over again she asked herself what else she might have said, but she could think of nothing. She'd told him the truth about everything, but maybe the truth was more than he wanted to hear. Time to think, he'd said, but he'd promised nothing. He'd driven off without a single glance back. Almost as if she were someone he'd already forgotten.

When Suzanna crawled out of bed Friday morning, her eyes were bloodshot and her nose puffy and red as a tomato.

"It's nothing," she told Ida. "A slight cold, maybe."

"Well, you look terrible. Go back to bed. I'll call Colette and explain that you're sick."

"No," she said. "I've already missed too many days."

Suzanna knew endless hours of lying in bed was the last thing she needed. She had to stay busy, concentrate on something other than Gregg.

She arrived at the shop moments before a thunderstorm rolled through and brought drenching rains. The weatherman had predicted it, saying it was a rapidly-moving cold front and he'd promised that by noon the skies would clear, but such was not the case. The rain continued throughout the morning and well into the afternoon without any sign of stopping. By three o'clock, only two people had come into the shop. The first was a sales rep looking to speak with Colette; the second was Misty Williams who plucked a simple black skirt from the rack and carried it to the register.

"Don't you want to try it on?" Suzanne asked. "I'm not busy and if it needs alterations, I'd be happy to—"

"No, thanks," Misty said. "It's my size, and I know it will fit."

After Misty left, Suzanna stood at the shop window and watched the rain. She felt sadder than she'd ever felt in her entire life. Sadder than when Bobby had passed her by in the school hallway; sadder than when her daddy called her a whore and threw her out; sadder perhaps than the day she'd watched them lower her mama's casket into the ground. Back then she'd been ten years old, too young to realize how long forever was when you've lost someone you love.

That evening after a dinner that Suzanna barely picked at, she sat on the floor of the living room helping Annie piece together a jigsaw puzzle, but her thoughts were a million miles away. After two hours, all they had done was the top corner.

"Maybe we ought to wait until Mr. Gregg comes back," Annie said. "He's much better at this than you are."

The problem was Suzanna didn't know if Gregg was ever coming back, but she didn't have the heart to tell Annie.

"Nonsense," she said. "We can do it ourselves." She picked up a piece of the puzzle then sat there holding it in her hand.

On Saturday, Suzanna arrived at the shop fearful that it might be another day of standing idly by, but before she'd hung her coat in the closet customers crowded the shop. The rush continued all morning, and it was early afternoon before anyone had time to eat. At three-thirty Colette ran down to the coffee shop and came back with sandwiches. Suzanna was two bites into hers when Misty Williams came in.

"I tried the skirt on at home," Misty said. "It's a tad too big, so if you don't mind I'd like to take you up on your offer to alter it."

Suzanna forced a smile. "No problem, I'd be happy to." She slid the uneaten sandwich into the cubby beneath the counter and followed Misty back to the fitting room.

At six o'clock, when the store closed, Suzanna still had to write up Misty's alteration ticket and two orders that were to be shipped.

"Go ahead and go," she told Colette. "I'll lock up."

In no particular hurry to leave, she finished up the paperwork, then basted the tucks in Misty's skirt. It was nearing seven-thirty when she finally snapped off the light and left the store. The sky had turned dark, and there were only a few cars in the parking area. She pulled the key from her pocket and hurried across the lot. She hadn't seen him standing in the shadows, so the voice startled her.

"I've been waiting for you," he said.

She turned and her heart quickened. "Gregg!"

He took a step forward. "I've given this a lot of thought, Darla Jean, and I've decided our relationship does deserve a second chance. My life has been far more meaningful with you and Annie in it than it's ever been before."

"Gregg, I—"

"Wait," he said and held up his hand. "Hear me out." He swallowed hard, then continued. "I'm normally not a risk-taker and I know there will always be the possibility that Annie's dad will try to push his way back into our life, but I'm willing to take that chance. I love you with all my heart, Darla Jean, and I believe in us. It won't always be easy, but I believe we can be a family that's strong enough to weather any storm. I may not be Annie's only daddy, but I can promise you I'll be her best daddy."

The tears Suzanna had been holding back overflowed her eyes and rolled down her cheeks.

"You already are," she whispered tearfully.

He held out his arms, and she moved into them.

"I love you too," she whispered. "More than words can say and way more than you probably realize."

He tilted her face to his and kissed her mouth. It was long and tender; the kind of kiss Suzanna had never before known. As they stood there in the dimly-lit parking lot, his hand strong against her back, their heartbeats mingling together and sounding as one, Suzanna saw forever. She saw them growing old together, sitting on the front porch of Ida's house with Annie and a cluster of grandchildren gathered around, and she knew at long last she had found the place her heart could call home.

Two weeks later, Gregg and Suzanna went to Alberto's for dinner. As they walked in, Gregg gave the hostess a nod and she led them back to the same booth they'd sat in the last time. A bottle of wine and two glasses were waiting on the table.

As Suzanna slid into the booth, he leaned close and touched his hand to her shoulder.

"Life doesn't give us a lot of chances for a do-over," he whispered, "so let's make this one count."

He poured the wine then lifted his glass. "A toast. To second chances."

Suzanna smiled happily.

"I'll drink to that," she said and did.

After dinner, he pulled a small box from his pocket, thumbed it open, and held it out.

"Darla Sue," he said, giving her new name the sound of familiarity, "you'd make me the happiest man in the world if you'd agree to be my wife."

"There's nothing I want more," she said. "Absolutely, positively, nothing!"

He lifted her hand into his, kissed her knuckles, and then slid a diamond engagement ring on her finger.

⚬⚬

Earlier that day, Earl Fagan was released from the Glades State Prison Farm. He'd spent the last four months thinking things over, and he knew exactly what he was going to do.

EARL

Finding Bobby Doherty

For four months Earl sat in a concrete cell thinking of Suzanna Duff. At night when the cell block was quiet and there was nothing to do but think, he'd wonder about the foolishness of pursuing her as he'd done. Twice he almost convinced himself that she wasn't worth the agony he'd gone through, but both times such a thought was lost when he remembered how it felt to hold her in his arms and breathe in the aroma of her strawberry-scented shampoo. He pictured her as she was in the early days, her breasts full, her stomach soft as a feather pillow. Back then, she was easier to get along with—more teddy bear and less mama bear—but she'd changed and he hadn't.

Now it would be different; he'd make himself into the man she wanted. A woman like Suzanna was worth it. He thought of how he'd explain the hardships he'd endured to find her and imagined the smile that would settle on her face. He'd hand her a bouquet of flowers, hold out a toy for Annie, then say he was a changed man and swear nine ways from Sunday that this time he'd absolutely, positively given up drinking.

On the day he was released, Earl was ready with a plan. His first call was to Jack Maloney at the bar. He explained the situation, then said he was stuck in the middle of nowhere and needed money to ransom his car from the impound lot.

"How much?" Maloney asked.

"A hundred and forty bucks."

"Whew." Maloney blew the word into a whistle. "That's a chunk of change."

"Yeah, but you gotta know I'm good for it."

"How would I know that? You haven't worked in months."

"I got a few bucks saved but can't get it until the bank opens Monday. I'll pay you back then."

"Fine, if you've actually got the money, but how do I know for sure you do?"

Earl was starting to sweat. He had to get the car. Without it, his plan was shot to hell.

"Okay then, how about this? When you bring me the cash, I give you a note saying if I don't pay up, you take my house. That sound good?"

When Maloney hesitated, Earl started to panic.

"Don't tell me you got a problem with that too," he said. "You done seen the house, you know I got it."

"Yeah, but..."

"That house's worth at least three grand, maybe four."

Maloney finally agreed to the loan, and Earl breathed a sigh of relief.

"I'll be waiting in the coffee shop," he said.

When Maloney got there, he slid into the opposite side of the booth and shoved a piece of paper across the table.

Earl eyed him suspiciously. "What's this?"

"An agreement. Before I hand over the money, you gotta sign it."

Earl read through the two typewritten paragraphs and frowned.

"It's more than fair," Maloney said. "I'm not charging you for driving way out here, and I gave you a full month to pay me back."

"I don't need no month. You'll get your money Monday when the bank opens."

"You've still gotta sign it. As soon as you pay what you owe, you'll get this back and we can call it square."

Earl begrudgingly signed the paper. Maloney pulled an envelope from his pocket and passed it across the table. "There's one-fifty here. I gave you an extra ten to get you through the weekend."

"Thanks," Earl said and gave a nod.

That afternoon he paid the towing and storage fees, got his car, and headed home.

He picked up a road map on the way, and that evening he sat at the kitchen table figuring how far it was to Atlanta. Over 600 miles; more than he'd thought. With a better car, he could make it in a day, but the Ford was 14 years old and when he pushed it past 45MPH it overheated. He thought about the problem for a while, then pulled out the bottle of Seagram's hidden beneath the sink and poured himself a drink. He'd planned to give up drinking, but it seemed foolish to let a perfectly good bottle of whiskey go to waste.

That drink led to a few more, and by the time he crawled into bed he'd decided to bring some traveling money. This road trip would be his last hurrah before he was forced into a life of abstention, so he needed to make the most of it. Once Suzanna was back, he'd be walking the straight and narrow.

On Monday morning, Earl was standing at the door of the bank when it opened. Once inside, he went straight to the teller's window and told Jeanine MacDonald he'd like to withdraw the $426.37 he had in his savings account.

"If you keep a dollar in your account, we can leave it open," she suggested.

Earl shook his head. "Nah, I might be needing it."

He'd earmarked $150 of the money for Maloney but his bar didn't open until noon, and waiting around was a waste of his time. He tucked the money in his pocket, figuring he'd hold onto it and pay Maloney when he got back. He had a month; he'd be back long before then.

He took the side roads across, picked up Route 75, and followed the northbound signs. Long about lunchtime, he stopped for a hot dog and two beers, then got back on the highway and kept going. He stopped twice more, once for another beer, then to buy gas and use the restroom. Once he was in Georgia, Valdosta seemed as good a place as any to spend the night.

A few miles outside of town, he found a road house that looked promising. The parking lot was jam packed with cars, and you could hear the music a block away. He pulled in, spied an empty spot on the far edge of the lot, and parked. Inside the patrons were standing three-deep at the bar.

He edged up alongside a full-figured blonde and asked, "How's a fella supposed to get a drink around here?"

She turned and smiled. "It helps if you know the bartender." She gave a wolf whistle and yelled, "Hey, Arnie, this guy needs a drink."

Earl ordered a whiskey, then asked if he could buy her one.

"Sure." She hollered for Arnie again and said, "Make that two."

They stood there talking; she said her name was Iris and that she'd lived in Valdosta for most of her life. He said he was traveling through on his way to Atlanta but didn't mention why. When the crowd thinned, they grabbed a spot at the bar and ordered another round. Iris had a nice face, but in the light Earl could see the crow's feet framing her eyes and the lines etched across her forehead. From the back he'd guessed her to be Suzanna's age, but up close he could tell she was closer to his own.

They danced a number of times. When she suggested they grab a booth and order dinner, Earl agreed. He didn't expect much more than maybe a free feel and a few laughs, but when he slid into the booth she slid in alongside of him and pressed her thigh up against his.

"This is cozier than sitting across from one another, don't you think?"

"Yeah," Earl said. "Definitely."

He'd planned to stay in a cheap motel over by the highway, but when the evening ended he went home with Iris. By then he was too drunk to do much other than fall asleep, but Iris didn't seem to mind.

The next morning, he woke with his head feeling fuzzy and only the vaguest recollection of where he was. He sat up, caught the scent of bacon, and followed it into the kitchen. The table was set, and Iris was standing at the stove.

"Good morning, sleepyhead." She poured a cup of coffee and handed it to him.

"Morning," he said and dropped into the chair. For a few moments, he sat there trying to recall what happened, and once he did he mumbled, "Sorry about last night."

"Forget about it," she said and laughed. "We had fun, didn't we?"

"Yeah, we had fun but—"

"Well, today's another day. Let's have breakfast and then—"

"I gotta get going," Earl cut in. "I should've been on the road by now."

"Aw, that's a shame. I was kinda hoping…"

Earl was already thinking about Suzanna and was anxious to make up for lost time. He folded three strips of bacon into a slice of bread, wolfed it down, then swiped the back of his hand across his mouth. "Thanks. That was good. Real good."

"I was gonna make French toast or an omelet." Iris gave a wistful smile. "Maybe next time, huh? If you're coming this way, give me a call." She jotted her number on a piece of note paper and handed it to him.

Earl folded the paper and slid it into his pocket. "I don't expect it to be anytime soon, but when I'm back here I'll call."

As he turned on to Route 75, Earl thought about the night he'd spent with Iris and began to wish he'd stayed the extra day. She wasn't bad looking and had a nice way about her. She made a man feel good about himself, which was more than he could say about Suzanna.

He could've delayed going to Atlanta for a day. What would have been the harm? It wasn't like Suzanna was waiting for him or had even done anything to deserve his loyalty. But after eight years of being together, he wasn't ready to give up. Yeah, Iris was fun, but for all he knew she took up with every trucker who passed her way. Suzanna was different. She was the kind of woman who made a man want to settle down.

It was almost nine o'clock when Earl reached the outskirts of Atlanta. His first stop was a roadside pub where he ordered whiskey with a beer chaser. After a long day of driving, he needed to relax. He downed the whiskey then went to the phone booth and searched the directory for the law firm of Greene & Garrett. The bold face listing all but jumped out at him. He tore the page from the book, tucked it into his pocket, then returned to the bar and ordered another whiskey. He made quick work of that one then sat savoring his beer and thinking over the possibilities that lay ahead.

When the beer glass was empty, he ordered another one and asked the bartender where Mitchell Street was.

"Downtown. A block over from City Hall."

"Any motels down there?"

The bartender shook his head. "No motels, but plenty of good hotels. Thing is, they're pricey. Some of them high as thirty to forty dollars a night."

"For one night?"

The bartender nodded, then handed Earl another whiskey. "On the house."

Earl grinned. "Well, then, gimme a beer to go with it."

He drank until almost midnight, then checked into the Lucky Motel two doors down from the bar. He'd planned to be standing in front of Greene & Garrett when Bobby arrived, but he slept until noon and woke up with his head feeling like he'd been kicked by a mule. Believing he'd be in better shape after some coffee and a bite, he headed out in search of a place to eat.

With getting a late start and needing a bit of time to pull himself together, Earl didn't arrive at the Greene & Garrett building until after four o'clock. He'd expected the building to be small, a two-story or private house maybe, but confronted with a 14-story glass structure he began to feel intimidated. He couldn't just walk in and demand to speak to Bobby Doherty. That was too risky. A place like this had security guards. Doherty could have him thrown out then call Suzanna and warn her to keep the doors locked. If something like that happened, it would be a cat-and-mouse game with Suzanna always one step ahead. No, the best way was to come at her with no warning. Catch her unaware with her defenses down; then she'd be more willing to listen, easier to convince.

After thinking it through, Earl decided to wait until Bobby Doherty left the office then follow him home. That way he'd find out where Suzanna was without Doherty being any the wiser. Instead of barging in, he'd wait until the next morning then talk to Suzanna after Doherty was gone from the house. Pleased with his plan, Earl chuckled. Sometimes he was so clever, he amazed himself.

He parked his car a short distance from the building entrance and waited.

At 5:15 p.m. Doherty came out. He was heavier than he'd been in high school, and his hair was a bit darker, but other than that he looked the same. Earl watched as he rounded the corner and headed for the parking lot. When Bobby climbed into the car, Earl eased his foot down on the gas pedal and pulled out. He followed one or two cars behind, always keeping Bobby's Lincoln in sight.

After they'd left most of the traffic behind, Doherty turned onto a tree-lined street and pulled into the driveway of a white colonial. Earl drove to the end of the street, rounded the corner, and parked. He got out of the car and walked back, passing Bobby's house so slowly a turtle could have outpaced him. Through the front window he saw a man and a woman moving about, but they were too far away for him to recognize the figures.

The street was quiet; too quiet. It was the kind of neighborhood where a stranger stuck out like a sore thumb. Wary of setting off alarms before he was ready to make his move, Earl walked by a second time, then left. He'd learned all he was going to learn tonight. Tomorrow morning, when Doherty left the house, he'd get his chance to talk to Suzanna.

With an evening to kill and nothing else to do, Earl returned to the bar where he'd spent the night before. He had two beers and a burger, then left and went back to the motel. He snapped on the TV, then stretched out on the bed and tried to relax but it was impossible. His thoughts kept jumping over to Suzanna. He could picture her a dozen different ways, feel the weight of her lying in the bed beside him. He could even hear her laugh, but the one thing he couldn't quite catch hold of was her face. It seemed blurry, out of focus maybe.

It's been too long, he told himself. Once they were together, everything would fall into place, for both him and her.

Throughout most of the night, he tossed and turned, and finally when the first light of morning was in the sky he climbed from the bed, showered, and dressed. He pulled a clean shirt from his bag, slicked his hair back, and checked himself in the mirror. Satisfied with what he saw, he got in his car and drove to Doherty's house. Most lawyers didn't start work until nine and it was not yet eight, so he had plenty of time. He parked three doors down and waited.

At 8:40 the Lincoln backed out of the driveway and drove off. As soon as the taillights were gone from sight, Earl got out of his car, walked up to the front door, and rang the bell. He'd expected Suzanna to answer, but when the door swung open it was a dark-haired woman who looked nothing like Suzanna. He stood there, his eyes wide and his mouth hanging open.

She was first to speak. "Were you looking for my husband?"

Earl shook his head. "Suzanna Duff. I'm looking for Suzanna Duff."

"Duff." The woman hesitated a moment then said, "Sorry, I don't think anyone by that name lives on this block."

"Tall, blond hair. She's got a daughter name of Annie."

The woman smiled. "No, now I'm certain. No one of that description lives anywhere in this neighborhood."

"Maybe I got the name wrong. She would've come here about nine months ago..."

"Sorry, I can't help you. If anyone like that moved into the neighborhood, I'd know. My husband and I are chairing this year's Welcome Wagon."

"What's your name?" Earl asked.

"Brenda. Brenda Doherty."

"And Bobby's your husband?"

A look of surprise lit Brenda's eyes. "Why, yes, he is. Do you know Bobby?"

"Not actually know him but know of him."

She laughed. "That's Bobby. I guess most everyone in town knows him."

"Further even," Earl muttered; then he thanked her for her time and left.

Feeling a bit flabbergasted, he got back in his car and sat there for several minutes. That's when it dawned on him. Bobby was seeing Suzanna on the side, hiding her from his wife. The thought of it made Earl's blood boil.

"Well, you're not getting away with it this time," he grumbled. He gunned the motor and headed back to the Greene & Garrett building.

This time he had no reservations about walking into Doherty's office and confronting him face to face. There'd be no more sneaking around. He'd come right out and ask, Where's Suzanna, and he'd demand an answer.

Earl parked the car, stepped into the lobby, and looked up at the directory. There it was: Greene & Garrett, 3rd Floor. He walked over to the elevator, pressed the UP button, and waited. Lost in his thoughts of what he was going to say, Earl almost missed seeing Bobby step out when the elevator doors opened.

He did a double take, then turned and yelled, "Hey, Doherty!"

Bobby looked back. "Are you talking to me?"

"You bet your sweet ass I am! I wanna know where Suzanna is!"

Bobby's eyes widened. He hurried across the lobby and spoke to Earl in a hushed tone.

"Suzanna who?" he asked.

Earl didn't lower his voice one iota. "You know who! Suzanna Duff."

He moved in and stood nose to nose with Bobby. Earl wasn't any taller than Bobby, but he was half again as wide, red-faced, and fuming. "I know you're the daddy of her kid, and she came here to be with you. Now either you start talking to me, or I start talking to your wife!"

"Who the hell..." Bobby suddenly smacked his hand to his forehead. "Oh, I get it. You're Earl, right? Suzanna told me about you."

"Yeah, I'm Earl. She tell you I been taking care of her and the kid ever since she was born? Suzanna owes me; she owes me big time."

With a sly grin creeping onto his face, Bobby gave a knowing nod. "I hear you, pal, loud and clear. I've had dealings with Suzanna too." He wrapped an arm around Earl's shoulder and said, "Let's go someplace and talk."

They went to a gin mill several blocks away and sat side by side at the bar. It wasn't yet noon, but Bobby ordered a martini straight up. Earl, who was beginning to feel wary of the whole situation, ordered a double whiskey and beer chaser.

"So, Suzanna told you about me, huh? What'd she say?"

"She told me how you'd been so good to her and Annie. Said she felt guilty running off the way she did."

"So why'd she do it? To come here and be with you?"

With an almost forced look of sorrow stuck to his face, Bobby shook his head. "Sorry, pal, it wasn't me. Sure, I'm the kid's daddy, but Suzanna didn't come here looking for me. I saw her and wanted to get back together, but she turned me down flat. Said she had something better lined up. She left me, the same as she did you."

Earl eyed him suspiciously. "I don't get it. Why would she do that? She was always talking about how you were Annie's daddy and ought to take responsibility for her."

Bobby shrugged. "Search me. The more I got to know Suzanna, the more I realized I never knew her at all."

"Me too," Earl said, then he ordered a second double and downed it. "You said you talked to Suzanna; when was that?"

"A month ago, maybe two."

"Was she here in Atlanta?"

Bobby hesitated a moment then nodded. "Passing through on her way to New York."

"New York? Why would she be going—"

"You didn't know? She married some guy with a ton of money, said they were going to spend the next few years touring Europe."

Earl's jaw dropped. "You're kidding."

"Not at all. The only reason she came here was so I'd sign a paper letting her take Annie out of the country."

"Did you sign it?"

"I didn't have much choice. She said it was either that, or she'd tell my wife I was having an affair with her."

"Damn, that stinks." Earl emptied his beer glass, then sat there shaking his head. "So if you wanna get in touch with your kid, how you gonna do it?"

"I can't. You know how Suzanna is; if she decides to disappear, that's it. You're never going to find her."

"And you've got no problem with that?"

Bobby gave another of those one-shouldered shrugs, then climbed down from the bar stool and stood. "At first I did, but now I'm doing the only thing I can do. Move on and forget about her."

"It ain't that easy," Earl said.

"It is if you put your mind to it. A nice guy like you deserves a good woman, not someone who treats you like Suzanna."

"Yeah, maybe." Earl swung himself down from the stool, and together they started to leave. They were almost out the door when he stopped and grabbed hold of Bobby's arm.

"Wait a minute," he said suspiciously. "How come you're telling me all this?"

Bobby grinned. "I owe Suzanna, and I figure this is the one way I can pay her back."

"Yeah," Earl chuckled. "Payback; that's exactly what she deserves."

Earl left Atlanta that same afternoon, and before he'd gone fifty miles he started thinking about Iris.

Good thing I hung onto that number, he laughed. Good thing.

WISHES COME TRUE

Spring 1961

A week after Gregg slipped an engagement ring on her finger, Suzanna filed the papers to legally change her name. She answered all of the questions honestly and accurately. When asked "Reason for Name Change", she wrote, New start.

Both Ida and Gregg were sitting in the front row on the day she stood before a judge to legalize her new name. Suzanna swore there were no pending bankruptcies or criminal intent involved then answered "yes" when he asked if she had met the publishing requirement for the intended change. By then most everyone in town was already calling her Darla Sue, and there was never any question that she was a true Parker. Ida claimed you had only to look at the girl's eyes to know that.

"Why, they're as much Bill as Bill himself," she said, and nobody argued the point.

The judge studied her application for a few moments then leaned forward and eyed her over the top of his wire-rimmed spectacles.

"New start is rather vague," he said. "Since Darla Sue Parker appears to have no relevance or connection to your given name, can you tell me why you decided to take it?"

Before Suzanna could answer, Ida stood up. "She didn't just take it, I gave it to her!"

The judge lowered his glasses and glared over at Ida. "And who are you?"

"Ida Parker, her grandmother."

He glanced down at the application, studied it a moment longer, then looked at Suzanna. "This says your grandparents are deceased."

"Those are my birth grandparents," she said. "Mrs. Parker is my adoptive grandmother."

"If this proceeding is intended to legalize a familial relationship, it needs to be refiled as an adoption. Simply taking the Parker name could imply fraudulent intent and—"

"Nonsense," Ida said. "Darla Sue doesn't need a piece of paper to make us family. We're already family. Not because of some piece of paper. We're family because we love one another. That's the true measure of what being a family means, and there's no court in the world that—"

The judge banged his gavel. "Mrs. Parker, this is a court of law. Sit down unless you're asked to provide relevant testimony." Once Ida sat, he looked back to Suzanna. "By changing your name, do you stand to gain something of value from the Parker family?"

"I already have, your honor. Ida Parker has given me a belief in myself, a place to call home, and her love. There is nothing of greater value."

The judge smiled and turned back to Ida. "Mrs. Parker, do you understand that even after I approve this name change, Darla Sue Parker will not actually be your granddaughter, that she has no claim on your assets, and you bear no responsibility for her upkeep?"

"Of course I do," Ida replied. "But what a person has to do and wants to do are not necessarily the same thing. I've lived long enough to both know and appreciate the difference, and as far as I'm concerned—"

"That's enough," the judge said and motioned for Ida to sit. "It seems apparent there is no malicious intent here. Darla Sue Parker, your request is approved."

⁂

That April, when the sweet scent of the magnolia trees filled the air, the azaleas were starting to flower, and people had pushed their heavy coats to the back of the closet, they celebrated Ida's seventy-fifth birthday. The party was a surprise Darla Sue and Gregg had spent over a month planning. They'd hired a band, ordered the biggest birthday cake the caterer could make, and told him it had to have seventy-five candles on it.

"A cake like that is gonna cost a pretty penny," he'd said, but neither of them flinched.

"We want the best," Gregg replied, and Darla Sue nodded her agreement.

Knowing full well that once a secret is out it can spread like wildfire, they waited until two weeks before the party to start inviting people.

On a balmy evening, when Ida was sitting in front of the television laughing at The Real McCoys with Annie, Gregg and Darla Sue strolled up and down the street, sliding invitations under the neighbor's doors. In bold strokes she'd written, The party is a surprise, so don't breathe a word of it to Ida. To make certain her message wasn't missed, she'd underlined the words.

Once the invitations were sent, she began telling the ladies who came to the shop and the merchants that lined the streets. On her lunch hour she went from shop to shop saying,

"It's the first Sunday in April at the Elks Club. Mark your calendar, but it's a surprise so don't mention it to Grandma."

On the Saturday before the party, she was on the telephone explaining to the florist that she wanted balloons as well as flowers when Ida walked in and overheard her.

"Balloons?" Ida said. "Why on earth…"

Before she could finish the question, Darla Sue fluffed it off saying that she was working on arrangements for the next holiday fashion show.

"This early in the year?" Ida asked suspiciously.

Darla Sue just nodded and ducked out, saying she had some errands to run.

Since Annie shared all her secrets with Ida, they held off telling her about the party until the day before, and then they only did so because it became a necessity.

"Mama, Lori's having a sleepover. Can I go?" she'd asked.

"Not this time," Darla Sue said.

Annie argued "why not" for the better part of an hour before Darla Sue pulled her into the bedroom and explained about the party.

"But," she said, "I'm warning you, if Grandma, gets wind of this, you're going to lose your allowance for a year!"

"That's not fair. What if she hears it from somebody else?"

Darla Sue eyed her with a raised eyebrow. "You're the somebody most likely to tell."

Annie pulled her mouth into a pout, sat there for a minute, then said, "If I don't tell, I'm gonna be breaking a promise."

"What promise?"

"Me and Grandma pinky sweared we'd never keep secrets."

Darla Sue turned away so Annie wouldn't catch her smile. "It's not really breaking a promise, because this is something that will make Grandma happy. Happy secrets are not really secrets; they're surprises, and those are okay to keep."

On Sunday morning, they all had breakfast together. Then Gregg said he had something to take care of and hurried off to check on the last-minute preparations at the Elks Club. Darla Sue then suggested she take Ida and Annie to Lady Anne's Tea Room for lunch.

"Let's dress up in something fancy," she said, "and make this a special girls' day out."

Annie giggled. "Yeah, Grandma, it's gonna be very special."

Darla Sue glared at her, expecting that she might say something more, but she didn't.

Ida wrinkled her brow. "That's a nice idea, but the tea room isn't open on Sunday."

That was something Darla Sue hadn't taken into account. With no more than a few seconds hesitation, she came back saying they'd just started opening and this was their first Sunday.

After a fair bit of back and forth, with Ida arguing they should at least call to check, and Darla Sue saying it wasn't necessary, they all climbed into the car wearing their Sunday best and started for Barston. When Darla Sue pulled up in front of the Elks Club and said she had to stop there for something, Ida offered to wait in the car. Poo-pooing such a suggestion, Darla Sue opened the car door and helped Ida out.

"There's something I'd like your opinion on."

Without finishing the statement, she hooked her arm through Ida's and started for the door. Annie followed along with a grin stretched clear across her face.

As they entered the building, Ida gave a nostalgic sigh. "The last time I was here was the day of Bill's memorial luncheon."

"I know," Darla Sue said. "I remember that day." She pushed the door to the ballroom open and stepped aside so Ida could enter first.

The moment Ida entered the room, the band broke into a rousing rendition of Happy Birthday, and the crowd of friends and neighbors shouted, "Surprise!"

Ida stood there looking astonished for a few seconds; then tears filled her eyes.

"So this is what everyone's been whispering about," she finally said and laughed.

When they returned home that evening, the grin Ida had been wearing all day was still tugging at her face. She kicked off her shoes and dropped down onto the sofa.

"I can't imagine anything better than this day," she said. "It was the best birthday ever."

"Really? The best ever, in your whole life?" Annie asked.

"Absolutely! Why, I never suspected—"

Not waiting for Ida to finish, Annie jumped up and started dancing around.

"I did it," she shouted. "I did it again!"

"You did what?" Darla Sue asked.

"I used my wishing power to make something else come true."

"Wishing power?" she repeated quizzically. "I don't believe there is such a power."

"There is, Mama, there really is. Remember in the Christmas movie, Susan wished for a house and she got it? Well, I did the same thing. I wished for a house and a grandma, and my wish came true. Then I wished the tree elves would tell Santa to stop at our house and bring presents, and that wish came true too. Last night when I was almost asleep, I wished Grandma would have the best birthday ever and she did. That proves I've got the same wishing powers as Susan."

Darla Sue laughed. "Annie, Susan was a make-believe girl in a movie. She was pretend acting. I'm happy your wishes came true, but there really is no such thing as wishing powers."

"Don't say that, Mama! You've gotta really believe, or your wishes won't come true."

Hearing the seriousness in her daughter's voice, Darla Sue smiled and said, "Okay then, I believe. I truly believe."

Annie gave a nod of satisfaction. "Good. Because I'm not done wishing."

☙❧

Darla Sue Parker changed her name one more time. It happened in June, a week after school closed for the summer and people had begun to spend their evenings sitting on the front porch or strolling into town for a soda or ice cream. That Sunday it was as if God were smiling down on them with the azaleas in full bloom and the sky an endless stretch of blue. The tiny church was filled to overflowing, and when she stepped out of the car a collective sigh rippled through the crowd. The gown, a silk taffeta with seed pearls scattered across the skirt, bared her shoulders, hugged her waist, then fell softly and danced about her ankles.

When Darla Sue started along the walkway, a springtime breeze ruffled the edge of her veil. Ginger, her matron of honor, leaned over and smoothed it. The gown had been a gift from Colette, one she claimed would be the perfect introduction to her new wedding collection.

As they neared the entrance, Darla Sue heard the organ sound the first chords of the procession music. Ginger stepped out to lead the way, and Annie followed behind scattering rose pedals from the basket she carried. She was wearing the gold locket Gregg had given her that morning. He'd knelt in front of her and asked if she would accept him as her daddy for now and evermore. As he'd hooked the clasp around her neck, she'd grinned and whispered in his ear that having him for a daddy was exactly what she'd been wishing for.

The strains of Wagner's Bridal Walk sounded, and Darla Sue moved to the entranceway. For a fleeting moment she hesitated, wishing her father were here to accompany her down the aisle, but he'd never answered any of her letters. She then thought of William, the grandfather she'd never known but had taken to heart. It was his presence she felt beside her as she stepped into the church and began her walk down the aisle.

With every seat filled and the congregation standing to watch her entrance, she could not see Gregg until she neared the altar. When she finally caught sight of him, he was standing side by side with Phil. A feeling such as she'd never before known swelled in her heart, and for a moment it stopped beating. She knew if she lived a thousand years or ten thousand years, she would never forget the look of love in his eyes.

As Gregg lifted the veil from her face, he whispered that she was so lovely she took his breath away. He took her hand in his, and they stood together as the pastor spoke of the responsibilities and joys of marriage. After he'd led them through the vows and exchange of rings, he spoke in a voice that could be heard by all.

"Today we are here to not only unite Darla Sue and Gregg in holy matrimony but to create a loving and enduring family." He turned to Annie and asked her to come forward, then handed each of them a small beaker of sand: Darla Sue's a snowy white, Gregg's a pearl gray, and Annie's pink.

"Each of you are individuals," he said, "as unique as the grains of sand you hold in your hand. Separately you are each a beautiful color, but blended together you will create a color even more beautiful. To preserve the beauty of this thought and create a lasting memory, we will now join the grains of sand. First, each of you will pour your unique layer of sand into this jar."

Gregg moved to the table and poured a layer of gray sand into the bottom of the jar; he was followed by Darla Sue, and when it came to Annie's turn he bent down and asked if she needed help. She shook her head and poured a thick layer of pink sand atop the other two.

"This represents the individuality that you each have," the pastor said. He then asked all three of them to pour their remaining sand in at the same time.

Annie looked up with a worried expression. "But it's gonna get mixed together."

The pastor smiled as a ripple of laughter came from congregation. "You're right, Annie, it will get mixed together. The sand will be blended just as your lives will be blended."

Annie eyed her mama and in a rather loud whisper, asked, "Mama, is this okay to do?"

Darla Sue nodded. "It's a good thing; a very good thing." She nudged Annie forward and then at precisely the same time, all three of them poured their remaining sand into the jar. Annie's eyes lit up.

"Look, Mama," she squealed. "It's beautiful!"

"It certainly is," Darla Sue replied as she looked at the soft rose-tinted beige their blended sands had created.

The pastor continued. "Love is a force more formidable than any other. It cannot be seen or measured, yet it is powerful enough to change your life and offer you more joy than any material possession you could ever own. You came here as three individuals, but love has made you one. You are now, and will forevermore be, a family, as beautiful and inseparable as these grains of sand. May God bless this union for now and forever."

A joyous "Amen" rose from the congregation.

Gregg bent and kissed Annie's cheek. Then he took Darla Sue in his arms and kissed her as never before. In that kiss she felt the forgiveness of the past and the promise of the future. As they turned and started down the aisle together, Annie was in front of them, dancing happily and scattering the remainder of her rose petals.

Somewhere deep inside Darla Sue's heart, a tiny piece of Suzanna remained, and she was smiling for she had never in all her life been this happy.

The following morning when Gregg and Darla Sue left for a two-week honeymoon in Virginia Beach, Ida and Annie stood on the front porch waving goodbye. When their car was gone from sight, Annie looked up at Ida and grinned. "I did it. I got another wish come true."

"You mean getting Gregg for your daddy?"

Annie nodded. "Uh huh. Now there's something else I'm wishing for."

"Another wish?" Ida said, sounding surprised.

Again, Annie nodded. "This time, I'm wishing for a baby sister."

Ida gave a big round laugh. It rolled up from her stomach and filled the air with the sound of happiness.

"I wouldn't be one bit surprised if you got that wish," she said. "Not one bit surprised."

A note from the Publisher...

If you enjoyed reading this book, please post a review at your favorite on-line retailer or social media site and share your thoughts with other readers.

If you would like to know more about Bette Lee Crosby's books, visit her website and sign up to receive her monthly newsletter.
https://betteleecrosby.com

Or follow Bette Lee on Facebook and join in her live chats.
https://www.facebook.com/authorbetteleecrosby/

Acknowledgments

When a reader holds a finished book in hand, they see only the face of the author, but in truth, many people contribute to the successful making of a novel. Even the most skilled storyteller is only as good as the people who support her. I am fortunate to have an advisory team that willingly reads through every draft, unflinchingly tells me where I have gone wrong, and then shows up with wine and a homemade cake to help me find my way to a new and more beautiful storyline. No words could ever express how grateful I am for my Port St. Lucie Posse, Joanne Bliven, Kathy Foslien, Lynn Ontiveros, and Trudy Southe. Such amazing friends are a blessing beyond belief.

I am equally blessed in knowing Ekta Garg, a superb editor, and extremely talented author, who somehow manages to catch my mistakes without ever losing sight of my voice. Ekta's attention to detail constantly pushes me to go deeper into the story and I believe I am better because of this challenge.

Thank you also to Amy Atwell and the team at Author E.M.S. They are like the proverbial Fire Department, always there to help put out the fires. Thank you, Amy, for turning my manuscripts into beautifully formatted pages and for being so wonderfully organized and dependable.

I owe a huge debt of gratitude to Sue Baker for reminding me of the *Miracle on 34th Street* quote that appears in the front of this book, and also to the gals of the BFF Clubhouse (Bette's Friends & Fans). Any author who has such loyal fans is truly blessed.

Lastly, I am thankful beyond words for my husband Dick, who puts up with my crazy hours, irrational thinking, and late or non-existent dinners. I could not be who I am without him for he is and will always be my sweetheart and greatest blessing.

Award-winning novelist Bette Lee Crosby brings the wit and wisdom of her Southern mama to works of fiction—the result is a delightful blend of humor, mystery and romance. "Storytelling is in my blood", Crosby laughingly admits, "My mom was not a writer, but she was a captivating storyteller, so I find myself using bits and pieces of her voice in almost everything I write."

A USA Today bestselling author, Crosby has twenty-two published novels, including Spare Change and the Wyattsville series. She has been the recipient of the Reader's Favorite Gold Medal, Reviewer's Choice Award, FPA President's Book Award and International Book Award, among many others. Her 2016 novel, Baby Girl, was named Best Chick Lit of the Year by Huffington Post. Her 2018 novel The Summer of New Beginnings, published by Lake Union, took First Place in the Royal Palm Literary Award for Women's Fiction and was a runner-up for book of the year. Her 2019 release, Emily, Gone was a winner of the Benjamin Franklin Literary Award.

Crosby currently lives on the East Coast of Florida with her husband and a feisty Bichon Frise who is supposedly her muse.

To learn more about Bette Lee, visit her website at:
https://betteleecrosby.com

CPSIA information can be obtained
at www.ICGtesting.com
Printed in the USA
LVHW050743300620
659360LV00002B/74